The Boy Who Made Music

A Novel by
James A. Costa Jr.

CCB Publishing
British Columbia, Canada

The Boy Who Made Music: A Novel

Copyright ©2004, 2021 by James A. Costa Jr.
ISBN-13 978-1-77143-500-0
Second Edition

Library and Archives Canada Cataloguing in Publication
Costa Jr., James A., 1931-
The boy who made music : a novel / by James A. Costa Jr. -- 2nd ed.
ISBN 978-1-77143-500-0 (pbk) – ISBN 978-1-77143-501-7 (PDF)
Additional cataloguing data available from Library and Archives Canada

Cover artwork and design by Joseph 'Zugs' Klein. A semi-retired artist, Mr. Klein resides in Monterey Park, California.

Publisher: CCB Publishing
British Columbia, Canada
www.ccbpublishing.com

For Mom and Dad

Chapter 1

On a long and sultry night in the heart of summer, one week after the boy's fourth birthday, the Garths came to full knowledge of their son's difference.

They had retired early that evening to escape the clinging heat of day. Through the window, thrown wide to invite a chance breeze, moonlight streamed across their faces and mottled the room in soft shadows. Garth tossed, straining against the stone slab he dreamed pinned his legs. He felt the sun burning down on his face and squirmed against the rock jabbing his ribs.

"Everett," she whispered, poking him again, "Everett!"

His eyes snapped open and he bolted upright. Then he heard it, too. Flinging himself from the bed he moved swiftly for the door. Padding behind, his wife followed him to the landing where she slipped off to the child's room. Everett Garth crept down the stairs to the parlor. He cocked his head, trying to identify the sounds that seemed to come from everywhere and nowhere. In the darkness his hands fumbled for the poker hanging next to the hearth. A bar of light angling in through the unlatched door fell across the kitchen floor. Soundlessly, his fist tight around the steel handle, he slipped into the kitchen and threw open the door. He peered out, adjusting his eyes to the moonlit night. Girding himself, he rushed onto the porch, a step or two ahead of his wife. She tugged at his arm, frantically, about to speak. He motioned her to silence.

Then she saw what he saw. Standing in the clearing of the yard with moonlight illuminating him to the whiteness of a star, was the boy. With his back to them and arms outstretched, he threw back his head and the music of violins flowed out, throaty and mellow and resonant.

The poker dropped from Garth's hand. Trembling, his wife stole forth to stand behind the boy. Her hand reached out, gingerly touching his bare shoulder.

"Child," she whispered.

He swung 'round to her, eyes wide, his face distorted as if in infinite ecstasy, or pain. Grasping her hand, he pointed with the other, his finger arcing across the heavens.

And he began to make music.

Garth approached and gazed up with them as a chorus of strings poured from the boy. Flutes and oboes trilled in. Woodwinds and brass melded with them in subtle and varied harmonies. Percussion marched in measured cadences and carried them out, reverberating, until the night was a symphony filling the world around them.

Abruptly it stopped. Mrs. Garth dropped to her knees behind the boy. She gripped his shoulders to turn him. Ancient, long-buried fears sprang up to haunt her as she looked fiercely into his face. Staring down dumbly, Garth shivered.

The boy pulled away and his head went back again. And again the music began, pulsing dimly in the night, like soft winds swelling in from the distant mountains, with echoes of muffled thunder out of some forgotten past, roaring and insistent as the timeless rhythm of beating waves on unknown shores. On it swept, like blowing sands gusting out of shadowed plains of ages long dead, gathering the infinite range of sounds and, by degrees, fixing, orchestrating and consummating them in majestic themes that leaped to new peaks erupting from the primal seas; the crescendos building, amplifying, piling out of the eternal night, spreading out to the heavens, a tide of music rushing to the ringing spheres beyond the sun into the eternal light beyond the stars.

To Garth it seemed as if the music was coming from without, pouring from the sky in torrents, cascading through the valley between the far mountains. The woman, bracing her child against her body, slipped her arms around to his naked chest. All three faced up. They stood as if frozen in a vortex of time and space and sound, sound rising concentrically from the center that they were. The music swirled and climbed and mounted, gushing from the boy whose arms were flung wide, as if garnering through his being all the music of creation and conducting it upward, a synthesis of harmonies and rhythms.

How long they stood there, neither could ever recall. They remembered only that the music ended gradually, diminishing in scope and power, the percussions fading first, then the brass, the woodwinds, and finally the dying flutes and strings which whispered off to silence, returning the earth, the moon and stars to the mute vacuum of space. Spasms racked the boy's body and he collapsed in his mother's arms. Garth's hands went out, but she interposed herself between him and the boy. Gently, she lifted the unconscious child in the iron cradle of her arms and carried him into the house.

She would carry him that way again when he was dead.

Chapter 2

Upstairs, she clothed the boy's cold and naked body and took him to her own bed. With her back to her husband, she lay with the child to her side, and for a long while gazed into the sleeping face, pale and still as the moonlight bathing it. Long after the heavy breathing of Garth had begun, she lay awake, stroking warmth into the frail legs curled beside her. Only then did the full terror of her own youth return. A time long past. She shuddered and clutched the child to her breast.

She remembered then an event of the previous year, one that also had awakened old fears in her. She had been standing over her ironing, pausing now and then to run her wrist across her damp brow while across the room Garth sat in his chair by the window, reading his newspaper. The warm breeze billowing the lace curtains brought little relief from the afternoon heat. In his out-of-the-way corner the boy straddled his mother's sewing box like a horse and rocked back and forth, laughing silently. He wore only a pair of shorts, nearly the whiteness of his skin.

"Good rains means a good harvest," Garth said, from behind his paper.

The boy stopped rocking.

"Yessir, I'm bettin' on lower prices this year. Be a heap o' help to us, for sure."

Shyly, as if from a distance came the wistful strains of violins. The music faded as suddenly as it had begun and the boy rocked again, cheerful and unaware.

Garth twisted around to the window, listening for the source of the sounds, then turned back to his wife, whose eyes searched the ceiling.

"Did you hear?" he asked.

She nodded, regarding the boy curiously, intently, as he lurched ahead in the frenzy of his ride.

Garth rose, throwing down his paper. "Maybe new boys is out to take up pesterin' us again after all these years."

He strode heavily through the kitchen to the porch, and in a few minutes returned, shrugging his shoulders. "Mos' likely, stray dogs is all," he said, and, satisfied with his conclusion, went back to his paper. His wife bowed silently to her work. A tremor shook her thin body….

Bethany Garth was no longer a young woman. Time had stolen from her any softness and spontaneity she may have brought to their marriage. It had burned down the candle of hope and left in its place a dark and brooding nature, a woman hardened by labor and tormented with thoughts of the child. Uncomplaining, she lived within herself, chasing thoughts and memories that scurried like shadows into the secret inner places where she lost them in the dark recesses of her mind.

For the first twenty years of their married life she had not conceived, and her barrenness had created between them a distance neither could bridge. In the early years she took Garth's long and sometimes moody silences as signs of his disappointment, which she interpreted as an accusation. She blamed herself and once offered him his freedom but he had refused, saying, "It's the will o' God, Beth; let no man question it!"

For a time she felt encouraged, forced herself to believe his words, but as the counted months turned into years she grew bitter. In the quiet of her days she nurtured a resentment toward the man eternally seated by the window, dozing or reading his paper or listening to the scratchy classical records he did not understand but which he enjoyed playing on the battered 'Victor-ola' he'd picked up at a bargain.

Garth himself was no longer the hard-muscled youth of time past, but was still strong at fifty. His red, unruly hair was thick, and his grit-dry skin seemed a permanent cast of green, the color of the marble dust that blew in his face at the quarry mill where he worked. Time had killed his ambitions. He no longer dreamed of what he might become and had resigned himself to his place in life, just as he had resigned himself to his place in marriage.

When not attending to his immediate needs, he spent his time in his chair, analyzing the daily news events out of which he would occasionally formulate a 'theory,' as he called it, which he would then offer up to his wife. She always paused to listen—he expected that—and when he was finished, she went solemnly back to her work and her own thoughts. He did not take to heart anything he read, however serious or close to home, and once he'd expounded his theory, he was satisfied and done with it.

The distance that lay between the Garths also separated them from the townsfolk. In the busy early months of their marriage, when there was so much promise in their lives and so much work to be done on the old house, they had no time nor desire to be with others. The few invitations they'd received and ignored soon ceased to come. They kept to themselves, putting in long, hard hours, content with the progress and the secure world they were building for their future. In time, when their greatest labors were over and the need for others arose, Garth invited several of his fellow workers and their wives to dinner.

All that day Beth fussed. With a vigor she hadn't shown in months, she scrubbed and scoured her house. She plucked and prepared the ducks, peeled a mound of potatoes, diced, sliced and cut vegetables. She pounded dough, whipped batter and turned her oven up hot for the baking. She scurried about, setting her table with her best linen and china and silverware, polished to gleaming brightness. Last, she dressed herself, meticulously, and came downstairs exuding a restrained excitement that did not escape Garth's eye. The starched white ruffles of her collar and sleeves were a sharp contrast to her emerald green dress and the dark sheen of her hair, immaculately combed and swept atop her head and held with combs.

"You're…beautiful, Beth," Garth stammered, embarrassed by his own words and hardly able to meet her eyes.

"And you're quite the gentleman yourself, Mr. Garth," she said, taking in his clean-shaven face and the neat press of his suit.

They laughed and talked as they hadn't done in a long time. Beth thought of things she would say and ask the ladies. They waited, anxiously anticipating the laughter and conversation that would fill the house that had been too long without it. They discussed what topics they would talk about, how they would answer. There would be no talk of children, they agreed, lest they encourage prying into matters too personal.

They fell silent, absorbed in their thoughts, half-listening for the approaching voices. Garth made frequent trips to the window. He sniffed over the pots. He paced. As the appointed time passed, their faces expressed worry, then disappointment, then hurt. No one was coming.

She turned off the stove. "Everett…."

Garth raged. He hurled a plate against the wall and the dishes bounced on the table when he brought his fist down like a hammer. Burning with humiliation he stormed through the house swearing oaths. Eventually he went to bed without eating.

For a while they had attended services at the town church where they would enter and shyly slip to a side-rear pew, he, hat in hand, wearing the same black suit he'd been married in, she, wearing the same brown dress she wore each week, and a plain yellow head scarf. They pretended not to notice the eyes surreptitiously regarding them and ignored the small children who stared and had to be cuffed back to courtesy. Perhaps it was the sight of the children, or unanswered prayers, or discomfort that finally kept them away. Months later, when the Reverend Hempstone called at their house to inquire about their lengthy absence, he was rebuffed at the door by Garth, who said, "We got all of God we need right here, Reverend. Without the hypocrites!"

No one saw much of them anymore, except when they went into town for provisions, or when Garth stopped at the post office for his newspapers. And, years later, though news of the boy's birth was spread by the town clerk who registered it, no one ever saw little Jonathan Garth.

It was on her forty-first birthday—which Garth had forgotten—that she became aware of her pregnancy. Nights, alone in her room, she would examine her body with trembling fingers and torture herself with the question of whether the poor soil she was could sustain the precious life beginning to stir within. For as long as she was able, she concealed the news and her excitement from Garth. She ate well and rested as often as her work would allow. She alternated between joy and despair. Days, while Garth 'slaved,' as he put it, she hummed almost forgotten tunes she had learned from her father, and sewed things the baby would need. And she prayed.

Then one morning at the break of dawn he came forth, beautiful and pink as the rising sun, his head a down of gold out of which opened vast round eyes bluer than a summer sky. It was, she thought, as if this one seed had taken nourishment from all the parts of her fallow soil and burst into the world a perfect flower.

For the first months of the child's life, she worked with an enthusiasm that amazed Garth. Each day she changed and bathed the child in the porcelain basin, his neck propped in the palm of one hand while the other gently ran the cloth over his half-submerged body, whispering and cooing softly as she looked into the blue eyes gazing back at her. She fussed with his fingernails, poked into his ears and his nose. She wrapped him warmly in white, sterile blankets and took him to nurse as she rocked and soothed him to sleep with caressing fingers. All these things she did in a secretive, possessive kind of way. Nearby, Garth hovered, shaking his head in wonder. In the background, always, played the blurry, sound-thin records.

Gradually, over time, a worry crept into her life, insidiously, like a disease slowly eating its way to recognition: the boy could not speak.

For a while she refused to admit to herself any imperfection in the child. She talked to him incessantly, trying to coax from him the word she desperately wanted to hear. In time she doubted herself. She tested him, thinking he might be deaf, and found to her relief that that was not the case. Finally, no longer able to bear her anguish alone, she confided in Garth.

"Ah, he's a happy one, Beth. Always smilin', ain't he?"

When she protested he put her off, saying, "He's still a tyke. And some parts don't always come along so fast as others."

As the months passed, Garth gradually came around to his wife's point of view. Evenings, when he would return from the quarry, he'd ask, "Anythin'?" And she, stirring her pots, always answered with a shake of her head.

Sitting next to the stove was the boy, sometimes helping his mother in some small way. At the sight of his father arriving home from work, his eyes would open wide and he would run to him, jumping into his arms, unmindful of the grimy hands lifting and clutching him to dusty, green clothes. It was on such an evening at the end of supper of meat stew that Garth spoke: "We'll have to get him to a doctor."

Her eyes darted quickly to the child, absorbed in spooning ripples across the broth in his bowl. Her face flushed. "What kind of doctor?"

"What kind o' question is that, Beth? A doctor's a doctor, ain't he? 'Course, it'll be the best I can afford, if that's your meanin'. No need to advertise, neither. Tomorra I'll head out for Torrence—find a good doc there."

The boy brought the Garths together in a way new to them both. They said little to each other still, but occasionally Garth would, as if reading her feelings, pat her on the shoulder or give her a gentle word without being forced to it by custom or manners. In the evenings, after the boy had been put to bed, he would retire with his wife instead of staying behind to finish his newspaper. Once in bed they would lie awake next to each other, neither speaking, but both knowing and understanding the fears gnawing at the roots of their private existence.

Often, when waking for work early in the morning, he would find her cradled in his arm. And as always he would ease himself out of bed without disturbing her, slip quietly into his work clothes and out of the room. He never descended the stairs without first peeking into the boy's room. In the dawn light passing through the shade, he could see the boy's face and he marveled that it should so resemble the faces of angels he had seen in religious paintings. Even in sleep the boy seemed to be smiling, as if seeing amusing pictures, the way he smiled when his mother thumbed through an old catalogue with him, pointing out items on the pages, speaking the names distinctly, though softly, then looking quickly to him, waiting for the sounds that would not, or could not come. He might speak someday, the doctor in Torrence had said. No reason he shouldn't, as far as he could determine. But doctors didn't know everything, Garth thought.

Chapter 3

The morning after the Garths came to full awareness of their child's difference, Everett Garth did not go to work. It was the first time in years that he had missed. Breakfast passed without even the minimal conversation that usually marked their meals. Their thoughts were of Jonathan, whose cheerful disposition revealed nothing of the events in the yard earlier that morning. Not until he had helped his mother clean off the table and gone off to ride his sewing-box horse did they speak.

"Others will know," she said.

He nodded.

"We must get away."

"To where? Besides, there's hardly no money."

"The house...."

"Who'd want it? The land is poor and it's too far from town to suit most."

"Soon he must begin school. They will know."

He nodded, staring down his crossed legs to his mud-crusted boots and listening to the music drift in from the parlor. "Never should've reported him being born. But who could've knowed or guessed such a thing as this."

For a time they went silent, but Garth could not ignore the pain in his wife's eyes, eyes imploring him for an answer he did not have. Days, he worked furiously at the mill, causing one the men watching at a distance to complain that he was killing the job and making the others look bad, to boot.

His newspapers piled up at the post office, and he spent his evenings hammering and sawing and patching up around the house. His wife worked without complaint, fighting the dust and dirt, but always with hollow-eyed watchfulness over the child, who played and sang close by. Her daily routine remained unchanged except that now, over her husband's protests, she took to rocking the child to sleep before putting him to bed, the way she had when he was an infant.

The days passed in slow and moody silence until late one evening when Garth stomped into the house wiping grease from his hands. Without looking up from the dough she was kneading on the kitchen table, his wife saw him drop the rag into the basket in the corner and hang his hat on a hook next to the sink. He said nothing, but she sensed something different in his actions, the way he poked around the bowl on the cupboard, searching for a suitable apple. Or perhaps it was the sureness of his movements, the lack of hesitation which had marked his actions during the preceding weeks. She felt a twinge of excitement when he pulled up his chair opposite her.

He polished the apple on his sleeve. "Sleepin'?"

She nodded, wiping the flour from her hands onto her apron.

Casually, he bit into the apple and contemplated his boots, considering his thoughts. "I'm gonna pass the word Jonathan's bad sick, Beth." Lately, he used her name so seldom that whenever he did, as now, it brought them together in a suggestion of intimacy they rarely experienced anymore. "But you're gonna have to keep the boy in the house, case anybody comes snoopin' 'round."

"What will you say?"

"Don't know 'xactly yet. Most anything'll work, I reckon. Nobody keeps track of us much these days."

"Is there no other way?"

"None as I can think of!" The doubtful tone in her voice made him firm, as if the firmness would allay his own doubts. "No money means we got to stay. The doc in Torrence didn't give us much hope neither, 'cept to say nothin's wrong that maybe won't fix itself in time. Just slow to talk, he says. Good thing the boy didn't start to singin'. Then he'd o' got an earful and knew." He glanced up between bites and read the misery on his wife's face. "Should have told him, maybe, but I couldn't. Would've called me crazy—or him a freak."

She winced.

"Tomorra after work I'll head into town, to the pharmacy, order some medicine. The clerk, you know, is gonna nosy over the counter, 'Wife sick? Boy sick?' That's when I'll drop it, real confidential like. Be all over the county in no time."

He tossed the apple core onto the table, with her eyes following it. "But you best keep him inside from now on or it won't work. Maybe if I think more on it I'll come up with somethin' better." The tight lines of her face did not slacken and her arms went stiffly back to punching into the dough.

The next day Garth tromped into the house carrying an armful of newspapers and a small sack of hard candy. He dropped the papers on the table with an abandon and lightheartedness that was contagious. The boy bounded across the floor and jumped into his arms, while Beth, encouraged, watched approvingly.

"For you, Jonathan boy," he said, shoving the candy under his nose. "But not all at once now." He tousled his hair, set him down and sent him along with a playful slap on the bottom.

"Just like I said, Beth, Old Nosey swallowed it all. Even made suggestions for medicine." He removed a small bottle from his pocket and poured it down the drain. From the parlor bubbled a bright and catchy tune.

At first Beth had difficulty keeping the child indoors. Each morning he would kneel by the parlor window and gaze out to the far mountains, the Timrods, his eyes watery blue behind his tears. And each day he sang the same mournful melody, rich and resonant as a lone cello bowing a wandering note lost on the wind.

Perplexed, she would lead him away and sit him on her lap in her rocker, where she would try to distract him with catalogue pictures and soothe him with gentle fingers stroking through the fine, golden strands of hair that never darkened. There, his music would gradually diminish to a measured breathing as he would fall off to sleep against her bosom.

Garth grew impatient with the boy's sulkiness. He shouted at him, threatened him with his belt and sent him to bed early. Whenever possible, Beth kept the child away from him. She took him upstairs to read to him or to play games she invented to amuse him.

Garth's anger eventually subsided and one day he brought home a wooden box filled with multi-colored marble stones, smooth and polished. For a while the boy took interest. Each evening when he came home, Garth would look hopefully to his wife's face, but found in it only a growing despair he could no longer bear. Pondering the alternatives, he decided to let the boy outdoors. "One hour at dawn," he said, "and one hour at dusk, when there's least chance of a traveler on the road."

There was no need for it. A change came suddenly over the boy when for the first time he seemed to notice the discarded newspapers stacked in the corner near his father's chair.

After work one evening, Garth listened to his wife's account of how the child carefully turned each page, singing softly as he pored over the print. Hearing of the boy's new interest was a great relief to Garth, who regarded it as a welcome solution to their problem. Once again their days became relaxed as the boy returned to himself.

In a way that neither Garth nor his wife could understand, the boy pried from them intimacies that recalled long-buried memories. Of the two, Beth felt it most keenly. To her, it was as if some unspoken thing, some undefined shame between them was being dissolved and transmuted by the child, a mutual deception, perhaps. She did not comprehend her thoughts, nor did she pursue them when they came to trouble her. Instead, she contented herself with the happiness of the child rocking nearby. Except for the stir caused by his recent insistence on removing all his clothes, their days passed peacefully, with music filling the rooms.

Chapter 4

For a year all went well. As Garth had predicted, word of the boy's 'illness' spread through the town, and curiosity seekers who had now and then passed on the road no longer craned their necks to see through the hedges bordering the property. By degrees the bond between Garth and his wife was strengthened by the boy, who spent his days singing over the newspaper pages he spread and turned on the floor.

Each day when Garth returned from work he was greeted by melodies flooding the house, and by his wife, whose faint smile put a light in her eyes he had almost forgotten. The dusty lines of his rugged face seemed to brighten too as a feeling of contentment grew in him. Occasionally he would come home with a bouquet of wild flowers, picked along the road, and offer them to her. The long-ingrained self-consciousness between them persisted, however, and he would say, "For the table."

Her head lowered in demure understanding, she always accepted them graciously and, cutting their stems, placed them in water in a canning jar on the sideboard. "They brighten the room," she would reply, fluffing them up.

"Child," she would then call. And through the doorway he would run, carrying another melody that suggested to Garth something very old, yet new, like raw marble taken and polished to a glassy finish. Into his father's arms he would jump, hugging him, his face alive with smiles and twinkling eyes.

Ruffling the boy's hair, Garth would sometimes pluck from his pocket a brown sack filled with hard candy. "For you," he'd say, holding it high. From another pocket he'd draw a package of medicine and say, "For the neighbors."

Then Beth would smile to his hearty laugh and they would sit to eat. A warmth filled the house and everywhere there was music. And the music was their words.

* * * * *

In the spring of the following year a pattern began to emerge, though neither Garth nor his wife was immediately aware of it. It was she who first detected the solemn, brooding music that came for only a moment to wrinkle her brow as she paused in her work to listen to her husband's latest 'theory.' But it was Garth himself who finally understood the significance of the dissonance, the unfamiliar strains of dark sound.

One evening after the child had been put to bed, she confided to her husband that this new music had an 'evil lurking in its passages.' For the next several nights Garth could not concentrate on his reading. He waited, listening for the 'evil' that had sent a shudder through his wife when she had spoken of it. But the evil did not come to intrude upon the ever-changing, infinite variety of melody that flowed without end. What he did notice, however, was a growing complexity of sounds he had not heard since 'that night in the yard,' and this he mentioned to his wife. She did not seem to hear. Old fears preoccupied her as thoughts crept into her mind and disappeared like shadows slipping into a dark forest.

"Gonna be a bad year for bill collectors, all this unemployment," Garth was saying over his paper one evening, when a single note, a far oboe, punctured the swell of music and scaled up through it until it was lost in a register beyond hearing. To Garth's mind came the image of an ivy vine climbing a tree and winding out of sight in the foliage above.

He stared at his wife whose face showed her thoughts: *Now you've heard it too.*

They turned to the boy, straddling his wooden horse, his head thrown back, eyes closed, his mouth open and silent. In a few moments the music returned, clear and sweet, while the boy rode vigorously on.

Two nights later the incident occurred again, with a minor variation in theme, but with the same sad intensity. The third night, again. On the fourth night Garth lowered his paper and watched the boy as he spoke. "Lots of strikes on the coast. Be outta a job myself if the mill closes." The boy's head went back and the doleful thrumming of a guitar vibrated the room. Garth felt sure then, but he said nothing to his wife until the end of the week when he returned home from work with a layoff slip. All that day a gloomy chord repeated itself.

"What does it mean?" she asked, after he had spoken.

"Don't know. And nobody to ask neither. That's the hard part. All we know's that he listens to me, and if it's good news he sings nice. Bad, well...." Garth saw her staring at the pink slip on the table and read her thoughts. "Don't worry, only temporary, I think. Till the new orders come in. Week, two at most." From the other room a viola called sonorously to singing strings that blended in and softened a run of tinkling piano keys. "Hear that? Good news."

Puzzling as it was, Garth was satisfied that he had solved the riddle of the boy's sad interludes and that he could again content himself with his paper. He felt relieved, too, to find no 'evil' in the music, and he chided his wife for 'losing sleep without good cause, and sulking 'round all day.' His words had little effect on her, however, and he, sensing her withdrawal, studied her with annoyance.

Second-guessing the outcome of news events was never more than a game Garth played to fill the quiet evening hours.

He had always expounded his theories off-handedly and, once said, dismissed them from mind. Until one evening when, after predicting a particularly ominous event, he noticed no change in the mellow music playing in the room. It was then that Garth began to carry a small pad and pencil in his shirt pocket. He confided nothing to his wife, who, self-absorbed, paid little attention to him and even less to the pad he held close to his eyes. Nor did she seem much concerned when he would suddenly drop his newspaper and thumb back through the pages in the pad to a certain place, stop and nod his head as if confirming something in his mind, or shake his head wonderingly and lick the tip of his stub pencil before adding something in.

Sometimes Beth would find herself staring at the boy, scrutinizing him, looking for long minutes into his eyes— neither the color of hers nor Garth's—eyes that seemed filled with love, or compassion, and which gazed back, searchingly, as if probing deep within her, beyond her, to some secret source of knowledge. At such moments his music came directly to her, grand and all-embracing, which both comforted and dismayed her.

Since the advent of the music she thought 'evil,' her face grew thinner, her hair grayer, her dark eyes more intense. To Garth she said nothing of her anxiety, for she had no words for it. Instead, she sought relief in the rigors of her labor and an insistence on orderliness that had lately manifested itself. Nothing moved that was not returned to its exact place, nothing dropped that was not immediately retrieved, nothing altered without her consent.

Her days were spent in unnamed desperation and, at night, after putting the child to bed, she would sit beside him, stroking him and gazing down at the placid face, studying the perfect upturn of his nose and the long golden lashes that curled to the outer corners where they touched his eyebrows, almost too faint to be seen. On one such night, as she sat running her fingers through his hair, she heard herself speak: "Child, who are you? What are you?"

Chapter 5

By the end of summer, conversation between the Garths had almost ceased to flow, like a stream going dry. She showed little awareness outside of herself and the child, who had given up interest in Garth's newspapers and rode his horse continuously by his mother's side. At times she would drop her sewing in her lap and lean over to whisper into his ear. His music would then rise to a sweeter pitch and she would return to her work, her features softened, her eyes shining out of the dark rings encircling them.

Squinting into the little book he meditated upon whenever he wasn't scouring his newspapers, Garth did not appear to notice or mind the ever-widening gulf between his wife and himself. The music was their only bond, the hub of their existence around which they orbited like silent, separate spheres.

*　*　*　*　*

October came not with the blue of sunny skies, but gray with rain and cold and with the shiver of approaching winter. Garth kept a hot fire on the hearth and sat close to it to drive the 'chill o' cold marble from my bones,' as he put it.

Sitting across from him, his wife rocked absently, her eyes dark on the child sitting at her feet. He had taken to staring into the dancing flames for long periods of time, and his music came low and cavernous, as if from a deep, subterranean place. From under her knitted brows his mother would watch the flames haloing his head, then call him up into her arms.

Curious at first, Garth soon lost interest and returned to the thoughts he had been so meticulously logging in his book. Unlike his wife's features that had of late grown more taut and pale, his had become animated. The green, ashen complexion that had for so long colored his craggy face was now brightened with a sanguineous tint. Had he noticed this in himself he might have attributed it to the steady slap of wind and rain on the job. And because his spirits were higher now, he no longer stayed up late to ponder his theories or study his newspapers, but went off to bed early, while his wife stayed behind, rocking the child as they gazed into the fire together.

One night when Garth came home from work, the house was particularly sweet with music and the aroma of bread baking in the oven. He shook the rain from his hat into the sink before hanging it on the hook. Next to it he hung his jacket. Grunting, he jerked his heavy boots off his feet and padded to the table, ready for the meat steaming on the plate. He sat opposite his wife, with the boy kneeling on his chair between them. Garth reached over and ruffled his hair. The boy sang out to him and reached back playfully. Garth ate hungrily, in silence.

The meal finished, the boy climbed off his chair carried his dish to the sink and ran off to play. Garth stared into his cup, watching the coffee slosh around with his rotating hand. His wife stacked several dishes, about to rise when Garth spoke:

"Sit, Beth."

She eased herself back and folded her hands in her lap.

"I think I got it figured, Beth. Don't know what it means, but it all makes sense 'cording to this here record." He tapped the little black book he slipped from his shirt pocket and tossed it on the table between them. Her eyes fell to it, then returned to him. "It's been hard on you, I know, my not saying much these past months, but I had to be sure 'fore I spoke." He gulped the last of his coffee and set the cup aside. Then he pulled his chair in close and leaned toward her, his voice low under the music drifting in from the parlor.

"Beth, the boy sees truth. I don't know how, but he does." He reached for the book, thumbed back through it and handed it across to her. "That page there is where I started, you check the date." She took the book and examined the page as he spoke. "Took me awhile to catch on. Like we noticed, ever' time I give out good news he'd sing prettier'n a canary, and if 'twere bad—" She tightened to hide her agitation.

"Now," he said, "that mightn't sound like much, but then I got to notice somethin' else. That's when I started keepin' that there record." He pointed to the book and leaned back, crossing one leg over the other. "Strange, awful strange, Beth." Her face twitched as if anticipating a new worry. "Couldn't tell right off, then I see it happenin'. Might be just dumb luck, I tells myself, or coincidence, so I gotta check around, wait to be sure." He stroked his jaw with his knuckles. "Well, tonight whiles I'm picking up my newspaper in town, I hear talk that Jackson's mill ain't goin' out o' business after all, only changin' hands."

"Everett—"

"Hold to it now, hold on, I'm gettin' there." He scratched the bottom of his foot. "Well, hearin' that cinches it for me, no doubt about it. For a long time I been noticin' how the afternoon train comin' along the spur past my place to Jackson's wasn't comin' so regular, and when she did, she weren't pullin' so many cars like before. Now you check maybe six, seven pages down and you'll see where I said Jackson's mill is closin' shop." She folded the book over, laying it on the table instead, waiting for him to finish.

Garth leaned suddenly forward with his hands flat on the table. "Don't you see, Beth? I was wrong, wrong as sin! You check me if you doubt my word. Check the paper inside my coat for news of what Jackson's done. The boy didn't sing sad when I spoke of Jackson's goin' under—like he knew better all the time. I tell you, Beth, the boy knew! Like he always knows. I make my theory and he listens. And he don't sing only to a thing's being good or bad, but to whether a thing's true or not. I don't understand how he knows, but he knows, sure as I know winter's comin'." He clenched his fists.

"You check back and you'll see he never misses. That's why I been followin' them newspapers so careful, always lookin' to see what comes true and what don't." He shook his head and his voice came low and forced. "That boy is always right and I don't know how he does it! It's a strange power he has, Beth, awful strange."

She lowered her head, staring down to her lap.

"Now there's no need for worry, Beth. I'm sure it's all a harmless thing with no hurt in it for him or us. Might even be some good in it somewhere...if we give it some thought." He watched her carefully, waiting for her response, while the music swelled and dropped in pitch for a moment before leveling off to its dulcet patterns.

After a few moments Garth began, hesitating, speaking in a hushed voice: "Maybe, just maybe—I mean, if Jonathan knows what's ahead..." She turned a stony face up to him. "...why not—"

"Use him?"

"Beth!"

"For profit?"

"No, Beth, but if we could know somethin' before—"

"Set him on your lap and take your notes so you can run off and make your bets somewhere?"

"For God's sake, woman, I was only thinkin' o' you." He raised his hands helplessly. "To get you out, to buy—"

"I won't hear of it!"

"For the boy then, Beth, think o' him. Them New York

25

doctors—"

"Never!" Her eyes burned into his.

"All right, Beth, all right. Just a thought. Anyways, I'm not keeping track no more. No need to." He started to push himself away from the table. "Listen to him in there, the way he sings so somber into that fire, like he's seeing things in it nobody else can. He's a strange one, he is," he said, fondling the little book in his hand, "awful strange."

She bore in on him with steely eyes. "Don't call him strange. Never call him strange again."

The force of her words startled him. "Why, Beth, I only meant to say—"

"He is blessed! Our son is blessed. Protect him, Everett. Protect him, or God help us all!"

Again they settled into the separate, silent pattern of their lives. He buried himself in his newspapers and she dwelt on thoughts of the child, on the frail, white body that seemed not to have grown in the past year. She felt his arms and noted the delicacy of the bones, stroked his cheeks and saw that they had lost their fullness. He was six years old now and should have been much taller, she thought.

Worried, she took to pressing larger portions of food on him, filling his plate half as much again. His bread she spread thick with butter and jams, and in between meals she tempted him with sweet pastries much to the delight of Garth, who would devour them all if she didn't hide them.

Her fears were allayed somewhat by the child's boundless energy, which displayed itself in his rocking and in the music that poured from him morning to night. Lately, too, he had taken to the polished stones Garth had brought home a year or two before. Each day he would take time to lift them from the box and let them sift through his fingers, like jewels in a treasure chest. He would study their colors, singing sweetly the way he did over the picked flowers his mother brought into the house in the warm months. Despite the nagging worries that would not go away, the woman found a semblance of peace in the passing seasons.

But it was not to last.

Chapter 6

It was in fact to last two years. On a quiet evening, as Garth and his wife sat entertaining their private thoughts, they were startled by the stomp of boots on the porch. Garth bounded out of his chair to the door, his wife an anxious and cautious distance behind. Amid the heavy-knuckled rapping, he threw open the door and glared into the bearded face squinting into the light falling across it. The man faltered a moment, then spoke:

"Mr. Garth—sorry for the hour, but we're here on business."

Garth appraised the face of the man, who grew suddenly resolute with the assurance of the men pressing behind him. "What business might that be?" Garth said, blocking his entry.

"Law business, Mr. Garth, law business."

Garth hesitated, then stepped aside.

His wife, standing in the archway between the rooms, watched them enter, single file, removing their hats as they came. She was grateful the child was asleep upstairs. She had lately added extra rest to the regimen designed to 'put meat on his bones.'

"I'm Kingston, Joseph Kingston," the bearded man began again.

"Councilman," Garth said coldly, "I know o' you."

"This here's Doc Waverly and," pointing to each, "Sheriff Longstreet; Josea Mackleroy—our next mayor; and Seth Lawson, Town Clerk." Each nodded in turn, but Garth gave no acknowledgment. The men's eyes darted furtively about the room.

"State your purpose," Garth said.

The councilman spoke again. "We've come to tell you, Mr. Garth—Mrs. Garth, with all due respect—" he nodded politely in her direction, "come to confirm—actually, to verify word of your son's infirmity."

Mrs. Garth inched closer to her husband, wringing the corner of the apron she still wore.

"Takes all o' you to check?" Garth said sardonically.

"Gus here is the one. Doc's got his orders from the judge to examine the boy. See if he's really too sick to attend school. Attendin' school's the law now, you know."

Doc Waverly slipped out from between them. "'Twasn't no more than hearsay, so far's the judge's concerned, Mr. Garth. Got to be legal and in accordance with the law. You can understand that, can't you—the law?"

Garth stood unmoving. "I know enough about the law to know you need a court order to come bargin' in here. Where is it?"

"Signed and sealed right here," the doctor said, drawing a long envelope from his vest pocket and handing the paper it contained to Garth.

Garth brought it close to his face, studied it a moment and thrust it back into the doctor's hands. His eyes fixed on each of the men, standing awkwardly, until each averted his face. "The boy's upstairs asleep. You'll have to come another time."

"I'll need but a few minutes to make my assessment," the doctor persisted, confident of his authority. "I think it best and in the interests of all that you let me see him now."

Sharp and dangerous as a shard of quarry marble, Garth's face hardened as he studied the older man before him, half his size. "Order or no, no man's got a right to enter my home!" He took a menacing step toward them.

"Everett!"

He turned to face his wife. "It's all right," she said.

Reluctantly, glowering, he stepped aside.

"Just the doc," he said, blocking the way of the others who had begun to follow. He listened to the footsteps going through the parlor. Out of the side of his mouth he called toward the stairs, "Only a few minutes, Doc, that's what you said."

Upstairs, Mrs. Garth lit the lamp and led the doctor into the small room. Gently, she tapped her son's shoulder and whispered into his ear. "Child?"

The boy twisted around and blinked against the light. His beginning smile faded with the sight of the man standing over him.

"This is a doctor," she said in a forced whisper. "Don't be afraid."

"Bring me a chair," the doctor said, his attention riveted on the face looking up to him. She brought the chair from the opposite corner and he sat, pulling it up close to the bed as he opened the bag at his side. He removed his stethoscope and, under the anxious eyes of Mrs. Garth, hovering close with silent prayers, proceeded to make his examination.

The boy lay still as the doctor checked his eyes, ears and throat, working down finally to the legs, which he tapped then elevated. He exercised the ankle and knee joints, rolled him over and tapped his back. He listened, looked and felt, and finally turned to the woman, puzzled. "I find nothing wrong with this lad," he said abruptly.

Trying to still her clasped hands, she glanced around nervously, as if for help. "He...something's wrong."

The doctor peered down to the boy, then back to her. "You mean his mind? Something wrong with his mind?"

She shook her head.

"Then what?" His tone hardened with impatience. "What's going on here, Missus? The lad's a might frail but he looks plenty okay to me. Good color, even." He adjusted his wire rim glasses onto the grooved bridge of his nose. "He can walk, can't he?"

She nodded.

"Word has it—well, look, something peculiar is afoot here. You'd better tell me what you think is wrong 'cause I have to report my findings. The law re—"

She strangled out the words: "He can't speak." She turned away.

"Mute?" He pondered the thought, then drew another tongue depressor from his bag. "Move that light here closer," he said, peering down the boy's throat. "Don't see nothing unusual here. A spot of redness is all." He pressed his fingers against the boy's throat, probing around to the sides. "Seems all right to me." He sat back, pursing his lips and tapping his knee. "'Course—did he ever talk?"

She shook her head.

"Ever any serious illness, fever and such?" He watched her closely as he spoke.

"No."

He leaned over the boy's face. "Say something, boy... Jonathan. Know who I am?"

The boy gazed up to him.

"Know who this lady is?"

The child smiled to her and she held her breath.

"Who's the lady, Jonathan, who is she?"

His smile widened, then faded.

"Least he hears. Understands too." The doctor snapped shut his bag, put his hands on his knees, pursed his lips, sighed and rose. He stood there a moment, silently appraising the boy before turning to go. "Might see what you can do about finding a specialist, Missus. Some fine ones in New York City." He glanced at the surroundings. "But they cost. Anyway, whatever his problem, he's beyond my help, that's sure. Meantime I'll make my recommendations."

"Doctor—"

He raised his hand. "Don't ask what they might be. You'll be knowing soon enough."

They were half way down the stairs when the doctor stopped suddenly, listening. A step behind him, she froze. A cry, sharp and keening carried in. "What in the name of—what's that?" he said, cocking his head.

"Cat."

"Mournful creature," he said, and started down ahead of her.

From the door Garth watched them troop down the path into the darkness, the low murmuring and the crunch of gravel under their feet fading into the night. He turned, confronting her agonized face.

"Everett...."

"Now, Beth—"

"Everett, I'm afraid."

"Nonsense, Beth. He didn't sing, I know. I think maybe ever'thin's gonna be all right."

"Everett, do something!"

"Anyways, what's to be done?" His anger erupted. "We're trapped! I can't take a pick and break us free like a piece o' them mountains out there." He gestured out to them and ran his fingers through his hair. Her eyes held him, imploring him. He threw out his hands, large and callused with a green tint to them. "I only got but these two hands. And they can just hardly keep our bellies full and a roof over our head."

He took her by the shoulders. "Beth, what can I do?" But her eyes were strong against him. He released her and dropped into his chair by the table. He laid his head over his arms. "Nothing to do but wait. The boy didn't sing, far as I heard, 'cept for that one sound." He lifted his head to his wife, standing above him, tall and still and cold as a statue. "He didn't, did he?" He sat back. "No, 'course not. Otherwise, the doc'd not o' been so calm leavin'. So there's a good chance the court'll see it our way yet and leave us alone."

He reached to touch her hand, but she pulled it stiffly into the folds of her apron. He turned away, holding his head. "Get some rest, Beth. It's been a hard day. No use to think more on it now."

* * * * *

Word was not long in coming. Beth was setting the table, the child helping, when Garth came in. His face, long as the envelope protruding from his pocket, put fright into her. The bowl dropped from her hand and cracked on the table. The music ceased, then started again, deep and brooding.

The meal went untouched except for the slice of bread Garth ate dryly. The letter lay on top of the newspaper on the drain board, and its message—the words he did not want to see or bring home—passed through his mind again: *...shall not be deprived... until more appropriate arrangements... enrollment... duly constituted....*

Sitting in the parlor that evening after the boy was asleep, they spoke—he spoke: "It's a fearsome thing, Beth, I know, and I feel it too, though you might not think it."

Head back and eyes closed, she rocked slowly to his words reaching out softly to her.

"But think on it, Beth. It mightn't be so bad. After all, we can't keep him cooped up and caged here forever. Where's the future in that? There's a point o' logic in what they say, too, 'bout the boy learning' though he can't speak." He leaned forward, earnest in his appeal. "Now listen, there's no harm can come of it if the boy don't sing. And he don't have to. You tell

him, make him understand, Beth. He listens to you. Ever'
word. I seen it. Seems he's listenin' to words you *don't* speak
sometimes, like he knows your thinkin'."

Garth fell back in his chair. "You got four days to get it into
his head that he don't never sing outside this house. You make
him understand that, Beth. You make him!"

Chapter 7

The morning soon came, bright with long rays of cold sunshine. In the kitchen Beth knelt before her child and buttoned the heavy brown sweater she had knitted for him. His eyes were alive and he was singing a repetitious little melody into her face, tilting his head from side to side as he did so. She ran her hands down his body, more as if to assure herself he were there than to straighten the lines of his clothing.

She gripped him by the shoulders. "Now listen to me, child, listen to me." He stopped singing and looked into her eyes. "You must never sing outside this house, never! Keep a silence like you truly have no tongue, no matter what." She stood up, searching him critically. "We've little time and a long walk ahead, so you keep up to me." From the table she took the small bag containing a sandwich, an apple and a biscuit, surveyed the room once and went out the door with his hand firmly in hers.

It was over two miles to the school house, a run-down, clapboard building housing two classrooms. As they walked she recalled the visions she'd once had of her child one day sitting in one of those rooms, learning to read, write and cipher. She remembered secretly running her hand over the swell of life stirring inside, and the deep sense of joy and apprehension she felt for it as she and Garth passed the school on the way to town. It seemed a lifetime ago.

She glanced down at the child, who every few steps had to run to keep up with her steady stride. The sun was climbing between the mountains and the air grew warmer. The brilliance of his hair in the sunlight surprised her. And she grew annoyed by the dust collecting on his shoes. "Pick your feet up, child, pick up your feet." Occasionally he tried to pull away from her, to reach the wild flowers growing along the road, but she held him tight to her side now. "No time for that today," she snapped. "Come along."

They were little more than half way there when the open yards of Burke's mill came into view on the right. The area was cluttered with shards and slabs and great blocks of white-veined marble stacked high, green as the ocean her father had once taken her to see. Burke's mill was Garth's place of work and she kept a watchful eye in that direction for him. Then she saw him, far off, where he said he would be, standing and waving to them from the top of a pile of marble rubble. She waved back briefly to acknowledge him, and pointed him out to the child, who could not seem to find him at first. She resented Garth's being there instead of with her, leaving her to shoulder the burden alone. But he had overridden her protests: "Can't afford to lose the time...." His excuses gave her little comfort.

Her breath came short and she felt tired. The walk was tedious and she had slept poorly. All night she had dreamed of music, mad, rushing music as from the big pipes of church organs that drowned her in sound, suffocating and tormenting her and calling up faces, faces of strange children swimming before her, with Jonathan in the midst of them, his tortured face pleading for her help, and she, paralyzed by a man's finger poking in her face, trying to call, "Everett! Everett!" who sat in deafness reading his newspaper....

At last the child saw his father, and music welled up, full-throated and sweet, then bursting forth climactically. She clapped her hand over his mouth and pulled his face into her skirt. "Hush, child!" she admonished, glancing around before turning his face up to hers. "Keep in mind what I told you!" When she was sure he understood, she released him and led him on, while he looked longingly back to his father, small and distant and dark against the mountains.

The schoolhouse loomed ahead, gray and scaling in the morning light. It lay caught in a fork of the road, which in one direction swept by it and around a pine grove into town. On the other side it cut a dark swath between barren fields where it ran straight to the vanishing point.

It was down that road, Barrow Road, she had come so many years ago, so full of hope and girlish dreams. She had been a little frightened then, and she remembered locking her arm into Everett's, listening to the confident drawl of his words as they rode. His character was strong as his arm and there was nothing he didn't know, nothing she would not have once he was out of the 'pits,' as he had called it. "Only a short while," he had said. And all his promises of "runnin' the mill, maybe ownin' a piece of it someday," were no more than the dust blowing out from under the carriage wheels carrying her to the miserable little house no one else would have—'Only temporary, o' course.' She thought of her father—

The child's tugging at her hand brought her sharply back. Together they crossed the road and went up the gravel drive toward the schoolhouse. Her eyes were on the building, much larger and more frightening up close, and she was only vaguely conscious of the sharp stones cutting into the thin soles of her shoes. When they were within twenty yards of the entrance, she pulled the child off the path into the shade of an old maple tree. She knelt without touching her knee to the ground and spoke in earnest whispers as her hands worked nervously over his clothing.

"Child, you must never sing. People—" The word caught in her throat "—people would not understand."

She slapped the dust from his socks and the tops of his shoes. "Hear me, child. There's nobody to hurt you and no need to fear. Just sit and listen and pay no mind to what some may say." She held his face and looked into the wide blue eyes, looking deep into her own. "In just a short while you'll be coming out that door and I'll be standing here waiting." She rose and took a deep breath. "Come," she said, taking his hand. "And remember!" She looked hard at him, as if to reassure herself, then started resolutely for the door, with the child in tow. "Don't waste none," she said, handing him his lunch.

As they reached the platform at the top of the steps, the door swung open and a woman, considerably younger than herself, she guessed, stood on the single step above the platform, bracing a book against her bosom. Her face was smooth and white as chalk and her hair was swept around to the side, secured by a thick-spined comb. The loose folds of her dress —of burlap color and texture— did not disguise her slenderness or her rigidity as she peered down as if from a pedestal.

"Mrs. Garth. We've been waiting."

"Well, you needn't wait longer. He's here now." She nudged him. "Go," she said. "And pay heed to what I said."

Turning abruptly and staring straight ahead, she descended the stairs to the path and down the drive to the juncture in the road. There she stopped, and only then did she look back to the gray wall that separated her from her child for the first and only time since Garth had taken him to see the doctor in Torrence.

For a long while she stood there biting her lip against the helplessness that threatened to overwhelm her. The door between them was closed and the long, rectangular windows glared back at her with the reflected light of the sun rising over the mountains to the east. The sun warmed her neck and though sweat beaded her forehead, her hands were cold. A chill ran through her body. "No music," she whispered. "Please, child, no music."

A prickly heat danced on her bosom and a dizziness swept over her. She thought she heard music and she looked anxiously to the door, waiting for the crying rush of children. None came and she admonished herself for her foolishness and her frailty. She tried thinking pleasant thoughts. She thought of Everett and she saw dust, brown and green; she thought of the child suckling against her, and she heard the wild rush of music pounding in her ears; she thought of her father, and she felt him tearing her hands from his coat. "Everett!" she cried, "Everett!" But only the sound of a silent world humming in her ears came to her.

She fell.

Chapter 8

Images floated up as if seen through water: her father's pendulous face, the cheerful eyes appraising her as she cuddled in the warm hollow of his lap, while his thick fingers rolled a lock of her hair between them. "Angel down," he said, and she heard his heart beat as she hugged his chest.

Her mother's face wavered up, first with tears in her eyes and pins in her mouth as she mended and stitched and talked incessantly, complaining of the 'the ruin'; then, uncomplaining, with the pinched features of her face relaxed and fixed in death, her rouged cheeks the color of the satin pillow caressing them.

And the big house loomed, peeling long, yellow flakes, the new sign nailed to the door, closed to her forever. And Everett, drifting in to take her away to a better life, shining and bright in his black suit, talking promises, talking dreams and finally pointing ahead on Barrow Road.

She saw herself again, a young girl alone, sitting near the stream behind her house. Fresh air, plenty of fresh air, the doctor had said after the fever that had held her so long had finally broken. It came gradually at first, like the humming of insects, sounds very much like those she had heard when in the delirium of her fever. For days it continued, and she listened to the buzzing that grew louder and seemed to come from everywhere, like vibrations, crude and undefined. She feared getting sick again, until one day as she grabbed for the elusive minnows in the water, she heard it, music sifting among the flowers. Unafraid she listened with curiosity and wonder.

She said nothing of the secret world she had discovered, and returned each morning to the same place, waiting for the music to begin anew. Soon she learned to distinguish between the sounds and could determine their source. The flowers sang lilting, happy notes, trilling in a way that seem to translate itself in her mind into the color yellow, so that the flowers and the sun were somehow one to her. From the grass came the quivering of strings, bowing up and flickering like stars, going beyond her range of hearing and back again. Out of the water leaped a rainbow spectrum of melodies, pleasing and bright. From the distant mountains, like a somber undercurrent reminiscent of the darkest of nights, swelled a brooding lament of bellows and horns and bass chords. Beneath the building symphony that lifted and carried her up, the earth itself pulsed a single motif, unifying the whole, far-reaching as the horizon circumscribing the earth. And the wind came to set the tempo, creating rhythms and carrying melodies mingled in blended harmonies, which suggested to her the joy of all living things for life.

She saw her father again, approaching, a huge man out of breath, with his deep concern for her flushing his face. "Bethany," he called, "child, it's growing chilly. Come inside. You are not yet well."

"Listen, Papa," she said, taking his hand, "listen. Can you hear it, the music?" She faced the wind, blowing out her dark hair.

"Music, Beth? Music?" She remembered him standing over her, a shaggy eyebrow cocked, gazing down at her with anxious eyes, the way she had seen them whenever he talked about business.

"Yes, Papa, can't you hear it, the flowers singing, the trees, the whole world?"

He looked off into the distance with her. "Like everything is singing for me, Papa—to me. Oh, say you can hear it, Papa, say you can."

"Yes, Beth, I can hear it now," he said, patting her head. "Come, come with me back to the house. You must not get sick again before you're well."

She remembered his telling her mother, and their somber faces as they put the questions to her: "Does the rose bush sing? Does the garden sing? And the stars, do they sing, too?"

She remembered too her discomfort when the admonishments came, gentle at first, and her anguish when they grew more severe: "You're twelve years old now, Beth," her mother said. "It's high time you set aside those childish imaginings. They're not healthy in a girl your age."

"But Mama—"

"Enough! People are going to start wondering about us. Bad enough your papa's business is lagging so, without your bringing suspicions to his house."

"Papa," she implored, pulling at his sleeve, pleading for his intervention, the final word in that house. He turned from her to gaze out the window. During the long silence she saw his worried hands squeezed behind his back and recognized the defeat in the slope of his shoulders.

"Your mother's right, Bethany. It will bring no good on our heads to go on telling that story. Let's hear no more of it."

"But you heard, Papa, outside with me, remember? The music of the flowers, of the trees. Tell Mama—"

He faced 'round to her, looking down into her eyes with his own, dark in his tired face, and she knew, knew he had been pretending all along. "Beth—"

"You lied!" she screamed. "You lied to me!"

"Beth!" He reached out for her, but she broke away violently, her words choked as she dashed from him out the door.

Thereafter she grew distant. Keeping to herself, she spent the hours wandering through the fields, sometimes sitting in the shadows of the trees spreading their low-hanging boughs over the stream. She knew she was not 'touched,' as her mother had suggested. And soon she came not to care what they thought. It was enough to hear the world singing, singing to her, beautiful melodies she could not imitate with her voice, but could hear in her head, even when she lay in bed late at night with the windows closed. Sometimes when it rained she would slip outside to stand in it and listen to its sad song drown out the music of the moon and the stars, cloaked in the darkness of the night. The poignancy and melancholy of the music soothed the unnamed disturbances of her soul.

One afternoon, still sleepy after the nap she had taken in the shade of the old hickory tree on the stream bank, she returned to the house. Upon entering she saw her father dozing in his armchair, and across from him, in the center of the parlor, a piano.

His eyes opened slowly. "Bethany?"

"Yes, Papa."

He nodded toward the piano, an ebony grand with polished ivory keys. "For you, child. Music you can make yourself."

She burst into tears, not knowing why, and rushed from the room, his voice calling after her, "Beth, wait—" and shut off with the slam of her door. She did not come downstairs until dinner time. Only her mother was there, as rigid as the straight back chair she sat in.

Beth sipped her soup quietly as her mother's eyes brooded over her, observing the sheen of her black hair brushed smoothly over her shoulders, and the fine black down beginning to emerge on her arms. "Cruel. You're a cruel one to shut your father out of your life this way."

"I—"

"And him, with money going faster than he can bring it in, going out to buy that piano—for you!" She sneered. "And this is his reward!"

Beth dropped her spoon, listening to the voice that cut like a knife. She could not speak, could not choose from the many words that rushed in to be expressed.

"So cruel! Don't you see his failing health? His color gone? His voice grown thin as his face? Working himself to death in a business already dead, which he should have been done with years ago? Heartless!"

So she agreed, reluctantly, to take lessons, but they never worked out. No sound could be coaxed from the instrument that could begin to emulate the music she heard in her head, not even the sonatas and waltzes her instructor played to arouse her interest. For hours she would sit there alone, staring down at the silent keys until, able to bear it no more, she would rush miserably to her room and bury her face in her pillow.

The piano had to be removed and like a bird set free she again flew to the fields. An immense silence settled over the house. No longer did her mother remind her that it was unnatural for a girl her age to be without friends. And, except for the occasional murmuring between her parents speaking out of earshot, conversations dried up at meal times.

Her mother's face, brooding over the table, seemed forever pinched in worry. But her mother could never touch her heart the way her father did. A permanent tremble shook his hands, and he carried his head obliquely, eyes averted, as if to conceal the thousand worries etched in his face. He became increasingly reticent, as if prey to an infinite melancholy that engulfed him like an endless night. All sighs, he moved sluggishly, an exhausted old man who seemed to live despite himself....

She saw herself, then, facing up to the strange man who kept poking his finger into her face. She could not remember his face, only the hard, colorless eyes and the dirty hairs sprouting from his nose. "Do you still hear the music?" he asked in his stern doctor's voice, and shaking his finger. "Tell me, do you still hear the music?" And next to him, always, stood the nurse with her plaster face and wooden smile. "How are you feeling today?" the doctor said, looking down his pointing finger.

"Fine," the nurse interposed, with her fingers gouging her shoulder, "just fine, wouldn't you say, Bethany?"

And she, Beth, would nod to the nurse's question that wasn't a question at all. Then they would go off to the side, the doctor and the nurse, glancing over their shoulders as they discussed her, and he would leave.

She recalled the terror of that first day when her father and mother brought her to the institution. She was going to the hospital, he had told her, for examinations, not long—a week or two.

Ahead, she saw it looming against the morning sky, dark and naked, a grotesque building of mortared brick and stone, rising like a castle fortress with iron bars gridding the windows. She cried out. They led her weeping up the long flight of stone steps, clutching her bag. Their footsteps echoed from the marble floor as they passed through the foyer to a cavernous room.

An oppressive gloom filtered in through the skylights of the vaulted ceiling. She wept. "Papa," she cried, clinging to his arm, "take me away, please, Papa."

And he, patting her head, not looking at her, said, "For a while, Beth, only a little while. Don't be afraid. Papa wouldn't let anything happen to you. These people are friends, here to help you."

"Mama," she begged, "Mama!" But her mother's eyes were dark before her.

The doctor and an elderly nurse with a shrunken face and

yellow-gray hair severely combed and tied in a bun met them in the center of the great room. The nurse took her bag and led her off by the wrist to the side, out of hearing range of her parents and the doctor with the hard, colorless eyes, who nodded judiciously as her father spoke close to his ear.

She grew dizzy with the mingled smells of medicine, dust and wax, and with the sight of an aged man shuffling across to a wicker chair which he eased himself into. He leaned forward, grinning a toothless smile and staring at her with dark, gaunt eyes that contrasted with the white skin of his fragile chest, exposed with his private parts when his green-striped kimono slipped open.

She struggled to free herself from the nurse's iron grip. Then she saw them coming to her, all together.

"This is your doctor, Beth," her father said in a hollow voice. "He'll be taking care of you and make you better."

"No, Papa, take me home with you. Please. I promise to be good, Papa."

"Now, Beth—" He could not look at her.

"Papa!" she pleaded, reaching for him. "Don't leave me here, not here. Take me with you. I won't be trouble to you anymore. Promise, Papa, promise!"

"For a while, child, only a while. Papa wouldn't lie. Trust me." His voice was choked. "You just follow doctor's orders."

"Bethany!" Her mother's eyes bore into her.

"Mama, why? Why, Mama?"

"For your own good. Listen to your father."

The doctor stepped close. "I think perhaps...."

"Yes," her father said, understanding. He bent down to kiss her goodbye.

She cried out, begging, clawing at him, clinging. Anguished, he tore her hands slowly free of his coat. He retreated a step and she flung herself at his feet, clutching his trousers.

The doctor nodded to the nurse, whose hands went around her arms like shackles. Backing away, her father faltered, as if unable to stand. He turned, his wife supporting him. His voice strained: "Pull yourself together, Beth. Behave." He hid his face. "Listen to the good doctor."

"Papa oh dear God no Papa not here alone please Papa don't leave me don't leave me here."

Horrified she watched them move away, receding slowly, as if in a dream. Her voice came as a whisper: "No, Papa." They drifted through the door, their footsteps dying away. Her scream, tearing off the last syllable of 'Papa,' rent the air. She remembered the hand clapped over her mouth and the room swirling inside her head.

The images flashed in disordered sequences after that, like fragments of an endless nightmare: the yellow tile walls echoing with cries that came like a madness in the night; her own stony silence against the poking finger; the little room where no flowers bloomed or sunlight shone; the ice-water baths; and finally the table where they strapped her down to receive the lightning that exploded in her head.

It was two years later that she walked down those same stone steps, no longer afraid or caring as she descended between her father and mother. She did not look at them, not at the stark, grim woman to her left nor to the spent, stooped man holding her arm. She did not know them anymore, nor did she know that the shine from her hair, her skin, her eyes was gone. The world did not sing to her. The music no longer came, had never come at all, she was sure now.

In the months that followed, she spoke little and kept to her room. She did not hear the ravings of her father, downstairs, railing against the steadfastness of her mother:

"It was a mistake," he cried, "God forgive us."

"We had no choice. People talking, saying how odd she was, that she—"

"Damn the people!" He raised clenched fists. "I've killed my Beth, my daughter, for their good opinion."

"Don't blame yourself. If it's somebody you must blame, blame me. It was my idea to send her there." Her chest heaved with her words.

"No, it was my word put her there, my signature. It was I who turned his back when she cried out for help. In my sleep I hear her yet, calling, 'Papa, Papa.'" He covered his ears.

"You didn't know. We didn't know. We did what we thought best for her, for us."

He pulled his hair. "We've lost her. Killed her. An angel who heard God's own voice in everything she saw and touched... Oh, Lord, what have I done?" He fell back in his chair, holding his face.

Tears dampened her eyes. "You must not punish yourself, Samuel." She came to him and put her hand on his shoulder. "You did what you had to do, what any man would have done in your place. It was a mistake born of caring, of caring too much."

Slowly he lifted his face. "I've murdered Innocence."

"Out of love."

"Then love be damned!"

She pulled his head to her skirts. "You must not think that. You wanted to save her. How could you know? How could anyone know?"

"I have taken a flower and trampled it into the ground. A thing of beauty and love and... she hates me."

"Someday she will understand, she will know your heart."

"No. She is a thing unfeeling now, cold and sterile. Do you see how she looks at me, the way she freezes me with her eyes? She does not speak, but I know her thoughts, her contempt, her—"

"It's not you, don't you see? The hospital, that is what has poisoned her." She dropped her hand and moved away from him to the window where she stood looking out. "When you are at the factory she is the same. All day she stands here, on this very spot, gazing out to the fields, seeing…I don't know what… standing so still, for hours unmoving, taking nothing to eat, saying nothing. I speak to her, but she doesn't answer, only stares ahead." She turned back to him. "If it is anyone she hates, truly hates, I am that one. She has hated me long before this…this. And I have never known why."

He started up, his mouth opening to speak.

"No," she said, "hear me. You were always too absorbed in her to see, or away to work, but she has long since put me out of her life. She has never allowed me to feel the mother that I am, the mother I had always hoped to be. Perhaps in my concern for her I was too demanding. I did not tolerate the frivolities in her that other mothers might ignore in their own daughters. I would teach her to be a lady."

"My dear—"

"No." She stiffened. "What I did I did as much for you as for myself, to make you proud of her. And I have endured her coldness for a much longer time than you have. I have learned to live with it. It has not been easy but I do not punish myself. Whatever I have done, right or wrong, I have done with good intentions…."

And Everett again floating in, he the last of many brought in as possible suitors, the only one who hadn't been driven off by her melancholy, working for her father, helping to hold the business together, at the end working only for his keep. Everett there, encouraging; Everett there, understanding; Everett, always there with his plain smile and his hand extended….

Chapter 9

Bethany Garth was surprised to find herself lying on the road, her cheek in the dust, staring through the shimmering heat waves to the pointed end of Barrow road. Climbing steadily, the sun was high in the sky as she staggered to her feet and swayed in the hot light. Everett's face was still in her mind and she contemplated it bitterly as she spit the dust from her mouth and wiped it from her face and brushed it from her skirts. And when school let out she was there, stiff and straight, a dark shadow waiting beneath the spread of the old maple tree.

That evening Garth sat across from his wife, watching the boy ride his horse. "Listen to him sing, Beth. Just like I said, no cause for worry."

She rocked slowly, her attention riveted on the child, who was singing for her, to her, she was sure.

"Still think you should o' stayed to ask how he did. I suppose ever'thin' went just fine though or he wouldn't be singin' so nice. And look how he's aclutchin' that book." Garth folded his paper on his knees. "Sure wisht I could o' gone along this mornin'," he said, half-apologetically. "I know it was hard doin' it alone but, see, you didn't need me after all." He was studying the boy as he spoke, contemplating how he might build him something bigger to ride than the sewing box, and did not see her face turn to ice.

* * * * *

For the boy it had gone well. Miss Lapham, his teacher, had led him to a seat directly in front of her and, after a long, imperious look down at him, returned to her task as though he were not there. Rumors of course had preceded his coming and she had to rap her ruler sharply against her desk to quell the excitement. The boy seemed unaware of the curious eyes on him and, with hands folded on his desk, fixed his attention on Miss Lapham, who grew irritated by his steady gaze. At recess he was left to himself while the other children, under the stern eye of their teacher, huddled together whispering secrets. Though she had warned against maliciousness, trouble came to visit on the third day.

Miss Lapham had turned them out to play behind the schoolhouse and momentarily absented herself. Sitting on one of the stumps cut from a log that had been placed around, the boy watched the activities in the yard. Two boys playing leapfrog worked their way close to him. The boy recognized the redhead as the one who had jabbed his elbow into his ribs the previous day.

When they were near him they stopped. The redhead faced him, hands on his hips.

Behind him stood his friend, slightly smaller, with large ears and light hair that fell over his eyes. He too stood with hands on hips.

"Why don'tcha play?" the redhead said.

"Yeah, play," his friend repeated.

A humming began in the boy's throat.

"Whatsa matter, cat got your tongue?" the redhead said, his fake smile revealing the gap where his front teeth were missing.

"Yeah, your tongue?"

The boy watched him, feeling danger creep out to him.

The redhead circled him warily. "Don'tcha like us?"

The boy turned on his seat with him. He smiled.

"Hey, Leroy," the redhead called over his shoulder, "he's

51

smiling and I didn't even tell a joke." He worked his way in closer. The boy leaned toward him and he backed off. "My pa says your folks is haunted."

"Yeah, haunted."

"Are you haunted too?"

The boy's smile faded.

"Boo!" The redhead laughed and circled in again.

"Boo!"

"Look out, Leroy, I think he's getting mad. Maybe he's cuckoo like my pa says his folks is." He stepped in, shoved the boy and jumped back.

The boy stood up, facing him. He did not like the feeling coming from the redhead nor the unfamiliar feeling growing in himself. He glanced around for Miss Lapham, but saw only the other children playing. He was not sure of what to do. He had never felt fear the way he felt it then, but he knew he could not run from it.

"Pa says your ma's a witch."

"Witch," Leroy parroted.

"A witch with horns." He laughed through his gapped teeth. "You got horns too?" He dashed in, ruffled the boy's hair and leaped back. "Stay away, Leroy, I think he's getting madder. Look at his face now." He almost sang the words, taunting the boy.

"And she sleeps in the fireplace."

"Yeah, fireplace."

"Jonathan's ma sleeps in the fireplace." He started to chant. Other children looked up. A few started toward them.

"Jonathan's ma...sleeps in the fireplace." He started to clap and more children drifted in.

"Fireplace," repeated Leroy, shaking the hair out of his eyes.

"Jonathan Garth...sleeps on the hearth..." He sang louder

and the rest of the children came running.

"Jonathan Garth…sleeps on the hearth…"

Gathering round and clapping time, the children joined in:

"Jonathan Garth…sleeps on the hearth…"

"Jonathan Garth…sleeps on the hearth…"

Laughing, the redhead leaped out suddenly and tweaked the boy's nose. Bewildered the boy glanced around to the laughing faces taunting him.

Again the redhead rushed him but this time the boy caught him in his arms and carried him to the ground. The redhead struggled to free himself as the boy pressed down on him, burying his head between the flailing arms until his mouth was next to his ear. The redhead cried out as a low, deep hum reverberating through his body, vibrated his internal organs and sent his body into spasms.

The chanting suddenly turned to shouts as the children scrambled at the sight of Miss Lapham flying toward them brandishing her ruler.

* * * * *

Each morning and afternoon Mrs. Garth made the trip to and from school with her son. His spirits never flagged and each evening his music came richer and embroidered with overtones neither she nor Garth had ever heard before. Garth grew more relaxed with time, but she, though less tense, could not rid herself of the anxieties that grayed her hair further and deepened the ridges of her brow. Each night as she tucked the child's covers around him she pressed her warning on him, and again in the morning when she left him at the school.

The passing days cooled fast with autumn winds, and she dreaded the coming snow. The journey was long and tedious, especially those two each day she made alone. Occasionally

Garth could be seen waving from the distant marble heap and the boy would sing out to him. She no longer forbade it, for Garth had assured her no one else worked that section of the yard.

Chapter 10

In early November the boy uttered his first sound in class, a deep bass note that rose vibrantly to an upper register. Miss Lapham's impeccable fingers stopped the globe she had been rotating for the geography lesson. The class focused on the boy with an interest they hadn't shown since the day of his fight with the redhead in the school yard.

"What's that?" Miss Lapham said, zeroing in on the boy. "What did I hear?"

Entranced by the globe on her desk, the boy went silent. She approached him, tapping the ruler in her hand and asking again. The boy's eyes did not waver. Frustrated, she stood over him a long moment before returning to her desk and ordering the others back to their books.

For a time she sat erect at her desk, hands clasped beneath her chin, studying the boy, wondering what she had heard, if she had heard anything at all. Lately, she had hardly been aware of his presence. Nor did she worry anymore whether he was learning anything. She appraised him critically, noting his eyes, blue as the globe before her that so fascinated him, eyes seemingly as large; the purity of his hair, so like a mythological god; the cheeks, more colorful than they were the day he'd first come—deep-red summer roses—with a cherub's lips the same color; the wrists and neck delicately protruding from the homespun sweater he wore. She found him strangely appealing, if somewhat mystifying, and dismissed the matter from mind. If he could speak she would know soon enough. She would know if he was of sound mind, too. She rose and called attention.

The next morning as she was speaking of the United States,

pointing to it on the globe, the tapping of snare drums and the trill of flutes escaped the boy. Miss Lapham turned sharply. Her breath caught in her throat. She stood rigid, unable to speak. The children erupted from their hush and tumbled in their seats. Miss Lapham ordered them to silence. The music had come only as a short burst but she was certain now that what she had heard—what they all had heard—was no quirk of the imagination.

She walked the aisles, enforcing silent work. Her hands fidgeted with the ruler. She paced, trying to understand, unable to concentrate on her duties. Many small transgressions escaped her notice.

After school had let out she stood in the window and watched the boy run to greet his mother standing beneath the old maple tree. She considered talking to her but she remembered the coldness of their last meeting and decided against it. It wasn't until several days later, when she heard the unmistakable fragment of a hymn accompany the word 'Bethlehem' that she decided to act.

* * * * *

At the appointed time two evenings later, Miss Lapham sat in the office of Mr. P.R. Jennings, town father in charge of sundry affairs, Education included.

"Really, Miss Lapham," he was saying, "a mute who sings!"

"Not sings, exactly, sir. It's more like…musical instruments, real musical instruments."

He leaned forward on his desk, smiling benignly. "You mean he can imitate the sounds of musical instruments." He leaned back. "For a mute I suppose that's a considerable accomplishment, and perhaps we should reevaluate his medical condition. However, it takes no great talent—"

"Sir, it's more than simple mimicry. The sounds are distinctly those of *real* instruments. Forgive my seeming immodesty, but my musical training—"

"Miss Lapham," he interrupted, "how many pupils are in your charge?"

"Sir?"

"At any given time how many children are under your supervision?"

"Twenty, sir."

"Of several ages?"

"Yes, sir."

"Miss Lapham, much mischief can occur when twenty children are thrown together. I must confess," he said wryly, "as one who was once a boy, I know whereof I speak."

"Sir, I can assure you—"

He turned brusque, intimidating. "Surely, Miss Lapham, you're not insisting I take this seriously."

"Sir, I understand your skepticism." She avoided his narrow gaze. "With all due respect...I know it sounds incredible," she faced him directly, "but I am absolutely certain of what I say."

He raised a weary hand. "Miss Lapham, you're not the first to report strangeness in the Garth family. For years, twenty at least, rumors have circulated regarding them—witchcraft, hauntings, Devil worship—none ever substantiated, to be sure. But this... this, whatever it is, defies reason itself."

"Sir, believe me, what I say to you here is God's own truth. And I am not overwrought as you may suspect, I assure you."

Sighing, he leaned back, tapping his vest and contemplating the sensitive features of her face, the determined and delicate curve of her jaw. He noted the tremble of her clasped hands, and wondered why so attractive a woman wore no ring. "The children of course heard this… this phenomenon?"

"They have been speaking of nothing else these past two days."

"Yes, well, I imagine they would, wouldn't they?" He pondered a moment. "Have you mentioned this unusual affair to anyone else?"

She glanced away. "To my gentleman friend, sir." She looked back to him. "Mr. William Hathoway. We hope to be married when…" She altered her words, fearing she was telling too much "…when we are able."

"Ah, yes, the bank clerk. Fine young man. I know him well enough to say he's a credit to the institution and will go far." He patted the contented bulge of his stomach. "And if I'm not being too personal, might I ask how your Mr. Hathoway reacted to this account of yours?"

"He listened, sir. Said nothing."

"He didn't laugh or ridicule you?"

"No, sir."

"Or call you mad?"

"Oh, no, sir."

He paused. "Only during geography lessons, you say?"

"Sir?"

"The music. It comes only during geography lessons?"

"And his eyes never leave the globe."

He grasped the arms of his chair and stood. "No, no, this is preposterous. Impossible!" He rubbed the watch chain slung from his vest; then, glowering under the fallen hank of white hair at the woman nervously perched at the edge of her chair, he said, "This will not go at all favorably on your record if you are mistaken, Miss Lapham—and I'm afraid you are. However, speak of this to no one. The years have perhaps softened my mind and I'd not care to have news of it bandied about."

"Then you'll send someone to investigate, sir?"

His voice boomed. "I'll come myself!"

He saw her to the door and closed it behind her. For a moment he stood there wondering if he were as mad as she.

The following morning Mr. P. R. Jennings found himself feeling somewhat ridiculous on the long narrow bench in the rear of the school room. Curiously polite and politely curious, the children filed in past him to their seats. The younger ones giggled and snickered until Miss Lapham's ruler cracked sharply on the desk.

"We have a visitor with us today, children," she said, "Mr. Jennings. And we do not wish to offend him with rude behavior, do we?"

Heads swiveled in awe of the figure, whose stature seemed to grow with the mere mention of his famous name. The boy did not turn.

Heart fluttering, she launched ahead, her concentration torn between Mr. Jennings, whose threat she painfully recalled, and the boy, who watched fascinated as she slowly rotated the globe with her fingertips.

"…United States of America…the United States is where we live," she said, and her eyes flashed to the boy. He remained silent. "Europe…is where our forefathers came from many years ago." No sound came but that of her own hollow voice. Restraining panic, she continued, calling names and naming places. "The world…" she spun the globe rapidly, "…the world is where all the people live."

Desperately she tried, even as Mr. Jennings without a word or glance in her direction moved ponderously over the wooden floor that squeaked under his weight.

"The pyramids," she cried as he approached the door. "Bethlehem," she pleaded, tugging at the high-necked collar choking her. "The Red Sea… Paris… Rome…."

Her hands shook, her voice faltered. She ordered the children back to their books. She sat rigid and flushed at her desk, with eyes fixed maliciously on the boy, whose eyes were fixed unwaveringly on the globe. A nearly silent hum vibrated in his throat.

* * * * *

The weeks passed. No word came from Mr. Jennings. The sympathy and understanding of her William Hathoway helped to allay her fears and her humiliation. Dispirited and with a monotony to match the dark autumn days, she droned through the daily lessons.

Snow fell, a little more each day, measuring the season with growing drifts against the building. No longer able to stand beneath the maple tree, now shorn of its leaves, Mrs. Garth stood in the path, dark against the snow, in clothing covering all but her eyes.

* * * * *

Not until the day before Christmas recess did the boy sing again. All week, alive with anticipation of the holidays, the children busied themselves, singing carols and making presents out of construction paper and buttons, ribbons, string and paste. On the final day they wrote and recited poems.

Miss Lapham passed slowly down the aisles. Here she encouraged one, there she praised another. She stopped at the boy's desk. It disturbed her that he had shown no progress at all. Except for his Christmas project— a manger scene brilliantly done with beads— he only listened and watched, had not even lifted a pencil, despite her prodding. Perhaps his mind is deficient after all, she thought, but his alertness and rapt attention seemed to belie that notion.

She remembered again that afternoon a month or so previous when she had gathered her courage and called after the boy's mother, who was already walking down the drive with the boy in hand. She had taken Mrs. Garth aside, whispering softly, hurriedly, voicing her concerns, and she recalled with bitterness the bitterness of her reproach:

"Well, you asked to have him here, not I!"

And now the boy was writing. She touched his shoulder to move him back and peered down at his paper. But she saw no words, only dark symbols so ornately drawn they appeared at first to be pennants and flags. Curious, she took up the paper, studying what she now recognized as intricately wrought musical notes. She drifted toward the time-worn piano in the corner and pulled the bench forward, smoothing her dress beneath her. Hesitantly she began to play.

The melody tinkled out, winding sweetly between the warm bass clef notes. The children stopped work to listen. Excited, bewildered, she played through to the end, marveling that, though she had never heard this beautiful melody before, he had somehow discovered it somewhere and memorized it.

The room fell silent as she began again, this time with greater sureness and facility. The unexpected accompaniment slowly issuing up startled her. Her fingers faltered, then she picked up her place, confidently, hearing the deep and somber chords surround the music, embrace and hold it as a central theme, while the enveloping harmonies expanded, filled and lifted it to a spiritual loftiness. They finished together on a rich, resonant chord that dissipated into a silence.

Stunned, unable to believe what she now knew with absolute certainty to be true, she faced the boy. He smiled out to her, then to the other faces beaming back to him.

During the holidays Miss Lapham agonized over the

mystery she could not fathom. She confided in her fiancé William, who reassured her, despite his private doubts. The children quickly spread news of the phenomenon, as they had several months earlier, but their accounts, so varied and distorted, were discounted by most as 'childish fancies.'

Several townspeople believed, however. They whispered of the 'strange goings-on' at the school, and those Few suggested that the Garths be driven out before they bring ruination to their community. Even Miss Lapham fell under suspicion. They could do nothing yet, these townspeople knew, but they would be watching closely. Very closely.

Chapter 11

The new year began with gloomy days a sad contrast to the bright holiday posters still decorating the drab walls of the schoolroom. Now the boy became a delight to his classmates and a source of unending wonder to Miss Lapham. He began to sing, cautiously at first, but gradually with greater abandon. Whenever something pleasant occurred, syncopated melodies broke from him, chiming clear as bells. Unpleasantness brought dreary tones, as from bassoons and French horns. He pumped fresh life into the lessons and created for the class a new and private world. He drove the darkness from their spirits, just as the cherry-bellied coal stove in their midst drove the cold from the room.

Rekindled rumors spread through the town. Among the Few, tempers flamed anew as they spoke of the 'Devil' living among them and the contamination of their children. They demanded action and a committee was finally formed to investigate the charges. For five consecutive days they came, four men and two women bundled in their greatcoats and silently squeezed together on the bench in the rear of the room, waiting, just as P. R. Jennings had waited before them.

They too waited in vain. The boy's long silence had pleased Miss Lapham, though she wasn't sure why. She had of course been questioned prior to the observation. In the presence of Mr. Jennings, who had been summoned to chair the hearing, she admitted she had indeed heard music, or thought she had, "but," she added coyly, glancing to Mr. Jennings, "much mischief can occur when twenty children are thrown together."

News of the events did not escape the ear of Garth and, reluctantly, he brought the latest home from the post office each evening to his waiting wife. Distraught, tormented, she did not sleep; she raved aloud. Her dress hung and the dark circles under her eyes widened their spheres. Her complexion turned the color of ashes and the rumors Garth reported nightly pinched her mouth. She despaired.

And her anxieties were not much relieved the night Garth came home smiling and buoyant. "It's all over now. No need to fret and hound me 'bout movin' away no more. The committee has disbanded and the disgruntled got nobody to rile 'cept theirselves. Most folks I hear talkin' think it to be no more'n crazy gossip, and harmless at that."

Bethany Garth no longer looked at her husband when he spoke. Occasionally she would lift her head from the skeins of yarn draped over her lap and, her face shrouded in shadows, turn haunted eyes to the fire. From time to time she would regard the child coolly, as if he had inflicted upon her a wound that would not heal, or had committed some inexpiable sin she could neither name nor forgive. In return the child offered up beautiful music to dissipate the chill in her heart.

Chapter 12

With the steadily rising arc of the sun, the snows receded from the school grounds until at last a wet, yellow-green swatch of grass lay exposed to the warming air. Inside the school, spirits brightened with the coming season and with the steady flow of music that bound and lifted them. Through the window Miss Lapham watched the ever-widening circle of matted grass. Soon, she knew, the tree would bud, and with the opening of its leaves would come Mrs. Garth to stand beneath them in the shadows to whisk her boy away. She knew too that with the coming heat, the windows would have to be opened. The winter and the thick plaster walls had kept the music from others sharing the building. She worried.

The days passed quickly, each more cheerful than the last. And as if to celebrate the advent of spring, the boy put music to their many drawings, crayon renderings and watercolors of trees and flowers and mountains and lakes. A few of these melodies Miss Lapham captured and played on the piano in a meager way, but harmonies sifted in to enhance them. All went well and, as if in anticipation of her fears, the boy sang softly, in tonal gradations that rose to a drifting silence out the open windows.

By now the townsfolk were accustomed to the strange tales coming out of the school. Most disregarded them or considered them exaggerated fancies that helped get the kids off to school without 'hittin'.'

The Few, however, expressed their views to any who would listen: 'That woman and that boy is working in tandem with the Devil,' they proclaimed, but in the absence of hard evidence, they were ignored and often ridiculed. If any were bold enough to accost Miss Lapham on the street, they were coldly referred to the 'investigation.'

* * * * *

Garth sat reading in his chair, with the breeze blowing the corners of his paper. With the passing of a hard winter and the dearth of rumors, he felt a cheerfulness he tried to share with his wife. She was unreceptive. Her energies went into her housework and in making warm-weather clothing for the child. She did not acknowledge Garth's latest theories and ignored his comments on her "brooding nature" and the "cold bed" she made for him. Through it all the boy sang melodiously and serenely, as if from far away, and in a fit of pique she once burst out: "Child, will you never stop!"

* * * * *

The class strained against their excitement as Miss Lapham spoke: "...an altogether successful year, delightful and, I might add, one none of us will ever forget." Heads swung to the bright-haired boy smiling in their midst. "Soon— much sooner than you can believe— we will be together again. Enjoy these carefree days as you will, but do not lose all we have discovered here." She drew herself up sharply. "Dismissed."

Cheering and tumbling over themselves, they trampled out the schoolhouse door where they fanned away howling. Miss Lapham looked down at the boy. "You may go too, Jonathan," she said softly. An aching chord that put a shiver into her escaped his throat as he rose—reluctantly, she thought—and walked slowly out.

From the window she saw him go down the path to the woman waiting under the tree. She contemplated him, this strange child who had touched each of them in an indefinably personal way, who in some mysterious fashion had brightened the dark corners of her soul. There was about him a purity, an innocence that eluded definition, an intangible something she could not name that seemed to reach out for, or to invite, communion. She watched them, strange son and stranger mother, walk hand in hand down the drive and disappear over the hump in the road.

Chapter 13

Behind the house, out of sight from the road, Bethany Garth tended her garden. She weeded and hoed and dropped seeds. Every vegetable her nubbed fingers could coax out of the stony soil was, she knew, money saved. She spoke to the child, helping at her side, teaching him. She allowed him to sing, but softly. As before, she warned, "People would not understand."

Occasionally he wandered off and she would struggle to her feet to search for him, her hand pressed to her back. Sometimes she would find him sitting in the field farther off, almost lost to view but not to hearing, his arms waving the long-stemmed wild flowers surrounding him. Or she would find him behind a boulder fondling in the cup of his hand some caught insect, a bee or butterfly, his head cocked, singing in tones almost inaudible. Once, as he stood a short distance from her, facing the mountains, music gushed from him and she crawled frantically on bruised knees to stop it.

The sun, fresh air and work improved her temper. Sitting in her parlor chair she rocked, less tense and more secure with the child home every day. Detecting the subtle change, Garth took advantage of it to open conversation with her.

"You notice the birds never fly when Jonathan walks up to them? Just like he's one o' them."

Still reticent, she at least faced him now as he spoke. He felt encouraged. "Lots o' work orders comin' in to the mill. Might even be a raise in it for me." A dizzy concatenation of notes scaled to a peak where they soared off and faded away. "See, Beth, he knows, he knows I'm right."

Apprehensive, she viewed the child, rocking on the new

horse Garth had built from old lumber, his eyes closed in the ecstasy of his music.

* * * * *

Early in June on a sunny morning full of summer promise, the boy wandered outside while his mother, weakened by the grippe, slept in her chair, her hands lost in the mending on her lap. From the road the boy stood facing the hazy peaks beyond. A short song broke from him, ponderous at first, then orchestrating itself to buoyant and joyous strains that diffused away in the cool morning air.

Finding a branch at the roadside, the boy dragged it along the ditch running toward town. He dallied on, digging up stones and watching the insects scurry away or bury themselves out of sight. He paused to smell the wild flowers and to listen to the buzzing morning sounds. A rabbit popped out of the weeds and sat up facing him with its nose twitching. It hopped away when the boy ran for it and he chased it, laughing silently. It stopped to look back, as if mocking him, then bounded ahead. He lost it in the rushes beside a seasonal creek where he squatted and watched the water funnel into a conduit beneath the road. Running his fingers through the cold water, he licked them and drank from his cupped hand. The sun warmed his back.

When he reached the mill he peered off into the distance where the rising stacks of stone towered like remnants of a shattered monolith. His music started again, flowing out like winds, gusting stronger, lustier and finally tapering off and diminishing in chromatic tones. His father did not appear.

At the juncture near the school where his mother had fallen, he paused to watch a twinkling flock of birds circle high overhead and sail away to the hills, merging into a black spot before disappearing. His head swam with the sights, sounds and fresh morning smells of damp plowed earth, mountain air and tender grasses.

A new music played in his head, unfamiliar and beckoning. Listening to its call, he did not hear the car approach from behind.

Chapter 14

"Hey, Sonny, looking for a ride?" The man leaned over to throw open the door. "I'm heading through Bainsville," he said, pointing ahead on Barrow Road, "...if that's your direction." He pushed his hat back and chewed on the stogie clenched between his teeth. "Watch your step on the running board, she's cracked....

"...'Brewster,' my wife sez— she always calls me by my last name— 'Brewster, it's about time you retired. A man your age can't go traipsing around the country forever.' Oh yeah, I sez, and how do you suppose the bills will get paid? No such thing as a money tree, I sez. If there was I'd have found it long ago, traveling these back roads the way I do." He flicked his cigar ash and his grin showed stained brown teeth.

"How about you, Sonny? What's a kid like you doing out so far? Not that it's my business, understand. Learned long time ago not to ask questions. Avoid a lot of trouble that way. Still, can't say I wasn't glad to see you meandering ahead. Pretty lonely, a job like this, selling. That's my game, selling." He kept glancing over to the boy and back to the road as the car jounced over the ruts.

The boy studied the man's mannerisms and listened to the strange cadences of his speech and the pattern of words that opened a new dimension of his consciousness.

"Don't say an awful lot, do you, Sonny? Just as well by me. I don't get the chance to yak much, being on the road all the time." He put another match to his cigar and blew out the smoke.

"Kinda lonely being a salesman. Tell you the truth though—wouldn't admit this to the wife—but I don't know as

I'd retire if I could. Staying home every day just laying around looking at the walls ain't exactly my measure of a good time. Tell you something else. I don't think the little lady would be none too happy, neither. She's got her life set up and organized just like she likes. I'd only be in the way. Oh, I've seen her fidget and fuss when I've been around too many days in a row, and I've seen how she kinda relaxes the minute I'm set to go, even though she does shed a crocodile tear or two. I don't hold it against her, though. That's just the kinda woman she is. A person can no more change their ways than a leopard can change its spots, now can they?" He removed his cigar and, scratching his ragged mustache with his little finger, contemplated the boy.

"If you're a little scared of me, you don't need to be. Got a couple kids of my own. Of course, they're all grown up now, married and flew the coop to make their mark in the world. Couple of nice boys they were. Still write to their mother once in awhile, mostly on holidays. And hardly ever fail to ask how the Old Man is doing out on the road. That's my one regret, I guess, never getting to see much of them growing up. Too busy making a living." He choked up. "Boy, how they'd come running outside to meet me when I pulled in with the old jalop!" He massaged his neck. "But you can't have everything in this world. First things first, as they say."

The car rattled as they drove along. The boy watched him light another cigar and fling the match out the window. Music played in his head, discordant and alien. He felt uncomfortable.

"Yesiree, money is all it takes. Some say it can't buy happiness, but I say, what it can't buy I can do without. If I had enough of the green stuff things would be a whole lot different, I guarantee you, a whole lot different...nice clothes, trips—California, maybe, bask in sunshine year 'round. Not have to look at those same old mountains out there, same boring road winding through the same boring towns with the same boring people who wouldn't know a bargain if it fell on their head."

He drew a flask wrapped in brown paper from his side pocket and held it between his thighs to unscrew the cap. He rubbed the bottle mouth on his coat sleeve before tipping it up. "Whoooee," he gasped. "Now that's what I call real first-class rot gut. Eats out the lining of your stomach, but it sure does get your heart started and paints the world rosy." He offered the bottle. "Have a swig?" The boy sidled away and Brewster laughed as he replaced the cap and stashed the bottle.

"Yesiree, one of my boys is off in Australia someplace, selling for one of the big companies. Took right after the Old Man." He beamed. "Heavy equipment. Big money in it. Maybe someday he'll strike it rich. No reason why he shouldn't."

He shook his cigar at the boy. "Don't ever underestimate the power of selling, Sonny. True, some people look down on it, but they're fools. You just think about what it means. It's selling that brings the creature comforts to your doorstep. Yesiree, that, and at the same time keeps the economy viable— healthy, that is. And jobs. Things are a bit tough now, I admit, but it keeps more people working than they otherwise would be. I drive along sometimes thinking of the whole chain of folks bringing home the bacon because of me.

"People just ain't believing today, that's the trouble. No faith. But here I am plugging along. Farm equipment. Books is all in the back seat if you care to have a look-see. It's a hard life a traveling salesman leads. Some people wonder why we do it. Well, it's not so much that we like people. We do, generally, it's true, or you couldn't ever take it, but that does lose much of its shine after a while. What it is, I guess, is the dream, the dream that someday that sale will come along, that one big order that'll put you over the top and land you on Easy Street." He drove along trying to watch the road and the boy.

"Not much of a talker at all, are you, Sonny? You're a quiet one. Not much for smiling, neither, I see. Never make a salesman. Well, maybe you can sing." With that he broke into song:

"Oh, the salesman's life's a desperate one,
He goes from town to townnn,
And even if they kick him out,
They cannot keep him downnn."

He drew out his bottle again. "How's that? Pretty good, eh? Talk to yourself and everybody thinks you're crazy. But if they hear you singing, why, they say, 'Now there goes a happy man.'"

The boy watched him lick the drops from his mustache and run his hand over his mouth.

"Yesiree, Sonny, I ask you to think about it. People can give all the credit in the world to the man who sits down and invents the fancy gadgets. But who is it that gets them into the houses? Why, the salesman, that's who. He's the one who works up the spiel and an appetite enough to make people's tongues hang out for things they didn't know existed. Create a need and feed that need. And everybody's happy." Music played around images of cogs and wheels in the boy's head.

"Ready again?" Brewster said, pulling himself up:

"Oh, the salesman's life's a lonely one,
He's on the road all daaayy,
He lives to sell his pretty wares,
For a pittance of a paaayy."

With the last verse the boy joined in with a simple harmony. "Atta boy, atta boy. Now you got it. Here we go again—ready?

Oh, the salesman's life's a weary one,
He's always on the goooo,
He sleeps in flea bags every night,
As he wanders to and frooo."

He laughed harshly as he unscrewed the cap and gurgled down the contents of his bottle. "Hahhh," he breathed, tossing the empty out the window. "You don't say much, Sonny, but you sure do hum a pretty tune." He slapped the boy's knee. "You make me sound better than I already do." He lifted his head high, beginning again:

"Oh, the salesman's life's a troubled one…"

The boy stiffened and swung his head toward a line of brush angling toward them.

"But he never tells a sooouul,
He wears a bright smile on his face…"

A rush of sound tore from the boy's throat, a wild cacophony of crashing cymbals and brass. Brewster slammed on the brakes. "You crazy little bas—"

The engine thundered out from behind the blind formed by the brush and roared past, a few feet ahead. Brewster gaped as the freight train hurtled by, drowning them in sound and rocking the car in its long, trailing wake. He spoke to himself, watching in amazement as it sped down the track and disappeared from view.

"No whistles, no bells, no—" He turned slowly to the boy. "But you knew it was coming. How'd you know, Sonny?

Couldn't see it, couldn't hear it, not with the singing and the rattling of this Tin Lizzy." He started out again with a lurch. "And that's some trick you got, that screaming noise. Like nothing I ever heard, especially out of somebody small as you."

Deep in thought he drove along trying to remember something he'd read.

He stopped when they reached Bainsville. "This your place of residence, Sonny?" He pantomimed, twisting his lips ludicrously. "You live...stay..." he pointed to the ground "...here?" The boy shook his head and Brewster shifted into gear. "Okay by me. Just as well."

The boy gazed into the storefronts, houses and markets as they passed slowly through the town. New impressions of people and streets assailed him, shaping new music in his head and reinforcing the old that came in dim remembrance of Torrence.

The countryside opened up again, brilliant with sunshine and refreshing with the cool air blowing in through the open windows. Brewster was speaking again and the boy's music played to his words, silently forming and redefining itself.

"Ever hear of phychical phen...phem...psychical people, Sonny?" He chewed the tip off a new cigar and spit it on the floor. "Been reading about it. Just lately. Seems there's certain people able to...to, well, they can tell what's going to happen before it does. Sort of like a fortune teller but without the cards and crystal ball." He sucked flame from the match to the cigar. "Sounds screwy, I know, but this New York paper I was reading told all about it." Blowing out a cloud of smoke he glanced toward the boy. "Of course, being a businessman of sorts and after forty years in the selling game, I'm a hard man to convince. Could be you had no more than a hunch. Have them myself now and again. Still—"

A shimmering haze rose above the city ahead. "No sir, I'm not an easy sell. That's what I've been telling myself driving along now this past hour or so. But I am not averse to taking a chance now and again, either, but some things you want to be more certain about, if you follow me." He paused, as if reluctant to go on, then said, "I'll let you in on a secret, Sonny…I got a weakness for the ladies." He glanced over for a response.

"I don't expect you to understand that fully. You don't have to, actually. But in this case there's a special certain lady friend I have hereabouts, who's been wanting me to…well, let's just say she wants us to be a bit more friendly, a little closer in our relationship. Of course that would mean a whole gang of trouble, being as, like I told you, there's another got me tied down on paper. If I could be sure…that is, if you could look into that crystal ball you carry in your head and tell me what my chances are to…well, like I said, California and all that, those are her words and her ideas. Mighty appealing to me, too, if I had some assurance of it working out for us. Now maybe you're just the rabbit's foot I need to sweeten my chances—I mean, with that train and all…."

The coughing engine noises swallowed the ominous undertones playing to his words.

Brewster leaned back and blew out a long puff of cigar smoke. "Ah, I can smell those ocean breezes already. And sunny skies year 'round…."

Chapter 15

They rode into the city outskirts just past noon. When they reached the city limits they crossed an iron bridge and from its crest the boy saw the shining rooftops in the distance. Farther on, in their midst, he saw the towering outline of clustered buildings. New music started up in his head, lively and spirited and exciting. Below, he saw the silver span of water stretching away, with boats large and small cutting white trails over it. His music dropped several octaves, broadening on quivering strings.

Brewster shot along the main boulevard, busy with traffic, while in the boy's mind music flashed in jarring rhythms. Weaving through several intersections, he turned down a quiet side street lined with modest homes that ended near a park.

"Here we are," Brewster said, pulling up to the curb. Climbing out, he lifted his hat to wipe away the sweat on his forehead and shook the stiffness out of his legs. He stood a moment looking up to the house set back on the lot and surrounded by trees before coming around to the passenger side of the car.

He bent low to speak to the boy through the open window. "You wait a few minutes till I run inside and make sure everything's okay. She can be a touchy one sometimes, Suzie can, but ain't they all?" he said, spitting out the tip of another cigar. "Just sit tight." He turned away and started up the sidewalk.

When he was out of view, the boy slipped out of the car and stood a few moments, taking in his surroundings and trying to get his bearings. Seeing the park ahead, he crossed the street and scampered toward it.

Chapter 16

By the time Brewster returned, the boy was already through the park and wandering down a busy side street, garnering and storing a new repertoire of sounds assailing him from all sides: voices crying, hawking and shouting; jingles and squeals; scratchings and gratings; whistles, horns and pipings; slappings and thumpings; screeching, hissing, banging....

He loitered, stopping here and there to absorb the sights, sounds and smells of life flooding over him. People hustled in and out of little shops, or hovered and stooped over the bushels and crates of produce crowding the walks. The fragrance of oranges and apples and lemons filled the air. He saw the pyramids and mounds of fruits and vegetables set on stands with the yellow sunlight washing over it all. And though he recognized the language of the people, the rhythms of the dickering were strange to his ear.

A wild cry startled him. He turned and saw a shopkeeper flying from his store and brandishing a meat cleaver at a black man who rushed up on the boy and knocked him over before he himself crashed into a vegetable stand. Potatoes spilled and rolled into the street.

Picking himself up, the boy gave chase, weaving and dodging between the throng. A block ahead, he saw the black man dart to the right, out of sight. He ran hard to catch up.

He slowed at the entrance of a cobblestone alley faced on both sides by the back ends of garages and narrow walks lined with trash cans and empty crates. Stagnant water stood along the curbs. Seeing no sign of the man, he walked cautiously ahead, offended by the dirt and the rank odors clinging in the air.

Suddenly an arm shot out, grabbing him by the neck and dragging him behind a trash heap. "Who are you, boy? What you chasing me for?"

The boy struggled to pry away the clamped fingers.

"Who set you on my tail?" He hauled the boy in close and seated him roughly. His eyes burned down to his face. "You tell me or I'll rip you up in li'l pieces and leave you for rat meat."

He peeked over the rubbish down the alley. "That crazy man somethin' to you? Maybe your daddy?" He forced the boy's head back by the hair. "That fool ready to chop me up with his meat ax for a loaf of bread—he special to you?"

Dolefully the boy faced up to him. The black man pushed him out to arm's length, scrutinizing him. Then he threw his head back and laughed. "You be a mighty brave tadpole, the laks o' you, to split out after a shark lak me."

Releasing the boy's hair, he peeked out again and ducked back. His smile faded. "How come you not scared o' me lak everybody else 'roun' here? So scared won't none o' them even give me a place to sit an' rest, much less a job." His nose almost touched the boy's. "And they's right 'cause I'd jes' as soon chew them up, every damn one, and spit them out lak jes' so much bad meat!" Still glaring, he eased back against a soggy carton box. He wore khaki pants and a torn short-sleeved shirt of faded blue, out of which his arms protruded lean and supple. Looped over his shoulder was a small canvas sack.

"You don' know, boy, you don' know how close you come to gettin' your fool head tore off, chasin' after me...and you can quit your fool smilin', too, 'cause I ain't sure I won't damage you some afore I buzz on out o' here."

The boy listened curiously, absorbing the peculiar rhythms and inflections of his voice. He reached out and the man pulled back.

"What's the matter, boy, you crazy? Don't you touch me. I

don' know you. You nothin' to me." He half stood, peering over the pile, then lifted the boy to his feet and rose with him.

"Okay, boy, you bes' be on your way. I won't hurt you none. I reckon you was jes' lookin' for some 'citement. Go on now, hustle on home and be glad you're lucky to have one."

The boy stepped close to him and he backed away. "Don' you be crowdin' me now. Jes' beat it on out o' here home. You mama's goin' to be worried."

The boy stood looking up to him, taking in the clean smooth lines of his face, the wide-spaced eyes alternating between anger and warmth.

"What *is* the matter with you, boy? Cain't you talk? Swallow your tongue when I grabbed you?" He eyed him suspiciously. "Open up," he said, grasping his chin. He peered into his mouth as if into a key hole, reminding the boy of the doctor who had once done the same thing. "Seems lak ever'thin's there that s'posed to be, and nothing there that ain't." He stood up, rubbing his neck.

"You simple?" He pondered. "No, you looks too bright for that. Maybe a sore throat took your voice away temporary. That it? Sore throat?" The boy smiled up at him. "I knowed it must be somethin' lak that. Well, you be gettin' on now. I got to get me some grub and I don' need no tadpole tailin' along." He began to walk. The boy edged after him.

He stopped and swung around. "You deef, too? I said get on afore I whup you." He raised his hand as if to strike, but the boy faced him, unblinking.

"Well, ah be——." He scratched his head. "You lost? That your problem?" He bent down, aiming the boy in the direction of his pointing finger. "Look, you jes' waltz straight on down to that corner by that ol' pole. Turn left. Pretty soon, maybe two blocks, you come to a po-lice station. They'll take care o' you. Cain't take you there myself. Wouldn't do *me* no good, but you'll find it, no trouble. Now go on." He nudged him. "Go now, y'hear? Move on out!"

A few minutes later, exasperated, he finally gave up. "Okay, Tadpole. I reckon you got your reasons. You can tag along if you want, but bes' you steer clear o' me if'n things start hap'nin', 'cause when Charles moves, Charles moves!"

From his hip pocket he pulled a ragged black hat, its broad brim mashed, and jammed it on his head. The boy ran to keep up with the long, loping strides.

They wound through a network of alleys to a small park where they circled wide, skirting a number of benches occupied by a handful of old men who dozed or warmed themselves with war stories. Finding a private spot near a cluster of sumac bushes, the two dropped to the grass. Charles fanned himself with his hat and the boy imitated him with his hand. Charles laughed, a rich, deep-down throaty kind of laugh, and he slapped at the boy with his hat.

"We'll rest here awhiles," he said, stretching out. "Then we'll get us some eats." He put his hat over his face.

The boy sat awhile studying the man. In his head his music tried to fit itself to the figure lying on the ground, tried to accommodate itself to its dormant power, its contradictory nature. He was not dangerous, the boy knew, no more so than the thunder that growled beyond the mountains. He felt the sadness of the man and tried to probe its source. A fugue played in his head and drove away his thoughts. He lay back then, but he did not sleep....

Charles squatted on his haunches, facing the boy. The sun hung over his shoulder. "You got any money?" he asked, looking the boy over sharply. The boy shook his head. "I thought not," he said, rubbing two soiled dollar bills with his thumb. He knelt and tucked the bills back in his pocket. "Well, I sure ain't spending these." He leaped to his feet. "But that don' mean we's gonna starve. C'mone. And stick close."

They took a narrow street, quiet now with the lateness of the day. Charles grabbed the boy by the arm and stopped him. His eyes were fixed on a poultry store ahead. On the walk in front of it stood stacks of crates alive with chickens.

"Now look, Tadpole, I sure am hopin' you can keep pace once I gets movin'. If'n you wants some dinner, best you do." His voice was hushed. "You go on ahead now. Jes' walk real natural and keep on walkin' till you see me comin', then run like the wind."

The boy walked on, with Charles sauntering behind, feigning the slow shuffle of one with no particular purpose. He stopped near one of the crates and bent down, as if deciding which to buy. A few feet beyond, the boy stopped. Frowning, Charles waved secretly, urging him on, his face distorted with the silent shaping of his lips. Sweat beaded his brow as he peered around the coops to locate the proprietor. Cautiously his hand crept out to slide back the gate. The chickens squawked and burrowed into themselves to escape his reaching hand.

He snatched a leg at the same time the crates fell crashing around him. Startled, he lifted his head, heard the shouting and tore away when he spotted a bald man rushing from the store. Climbing out from under the crates, the boy scrambled to his feet and darted off after Charles, already in full gallop half a block away. Flapping and ruffling their wings, the freed chickens clucked and strutted over the sidewalk and street.

"Boy, I swear you did that on purpose," Charles complained when they had finally reached a small bridge beneath which they had hidden themselves. "Dang near almost got us caught."

The boy's head lay over his knees. A dim harmony rumbled in his throat.

"Yeah, you go 'head and groan all you want. That ain't

gonna fill our bellies none." He glared. "What's the matter wid you, boy? How come you held back lak that, agin my word? Don't you know I could this minute be flat out on some hoosegow floor?" He took in the gloomy surroundings.

"Maybe wouldn't be so bad at that. Be dry at least. And they got to feed you, even if they don' lak you." He lay back against the stony bank, cold and damp. "We'll jes' set awhiles till I'm sure they ain't nobody out lookin' for us. Dang, I'm hungry. So hungry I could eat the timbers right out from under this here ol' bridge. Nails and all."

The hours passed and at dusk the boy followed him out to the edge of town where they crept on hands and knees along a hedgerow bordering a farmhouse. Charles parted the foliage and peered across an open yard to the house. The lights inside made yellow squares of the windows. The boy hung over Charles's shoulder to see.

"Okay, Tadpole," he whispered, "you jes' stay put. When I gets us one o' them chickens there," he pointed, "we takin' off thataway." He pointed again. "And that ain't all. Squeeze in closer and look 'round there. You see them bushels on the vee-randa? Taters in one that I can see, and I intends for us to have us a few. Lak my mama used to say, 'Chicken don' taste good less'n they's taters on the plate.'" He chuckled to himself.

With that he slipped through the hedges. The boy watched him crouch to a compost heap where he lost him momentarily in the shadows. Then Charles crept around it, moving stealthily toward the porch. He was on the steps, almost there, when a dog began barking.

Charles froze. Inside, he heard voices raised as the dog battered itself against the door. He heard the deep growls and the thumping feet growing louder. Wheeling, gripped with fear, he sprang across the yard and, half-turning, saw the dog, a huge German shepherd, released and bounding off the porch, snarling through its bared teeth. A sudden anger drove off his terror as he swung around, girding to meet the attack. He couldn't outrun the dog, he knew, and he had to take its throat before its fangs could take his own.

The boy saw all, and from his throat came a shrill, piercing note that rose instantly beyond the range of human hearing. The dog whirled in the air and struck the ground writhing. Howling and whimpering it charged back to the house. They were charging away, too, Charles and the boy, with shotgun blasts reverberating across the countryside.

At the edge of a pine forest they squatted on soft needles. "It ain't chicken but it's good," Charles said, slapping the ham between two slices of bread. "Sure did hate to bust into that money but sometimes a man don' have no choice."

He watched the boy nibble off the crust before taking a bite of his sandwich. "You sure is a delicate eater," he said, tearing away half his own sandwich in one bite. He chewed slowly, thoughtfully. "Sure is pee-culiar how that dog jes' turned tail and run. Didn't think I was that ugly." He laughed, shook his head, then devoured the rest of his sandwich. "Sure wish I had me some may-yo-naise."

When he had finished his fourth sandwich he lay back sighing. The boy imitated him, lying down next to him with his arms akimbo behind his head.

"Funny," Charles said, gazing up, "most folks is happier in the morning with the sun coming up bright and the whole busy day ahead. But not me. I lak it best at night, lak now. Peaceful. Can almos' feel the world slow down, trouble dyin' away. Maybe it's the dark they's afraid of. Dark never scared me, even as a li'l chil'." He patted his canvas sack and adjusted it under his head.

"Ever wonder what it mus' be lak, Tadpole, way up there? Jes' look at them stars. Millions and millions floating in a sea o' milk. Some say they ain't no end to them, neither. Say, too, they's worlds up there, same's ours, but I hope not too much so." He chuckled softly. "You's young yet, too young to know what I'm talkin' 'bout. Someday you'll know.

"Wonder what it mus' be lak, so free and uncarin'— the stars, I mean. Lookin' down so, so lak my mama's eyes used to look down on me. Maybe those is the eyes o' the dead, watching us. Or saints maybe—You listenin' to me?" He turned and saw the boy, looking up, silent and still, eyes wide. "Well, I don' mind if you don't. Esther—she be my wife— when we'd sit out under the stars, she'd say to me, 'Charles, now there you go again, talkin' that crazy talk.' I knew though that she was right pleased wid it 'cause sometimes she'd say, 'Charles, maybe you should turn your hand to pomes.' And maybe if'n I could write I would. I'd say something lak—you won't laugh now—well, I'd say them stars is lak a...a scatterin' o' ice—no, that no good...lak the sheddin's of angel wings. No, that neither. Maybe that God jes' dipped his big ol' bucket in a mountain o' diamonds and jes' kep' flingin' them out till they filled up most all the black up there... Oh, shecks, seems they jes' ain't words made to reach down far enough to say what I feels."

He spat off to the side. "Ah, jes' crazy, like Esther says. But I might've learned writin', maybe caught some o' those wild idees sliding 'round in my mind all the time. Startin' to learn too, 'bout the time it happened. Little Negro man, edjy-cated, was gonna teach me. On my way there one night—nice night lak tonight, wid stars budding out—when I hears this scream. A lady's voice. Tell the truth, I held fast. Could be some ol' man beatin' on his woman and none o' my business. Then I realizes it's comin' from the widder Marsh's house. Used to do yard work for her off and on. Nice lady. Let me sit at the table wid her for lunch, even.

"So off I tears. Ain't nobody else around to help, lak the way it always is when trouble breaks out. Got there in time to see somebody cuttin' out the back way, couldn't tell who. Well, I got to stop for the widder, see if she's okay, and there she is, laying on the floor wid a big gash in her face. I called out, 'Widder Marsh, you okay?' She jes' looks at me and faints dead away. I know she needs a doctor mighty bad so I cut out fast, no good I could do there.

"Well, don' I run smack into the arms of a whole gang runnin' up to see what's wrong. I try to explain, tellin' them the widder's hurt and needs a doctor. They believe she needs a doctor all right, but they sure don' believe I had no doin's in the thing. Don' mind admittin' I was right scared 'bout then and talkin' up a blue streak. But the more I tried the meaner they got. They was a whole riot o' them. 'Lynch him, they was hollerin', 'lynch the nigger.'

"Would've, too, but Mr. Hyden, he says they got to be sure I did what they think I did and they hauled me back to the house. When they drags me in, the widder's standing there holding her face. They got my arms behind' me, and one's got a tight squeeze on my face, holdin' it up wid a lantern light aside it. 'This here the one, Emma?' they says. Her eyes peek out behind this towel she hugging and open wide. 'Give us a sign, ma'm, this one here do it?'

"She didn't have to point. Jes' gives a big whoop and don' she faint dead away once more. Thought sure my time was up when they haul me out, crying, 'Hang the sombitch, hang his black ass!' Fortunate the sheriff got to 'em in time and pokes me on to the jailhouse at the end of a shotgun.

"One thing an' another happens and comes the time o' my trial. I never been no angel, I admit, and that don' look good on my record. The widder says it was me, then not. She jes' can't be sure no more. Oh, they was mad enough to chew nails 'bout that. I was already smellin' free air, ready to clear on out, when they comes up with crimes I never heard no names put to before. Ten years on the chain gang they give me. Ha! Didn't stay but three. Bust out."

He sat up suddenly. "See this?" He lifted his pants cuffs. "Glowin' in the dark, scar tissue skin whiter'n yourn. Put shackles on so tight they was bloody six months afore they healed, burnin' and painin' even in my sleep." He sat rubbing his ankles.

"Never hurt so much though as that pain I saw in Esther's eyes when they was takin' me away...holdin' so tight to our boy, lak he was me. Same kind of pain I sometimes seen in the widder's face lookin' across the table watching me eat, talkin' 'bout her man. Thought I understood her feelin's then, but I know now I didn't till I seen Esther there, watchin' them drag me off. I felt it, too. It weren't no fear o' jail that hurt so. And even did I know the kinds o' things they knew to do to hurt a body, it wouldn't match up wid the hurt o' that one minute.

"Didn't come to me till a long time after—diggin' up a road bed, sweatin' to beat all, lak a pig under a hot ol'sun. Guard standin' there, black against the light wid his gun barrel aflashin' —it come to me then what it was: separatin'. That's the real sentence, I tells myself. That's the pain I seen in Esther's face and felt in my heart, same's the widder must've felt when her husband passed on. A body can take anythin' no matter how bad, if he's wid the people he loves. But alone, anything can do him in, mos' anything a-tall. Made up my mind then and there they wasn't keepin' me, 'specially for somethin' I never done, so I run. Ain't stopped since. Not so bad now, but Esther, my boy...' bout your age now, I reckon...." He flung himself away and stood up.

"I mus' be goin' crazy talkin' to you this way. None o' your business. And besides, you don' even know what I'm talkin' 'bout. First thing in the mornin' I'm headin' out—alone. Hear me white boy? Alone!" Nostrils flaring under his blazing eyes, he threw himself down and buried his head in his arms, trying to drive away the images that remained even after he had fallen asleep.

Chapter 17

When Charles awakened in the early light, his eyes opened to the boy, sitting next to him and looking down into his face. He did not understand the boy, did not know that the boy was trying to understand the strange mixture of moods that shifted in him like the winds, winds that seemed to carry in them the weight of chains and the flight of birds. The boy's thoughts were not framed in a verbal way, but in the music that played in his head, had, in fact, played all night long. The man was a new composition, capricious and unpredictable, serene as waving palms or jarring like a sudden clap of thunder. Beating like a far-off tom-tom, his music probed and searched, slithering its way like a silent stream in underground caves, seeking the essence of the man.

"You always stare at folks sleepin'?" he said, starting up. "And don't you be smilin' at me, 'cause here on out you're on your own. Been fool enough already. Promised mahself long time ago to do nobody no favor again, ever!"

He rubbed his eyes. "I gots to keep movin'," he said, glancing around. "Find a job. Not givin' no favors and don't want none. Jes' a fair chance. Is that too much for a man to ask, a fair chance to make his'n own way? Don' give a man a chance and soon you got to take your chances wid the man. You think about that, boy. Tell yo' daddy."

He stretched, yawned, then padded over to a shallow pool where he knelt down and splashed water over his head. "Yowee, that is cold!" Following him, the boy knelt beside him and did the same. Both drank from cupped hands.

Charles pulled his sack between them and opened it on the ground. "They's enough here for some breakfast, not much and no meat, but enough to take up both kinds o' the holler in our bellies." He tore off a chunk of bread, handed it to the boy, and stuffed a hunk in his own mouth. "You take that now, Tadpole, and be on your way. I'm headin' for the tracks. Jedgin' by the sounds las' night, trains pass here reg'lar. Now you git. Git!"

Slinging the sack over his shoulder, he rose and strode off. The boy hung back a moment then ran after him. Charles picked up a stick and turned to face him. The boy backed off. When Charles started away again, the boy kept pace, but at a distance.

The pine needle floor was soft and springy under Charles's feet as he worked his way through the forest. He emerged from its thin and ragged edge into the sunlight and pushed his way through a row of berry bushes that circled like a thorny collar around a flat, rock-strewn meadow. His stick chopped away the last of them and he squatted on the far side, where he wiped blood from his scratches with his hat.

Moments later when the boy appeared through the opening, Charles's hand flashed out and caught him by the shoulder. Glowering, he sat him down. "I gotta min' to gib you a sound thrashin', maybe put some sense in your haid, but I'm afraid you'd fall apart. Now you listen real careful." He gripped the boy's arm. "You ain't nothin' but bad luck. Have been since the first I laid eyes on you. I got all the troubles I can use widout you to add. Besides, you got a mama and daddy worryin' someplace."

He lifted the boy's chin and stared into the blue eyes fixed on him. "I got to make a life for myself, get back my fambly, you understan'? Got to find a fair chance and prove myself a man. You being along won't make it easier for nobody. So you be gone now, hear?"

He stood, hoisting the boy with him. "Best you head out now jes' the way you came. You small 'nough not to get all scratched up. Road's not far off." He pointed. "Thata way, straight on through. It ain't far to town. Go on now." He pushed him. "Go on. Scoot!"

The boy ducked through the thicket, stopped on the other side and looked back.

"Thass right, keep right on agoin'." Slapping on his hat, he took up his stick and picked his way between the rocks until he came to the edge of a bluff. He looked down at the tracks, about forty feet below. It was a steep slope, almost vertical, but with enough vegetation sprouting from its side to allow a reasonably safe descent. It wasn't a natural bluff, he knew, but one made by a cut through the hill for the railroad. The track curved around it and he knew too that the train would have to slow to negotiate the bend.

The sun climbed in a clear blue sky and warmed the air as Charles sat on the edge of the bluff tossing stones. He thought of the boy, who didn't look or act sick, yet who couldn't talk. He wondered if something more were wrong with him and what it was that could drive a boy so young away from home. The thought occurred then that he might be an orphan, and his thoughts turned to his own boy.

He'd been in prison three years and one now on the road. Four years he hadn't seen him and he wondered if he looked like him, how he'd grown and whether he'd been getting any schooling. And Esther, would she still be there waiting? Did she find another man?

He stood up and flung his stick across the gap. He didn't want to think anymore, but her face rose before him, her quick, black eyes, the soft turn of her lips smiling up to him. It would be better if she did find another man, he thought. Finding a place for her beside him, her and their boy, seemed hopeless. He lifted a small boulder, hurled it over the side and watched till it slammed to the ground below. For a moment he thought he might throw himself over too.

Then he heard it, the high, thin whistle, far off. He slipped his arm through his sack loop and, shading his eyes, peered into the distance. Near the horizon he saw a long, dark line trailing a wisp of black smoke.

Squatting, he watched the train grow larger as it approached. He scooped up a handful of stones and dropped them over the side. They clattered down, kicking up little clouds of dust. Readying himself, he folded his hat and tucked it away.

Cautiously he eased himself over the edge. His feet digging in for toe holds in the loose soil started small avalanches. Pressing in close he lowered himself gradually and as warily as a lizard, grasping where he could the delicate necks of saplings arching up. A few tore out by their shallow roots, but he had been careful not to depend solely on them. Halfway down, fingers and toes dug in, he clung to the wall, waiting.

The whistle shrilled high and piercing, and he could hear the steady chugging of the engines as the train strained against the long grade leading up to the curve. "My luck's changin' awready," he said aloud, knowing the steep incline would slow the train and give him more time to get down and into one of the cars.

A rattling slide of stones swept past his face, hugging the wall. Clearing the dirt from his eyes, he looked up and saw the boy clambering over the edge.

"Go back, boy! You gonna get us both killed. Go on back! Get your leg over the top," he shouted.

The boy kept coming.

"Dang you, I said go back!"

The train approached, its steel wheels grinding the rails, squealing under the weight of the load. Another avalanche rained down on him and he buried his head in his shoulder. It stopped and he craned his neck. He saw the boy's feet slipping out and dangling overhead.

"Dig in, Tadpole! Dig in your toes! Don't trust them twigs—"

His words were lost as the train, horn blasting, thundered below. Black smoke and cinders huffing from the stacks billowed up, choking and blinding him.

He didn't see or hear the boy falling. Nor did he expect the sudden impact that tore his hands free and dislodged him like a stone. Together they slid, Charles on his back, the boy flung across his body. Flailing wildly, his arms reached desperately for something solid to grab as they plummeted. Hard roots gouged his back as bushes broke away beneath them, slowing their descent enough for him to grasp a jutting rock. It held briefly, swinging them horizontally before ripping loose. Cascading, they tore through a dense cluster as they neared the base and smashed through some older growth until, finally, at the bottom, within inches of a low wall of boulders, a dwarf sapling snagged and held them.

Stunned and dizzy, Charles lay for a moment, his hand still gripping the boy's clothing. He felt the cool rush of air as the train creaked and groaned past, a few feet away.

"You all right?" he shouted. He lifted his head to see the boy tangled in his legs. "Me almost dead and you smilin'! Man, couldn' I jes…."

Holding the boy's head he sat up and rolled him for a quick check. "Look all right to me. Jes' some skinnin' here and there. No harm." He felt himself. "My ribs is cryin' but I guess I'm okay, too."

He wiped the side of his bruised face and staggered up. "C'mone," he said, yanking the boy to his feet. Keeping the boy behind him, he stepped over the rocks and edged cautiously onto the incline of crushed stone bordering the track, wary of the slip he knew could slice away his legs. The cars swayed and tipped past.

"Now listen, Tadpole," he shouted above the grinding noise, "you jes' relax." He picked the boy up in his arms. "Next open car, I'm gonna toss you inside. You hear me? Once in, you stay put. I'll grab me another down the line and work back to you. Don' worry none. Ready now?" He lifted the boy in the palm-seat of his hand and balanced his chest with the other. "Now!"

He heaved and the boy sailed into the boxcar on his belly. Charles stepped back a second. He could see the end of the train curving to him. Setting his feet, he waited for the right moment, then snatched at the ladder of a hopper. His arm sockets took the jolt as the train jerked him off his feet. Holding tight, he reached for another rung and pulled his legs up for a foothold. Clinging for a moment, he turned his head to blink away the blowing cinders stinging his eyes. Within minutes he was up and over the cars and lowering himself over the top of the door of the boy's car. He swung in and dropped to the floor.

"Dang!" he said, stretching out and breathing hard.

Out in the open country the train picked up speed. Chewing a straw from the floor, Charles rose and peered out before pulling the sliding door nearly closed. He turned, glowering down at the boy. "Dang!" He shook his head and eased his sore back to the wall. "Got me a boy I wants to see and can't, and one I don't want to see and can't not." He examined the cuts and bruises on his arms. "Too bad I lost my sack. Mighta had some bread in it left over."

Pushing some straw together for a bed, he eased his body down on it. "Maybe my luck ain't all run out yet," he said, absently chewing a straw. "Who knows, could be they's still a chance...find a job...settle someplace quiet and far away...get

a little house. Won't take much to fetch Esther. Henry too—
he's my son—get him off to school."

He lurched up and sent a handful of straw flying. "Jes'
dreams, jes' my crazy 'magination again lak Esther says.
Nothin' but. When I gonna learn!"

He reached out and grabbed the boy. "You unnerstan'
anythin' I say? It's your laks got me this way, your kind keepin'
all o' us this way, scratchin' jes' to stay alive, jes' barely. And
all that talk about *someday*. Seems all my life thass all I heared
is *someday*. Right now, this minute, you know how many folks
is settin' out on po'ches, po'ches o' shacks wid burlap bags
'stead o' glass for winders, talkin' 'bout *someday*. Ever' dang
one! Don' know the only *someday* they's ever goin' to see is
the one that gets them buried in a no-man's grave."

The boy reached out to touch his hand.

"Oh, yeah, you wet-eyed now 'cause you scared I's gonna
throw you out that there door." He sighed. "Well, you can rest
easy. Maybe someday you be lak the rest, but right now you
still a tadpole. I ain't mad at you. Ain't mad at nobody, really.
Jes' at things, the way they be. Truth be told, I don' know
whose fault anythin' is.

"Settin' out there awhiles ago, waitin' for this train, I
picked me up a big ol' stone. Threw it down over the side,
wantin' to see it smash in pieces. Now that stone didn' do
nothin' to me. No reason for what I did, but I did it. Maybe
that's the same kind o' thinkin' in them folk who tried to do me
in. Maybe it wasn't me personal they was hatin' so much. Don'
know what it was, but it was me they took after, jes' like I took
after that stone."

He pulled his legs up and wrapped his arms around them.
"Last night, first time in a long time, I dreamed o' my Esther
and my Henry. I s'pose it's havin' somebody around that
reminded me. Sittin' and wingin' stones, I got to thinkin', most

people in the world go fightin' and killin' and cheatin' and hatin' each other, and what for? They'd never find more riches than right there in their own house if they jes' look to see. Didn't know it myself when I had it. I knows it now.

"Tell you, too, Tadpole, I been feelin' sorry for myself. Blamin' ever'thin' on ever'body. 'Course, there's sure 'nough blame to go 'round, but what's the good in it? Leastwise thass what I keep tryin' to believe. So far I reckon I ain't done such a good job o' believin'.'"

The boy edged closer. His music flowed placidly with the liquid gush of the words. It was finding the man now, molding itself around his rooted melancholy, insinuating itself into the darkest fissures of his being.

"No, Tadpole, I guess I been doin' more sayin' than tryin', and more thinkin' than doin'. Seein' as to how you latched tight to me and never let go forced me to see that. A man's got to take a bite'n hold on. And even if he got no faith in the world, he got to have it in hisself. That's somethin' nobody can stop. Ain't nothin' in the world that stands still anyways. There's good times and bad times. Seems to me sooner or later things work out. Jes' a matter o' time. Ain't nobody got it easy, I don' think. Ever' man totes his own troubles and I s'pose every man thinks his tote's the heaviest." He sighed and went silent for a moment, listening to the rhythmic click of the wheels on the track, then started again.

"A man's got a right to earn his keep. Don't mean he'll get it, but he can try and keep on tryin' till he do. I don't want no man to *give* me nothin'. The way I sees it, when a man gives you something, he owns you surely as my granpap was owned. And takin' makes you hate the giver; mostly you hates yourself 'cause nothin's free and what you's tradin' is your pride and self-respect. I intends to make my own way. Ain't nothin' goin' to stop me." His smile glowed in the half dark of the car. "That rock I threw down didn't break neither." He laughed. "This here's one goddang uppity—"

The boy suddenly went rigid. From his throat issued the plangent thrumming of a guitar, deep and reverberating. Charles fixed his eyes on the boy, trying to see him clearly in the dim light and trying to distinguish the sounds from the steady rumble of the car, the clacking of wheels.

"You not settin' to throw no fit, is you, Tadpole?" He inched up on his hands. "Didn' mean you personal, boy. Shouldna done no talkin' lak that to you, jes' a chil'."

The boy snapped to his feet, his eyes closed, and swayed with the sway of the car. Fluttering woefully, flutes melded with the vibrating strings. Charles gaped as the boy lunged suddenly to the door.

"Get away from there, Tadpole! Wha's the matter, boy," he cried, leaping to his feet, "you gonna be sick?"

Again the music came, gushing with a force that froze Charles in his step. Wedging himself into the narrow opening, the boy pitted his strength against the weight of the door. Charles dove for him. "You crazy, boy?"

The door gave a bit more, and with the rush of smoky air blowing in rushed a screaming of brass, a wail of woodwinds, a symphony of booming rolls of drumming thunder crescendoing to a grinding collision of metallic sounds that vibrated the floor under Charles's feet.

Abruptly the music stopped. The boy clung to the door as Charles threw his arm around him and pried at his fingers. Below, Charles saw the gray-blue blur of the speeding right-of-way and, peripherally, across a clearing sliced for power lines through heavy woods, he caught the flash of polished metal about a mile distant. The bend of the cars ahead told him they were on a slow-breaking curve. What he had seen might be a standing train. Might be. And it might be on their track. Might be anything, they'd gone by the gap so fast, or nothing but a watery reflection. Probably no more than my 'magination, anyways, he thought.

The air blasted his face as he held the boy around the chest in front of him and held to the door for safety against the lurching car. He was trying to clear his mind, to understand what he had heard, when the music began to pulse again, a threnody of liquid sounds that evoked images of darkness. He remembered the music of moments before, unable to distinguish the horror of its effect from the mystery of its source. He saw himself tumbling down the slope, reliving the dizzy fall and wondered if he had injured his head. Confusion swept away his thoughts as he looked down at the boy.

Without warning, the boy suddenly locked his arm into Charles's and leaped from the train. Together they landed with a body-jarring impact on a weedy slope that pitched them forward and rolled them with the same dizzying momentum they'd experienced earlier. Arms and legs askew they spilled into a muddy ditch where they finally came to rest.

"Dang!" Charles eased himself to his knees. "I'm tellin' you, boy, if you ain't already bust up, I swear—" Looking up he saw the boy climbing onto the track, watching the last few cars fade around the curve behind the tree line.

A wailing horn carried back to them, a series of insistent blasts, then a long, screeching sound that rose in pitch, tearing apart the afternoon stillness. Scrambling up to the track beside the boy, Charles froze as images of a train wreck erupted in his mind, flashes of horror as he'd once seen when he was a child: Sparks flying like meteor showers as the shrieking wheels ground themselves flat against the track. Then the rumble, like that of an earthquake or the rippling thunder of a breaking electrical storm. He realized they were the same sounds he'd heard in the boxcar. He squeezed the boy's shoulder, trying to understand while bracing his mind against the metallic howl washing over them in endless waves, piling over each other in screaming succession.

Just as the music had moments earlier, all sound ceased, nothing moved or stirred.

"Wreck!" Charles cried, breaking away. "C'mone, Tadpole."

Chapter 18

Together they dashed down the track between the rails, Charles ahead. Rounding the bend they saw it, farther down, cars strewn everywhere, like the mangled and dismembered parts of a steel serpent.

"Watch your step you don' fall," Charles called behind, lengthening his stride. "Then again, might be better you stay back. This sure won't be pretty." The boy shook his head. "I'll come get you soon's I see if'n I can do any good up there." The boy shook his head again. "I'll say this, Tadpole, you sho do have a mind o' your own. Okay," he said, pulling out his cap and snugging it on his head, "don' say I didn' warn you."

Below, in a swale off to the side, Charles spotted the caboose crushed against the trees. He ordered the boy to wait as he began picking his way down the earth-scarred bank to it.

Several trees lay splintered at their base and one hung broken over a car. Moving around to the far end where one of its wheels was still spinning, he climbed up and surveyed the ruin. Near its caved center he found a hole punched in its side and lowered himself in. In a moment he was out again and climbing up to the track.

"Sad to say, Tadpole, we cain't do no more good in there. C'mone."

Treading cautiously, Charles led the way between the scattered debris, awed by the immensity of the damage. The air reeked with the acrid stench of hot metal, oil, and the smoking little grass fires burning along the right-of-way. Torn rails, sprung from their beds, snaked up and gleamed in the sun or twisted away beneath the wreckage. One car lay on its side, impaled by a rail that had pierced it and lay buried beneath the boxes of machine parts that had spewed from the rupture.

Slowly they wended their way around heaps and barriers of toppled loads here, or skirted wide the jumble of cars blocking their way there. Charles lifted the boy over dangerous obstacles and warned him of the treacherous footing. Then they saw it looming ahead, a mountain of cars rising like a monstrous head. From the first of two upended locomotives, fire spurted from the cab window with voracious tongues of red flame licking out of plumes of black smoke.

"Good Lord. Aint nothin' could be alive in that!"

Charles circled wide with the boy. On the far side they saw the wreckage of a passenger train, its cars flattened or accordioned, battered and torn. They picked their way closer, over jagged sheets of metal and wheels thrown free. Charles hesitated.

"Looks to me lak some kin' o' private train, Tadpole. Too short to be much else." He mopped his head with his hat. "Don' hear nothin'. 'Course—" He slapped his hat back on, pulling the brim low over his eyes. "None o' my business! Ask no favors, give no favors!" He turned. "Le's go, Tadpole."

The boy grabbed out to him. "Let go my belt, boy. We's leavin'." The boy held tight.

"You crazy? Now let go! Ain't nothin' there goin' to do *me* no good. Las' time—Hell, boy, you askin' me to risk my hide for—You see this?" He parted the tear in his pants, showing the bloody cut in his leg. "Got that crawling 'round in that cay-boose. Tol' myself then, Charles, you plumb crazy, man! What you owe anybody, 'specially after the widder Marsh? You forget so soon?" He tore the boy's hands away and stepped free.

The boy wheeled and darted for the car. Charles sprang after him and caught him by the neck.

"Hey! Better learn, Tadpole, before you gets yourself hurt

lak me. Ain't nobody goin' to ever know or care what you done or didn't do. Stay out o' it. Min' your business. Save you lot o' hurt, take my word.

"C'mone, now, don't you be lookin' at me lak that. I got no reason to feel guilty. Lookee thata way." He swung the boy's head around. "Ain't nobody can be alive in that, no how no way…Now I said…Oh, man! You quit lookin' at me." He crammed his hat in his pocket. "Okay okay. You stay put. Any part o' that gives and you be squashed lak a bug. And if'n I don' come back, you can thank yourself."

Gingerly he mounted a wall of razor-sharp sheeting and eased over it. He hurdled a short field of jagged rubble to where the track once lay but now stood like a massive fence of ties twenty yards long. Crouching through an opening to the other side, he saw a car hanging sideways on the embankment. The far end, though crushed by another car lying across it, was tilted higher than the near end. He crawled in through a gash in its side, pausing to let his sight adjust to the gloom. Pulling himself along, he felt for handholds where ever he could to keep from falling back. He edged in, as if along a steep wall.

He thought he heard a sound and held his breath to listen. "Anybody here?"

A groan, faint, almost inaudible reached his ears.

"Where you at? Speak."

Contorting and squeezing his way around a mangled heap of dislodged seats he forced his way in farther. In the dimness he could make out the fuzzy outline of a man pinned tight. Only his head and arm were exposed, the rest hidden by a sheet of steel that had been hammered in from the roof. Charles reached out, feeling ahead. He touched the hand, grasped it and, applying a steady pressure to see if he could free the man that way, pulled. Suddenly the severed arm broke free and Charles, recoiling, dropped it and heard it roll away with the pitch of the car. Shuddering, he crawled on, nauseated with the stickiness of warm blood on his hands and its cloying smell in his nostrils.

Squinting in the dark toward the raised end of the car, he flattened himself under a jagged tear in the steel roof and emerged in a hollow beyond, where he found room to kneel. A trace of light found its way in. "Anybody here?" he called out.

The voice, stronger than before, answered. "Here."

Charles crawled into a narrow tunnel of dark space. "I hears you. Hang on." His exploring hand touched the man's hand and the man gripped hard.

"…wife…my legs…."

"Okay now. Don' be doin' no talkin'. Your wife in there behind you someplace? Okay, we'll git to her, too." He paused a moment, trying to think. "You gettin' 'nough air?"

"…can't hear her.."

"She be okay, don' worry none. Jes' rest quiet. I got to go, but only for a bit." He pulled his hand free and eased back to the tear in the roof and lifted himself out. His mind raced ahead.

"Tadpole! Tadpole!"

The boy appeared from behind the fence of ties.

"Didn' I tell you to stay put! Look at your arm, nasty cut there." He inspected it on the run. "You lucky… C'mone, we's got work to do. People inside needs us. Probably more down the line, too."

The muscles of his arms stood out and perspiration wet his face as he worked the jammed end of a wooden tie free from the earth and grappled it over the rough ground to the car. The boy tried to help.

"You stay away now. I'll tell you when." The blood vessels swelled in his neck as he lifted the timber onto the car and slid it into the opening until it dropped all the way. Careful to avoid the sharp edges, he lay on his belly and reached in to position it. "Hold on," he called inside. "We's gettin' to you."

"C'mone, Tadpole," he said, jumping off the car. "Help me find a hunk o' rail for a pry." The boy tagged along, dodging with him around the obstacles.

"Worse'n any junk yard I ever did see." He stopped. "Here we go. Might jes' do."

A section of rail lay free. Except for a slight warp it looked perfect. "Now can I drag her? She gonna be heavy, boy, and goin' quite some ways back too." Taking an end, he lifted then dropped it. "Don' know, Tadpole, don' know."

He pulled his hat from his pocket, slipped it under the rail for a pad, then lifted again. Grunting, he turned sideways, bracing it on his knee, then clamped his arm around it like a vice. He leaned forward and pulled. Neck muscles stood out like cords and his body swelled with the strain. Teeth clenched, his breath came in short tight gasps. Inch by grudging inch the rail gave to his pull as he dug in and strained like an animal in harness. Under the beating sun, sweat burned over the cuts and bruises marking his body.

Fifty feet beyond he dropped the rail and fell to his knees. The boy squatted next to him, his chin propped in his hands.

"I'll say one thing, Tadpole," he said, sucking air between his words, "breakin' rock didn' do much for my mind, but it sure put muscles where they never was befo'." He stood up, weary. "Maybe not near 'nough, though. We still some ways off. Gonna take time. Don' know as we can afford it."

When he stood to take the rail again the boy tugged at his arm. "What is it, Tadpole?" The boy pointed back down the line. "We can't give up now."

The boy shook his head and pulled.

"Now you quit your messin'. Don' lak nobody grabbin' me. If'n you wants to go, go 'haid. I believes in finishin' what I starts."

The boy pantomimed working a lever.

"You see a pry better'n this'n?" The boy nodded, pointing back. "Got to be pret' near as long, and strong."

The boy tugged at him again.

"Well how come you didn' say so?" he said, letting himself be pulled along. "Lettin' me kill myself unnecessary lak that. How come you can't talk anyways? Do ever'thin' but. Eat my food and get on my nerves jes'fine. Make me do things I never intentioned." He laughed and scooped the boy up and over a piece of an undercarriage.

The boy pointed when they reached the spot.

"Oh, yeah," Charles said, climbing over to it. "Didn' see them past all this other junk here." He inspected the pile. "Jes' about right, I think, and not much more than half as heavy as I had." He patted the boy's head and reached down for one of the beams.

"Good work, Tadpole. Thass one sharp eye you got." He strained and started back.

"We'll get her now, Tadpole," Charles said, when they arrived. "We gonna do it." He lifted the bar until it touched the top of the car. Then he moved farther down and pushed it ahead, letting it slide on the metal top. When he had it raised enough, he climbed up and swung it onto the car, guiding it to the opening he'd squeezed out of earlier.

"Good thing this car's banged up, Tadpole," he shouted down. "She'd never stick in place otherwise, the way she's anglin'. He stepped over to the hole and stuck his head inside.

"Jes' hang tight in there and don' mind the noise. We's goin' fast as we can."

Scrambling back, he picked up the beam and worked it into the opening. The lower end of the car, with its roof relatively intact, posed a problem, and he had to work from the side to provide room for the lever.

He labored longer than he'd anticipated, cursing when things did not go well, and smiling when they did. Several times he called to the boy to hang on to the end of the bar with him for the extra weight he needed.

Gradually, reluctantly, the metal yielded to the steady pressure until the space below expanded. Bit by bit he pushed the tie in further as he gradually worked the beam in deeper. Back and forth he scurried, bearing down at one end, positioning and repositioning the tie and lever at the other. Inch by torturous inch the metal gave, widening and lengthening the channel.

"Thass it, Tadpole," he shouted back as he inspected the space. Hunched low, he crept in on all fours.

"Okay, mister, we got you now." He gripped the man under the arms and worked back. "You tell me if somethin' hurts." Straining in the cramped space, he tugged him along as gently as he could to the hole.

He poked his head up. "Tadpole, you see that board down there, off by the side o' them busted wheels up front? Get it and fetch it up here to me. Be quick."

Charles propped the man up. "Almost there, mister," he said, climbing out and reaching down for the board. "Good boy. That looks 'bout right." Positioning it over the hot metal next to the hole, he knelt and stretched his arms inside.

"Good," he said, grasping the man by the shoulders. "You comin' now." Rising, he hoisted the man clear and laid him on the board.

In the clear light Charles saw that this was no ordinary man. His clothes were of a material he had never seen before and on his hand, flashing like the sun, was an immense stone. Until that moment, Charles had never seen what he knew for sure was a real diamond.

The man was silver-haired and had the rosy complexion of a baby. His expression was grim and his jaw authoritative. A bluish lump bulged on his forehead, and the angle at which his legs lay told Charles they must be broken.

The man's eyes opened slowly, like doors, it seemed to Charles, church doors opening to some great reservoir of knowledge. The man tried to speak, but Charles cut him short:

"You gonna be okay, mister. Help be here soon and get you to the hospital. That smoke billering up is gonna call somebody shortly. In the meantime we'll take care o' you." He read the man's lips. "Don' worry, your woman comin' out right soon." He swung around. "Tadpole, your turn. C'mone."

Charles lowered the boy into the hole and followed him down. The boy crawled in ahead of him. Farther in, the space shrunk.

"Gettin' too tight for me now, Tadpole, but you can get back in there. No light hardly a-tall, so you gonna have to feel your way along. Not much air back there either, and it's hot, so don' waste no time.

"When you gets to her, jes' take holt under her arms if'n you can, anything else if'n you cain't. Pull easy, no jerkin', hear? Easy. You got some hard pullin' 'cause she's in tight and she's low, and no sayin' how big she is and how far to go. Get on now, Tadpole, you can do it. Didn' I see you push that big ol' boxcar door open, and break my grip to pull me off'n that train, too? Jes' drag her to me here till I can get a purchase on her." He lost the boy in the darkness and shouted after him: "And don' get yourself hung up in no bind!"

The boy bellied into the dark inner recesses of the mangled car. He stopped to listen then crawled on. The tunnel was clear but even more constricted. Feeling ahead he pressed on, finding it hard to breathe.

Then he touched her. He tried to reach in past her arm but

found it too tight. Grasping her wrist with both hands, he pulled with a steady pressure. She didn't move; he was too light. He tried bringing his knees underneath himself but lacked room. A wooziness touched him.

Still holding her wrist, he rolled to his side and brought up his knees, wedging himself in obliquely. Again he pulled. She slid a bit. Encouraged, he inched back, tugging with an even pressure, repeating the effort until he found room for a better hold. Her face was close to his in the darkness and he heard her breathing, shallow and whispering, like the susurration of the organ bellows playing in his mind. He worked her back, faster now, more confidently.

"I got her, Tadpole," Charles said, when the boy had dragged her within reach. "You slip on by me now, outside. My shirt's out there. Run on down and sop it up with water down by the trees and hurry back.

Charles brought her out and laid her on the plywood sheet next to her husband. She had a head laceration that looked serious but could be worse, Charles thought. And the way she groaned when he had picked her up led him to suspect her ribs were cracked. Her hair, silver-blue like her husband's, was disheveled on one side and matted with blood on the other.

She was a slight woman with a thin, fragile nose and chin. And like her husband, she wore an austere expression, but softened somewhat by a gentleness that seemed to touch the corners of her mouth. Around her throat her starched lace collar was dirty but still intact.

"Good boy," Charles said, taking the wet cloth from his hand as he climbed onto the car. "Looks lak you got to her jes' in time, Tadpole. Wonder she warn't suffercated way back in that hole. See how nice her color comin' back?" He dabbed at the head wound to clean it. "You be all right, ma'm," he said, sponging her face, "Charles here's makin' sure o' dat."

The woman's eyelids fluttered. In the distance Charles heard the cry of sirens. "You be all right, ma'm. Your man, too. Ever'thin' gonna be all right now."

The boy's eyes opened wide, taking in the three of them. In his head played a dulcet composition of interchanging harmonies. Easing back, he lowered himself over the side of the car.

Chapter 19

"Pssst."

The boy stopped on the road. Off to the side, through a tangled growth of wild raspberry bushes, he saw the bearded face of a man peering out sideways at him. One eye squinted, while the other opened wide, exposing a white eyeball that seemed to start from his head.

The bushes parted suddenly and the man stepped out grinning through a row of shattered teeth. He wore an olive-drab knee-length coat of old army stock, buttoned only at the collar and pulled tight around his sloping shoulders. Below, his tweedy pants bagged and on his head he wore a battered hat pulled tight over his ears.

He stooped over, hands on his knees. "Well well well well well, what have we here? Come to give an old-timer comfort, have ye?"

He knelt in the dirt, fingering his grizzled beard while his face twitched around his squinting eye. He beckoned with a stubby finger. As the boy slowly approached, the man suddenly grabbed out and pulled him in close. His hands rummaged in the boy's pockets.

"What, no candy? A lad with no candy stuck in his pockets?" Shoving the boy at arm's length and holding him there, he eyed him from top to bottom, his head cocked at a diabolical angle. He grinned. "Not affrighted of me, eh?"

He pushed the boy roughly away and stood up, wheezing. He was a ponderous man of great girth and relatively narrow shoulders and short legs. "Most unusual," he said, "most," then suddenly thrust out his hand.

"J. McCready Quisleby here." The boy shook his hand.

"Put a little force to it, son, a bit of strength. Measure of a man's will and determination. A man without a grip is a man without a backbone." The boy squeezed.

"Now, there you have it! And what might *your* name be?" The boy tried to free his hand.

"Out with it, out with it." The boy stood mute and Quisleby took him by the hair to tilt his head back. "Shy little dove, eh? Then give us a coo. Come on with ye now, coo." He threw back his head. "Like this: coo, coo, coo, coo, coooo." He laughed and flung the boy's hand away.

"Think *I'm* cuckoo, don't ye? Good. That's the way I like it and that's the way I'll have it. It's cuckoo I may be, but not cuckoo enough to care who thinks so— or who you might be. Now begone with ye!"

He crashed back through the foliage where he knelt to pack away his tins in one of the pockets of a canvas belt. He rose, short of breath, and slung the belt over his shoulder.

"Go on, little bird," he said, seeing the boy staring into the opening at him, "fly away." He lumbered out of sight behind a hedgerow. "I'm coming, Sadie, I'm acoming."

Moments later he reemerged atop a mule, its spindly legs splayed beneath his massive weight, and rode past the boy without a glance. Looking off in the distance to the smoke still darkening the sky, he sang:

"Lady bird, lady bird,
Fly away home,
Your house is on fire,
And your children will burn."

Roaring with good humor he rode off.

For three hours the boy walked the shoulder of the dirt road, trailing behind the plodding mule. Quisleby never stopped or looked back. Now and then he broke into a song and then went silent again. The air lay heavy, hot and still in the late afternoon sun, and the boy's mouth was parched with dust scuffed up by the mule's hoofs. In his mind he heard a scattering of notes, bubbly, fragile and insubstantial drifting aimlessly off.

At a small roadside clearing Quisleby finally turned in. Dismounting, he wiped the sweat from his face with a corner of his faded red shirt and yanked his coat off Sadie's back.

The boy stood watching him from the roadside, but Quisleby appeared not to see him as he hunted some tinder for a fire. From a trickling stream he filled his coffee pot and returned to set it beside the flames that were beginning to lick up. Dumping a bag on the ground, he picked the necessary utensils and wiped them on his sleeve. He polished a skillet with his elbow before spilling in a can of beans and placing it on the fire. Spooning them around until they were steaming, he lifted the pan and replaced it with the coffee pot.

He growled. "You're not going to stand there watching me to the end of my days, are ye? Eat!"

The boy edged up. His music had stopped and he struggled to understand this man who both attracted and repelled him. He tried to reason his thoughts with words, words that were beginning to shape and define themselves with greater clarity.

"Sit!" Quisleby commanded, shoving a tin of smoking beans in the boy's hands. "Drink your water from this," he said, tossing a canteen to him.

The boy sat cross-legged next to Quisleby, who alternately slurped and burped as he choked down his beans. He refilled his dish, threw the last few spoonfuls into the boy's dish without asking if he wanted more and proceeded to scrape up what was left of his own. When he had finished, he ran his sleeve across his mouth, patted his belly and released a long, deep, reverberating belch. For the first time since he'd met the boy he took a long, hard look at him, eyeing him severely.

"What do ye be following me for, Little Bird?" The boy, still eating, looked up at him. "You from that town I see burning, back past where the track bends around Sandow's Hill?"

Squinting suspiciously, he waited until the boy finished, then snatched away the empty tin and set it beside his own. From another canvas pocket he took a bottle of brandy, unscrewed the cap and measured a portion into his cup. He sipped it, smacked his lips and poured in the coffee.

He bellowed, "Well?" The boy recoiled. "Yes," he continued in a voice like a rough purr, "I see Old Quisleby has struck fear into your tender heart after all." Roaring with laughter, he stood up and carried the utensils to the stream where he sloshed them around in the water, shook them and returned. He put them away and sat down again, holding his cup in his hands like a libation.

"Now then, suppose you confide in Old Quisleby the exact nature of your business, particularly that disquieting business of stalking me like a shadow, though I may say I find it more to my preference than being shadowed by the Law.... Come now, Little Bird, speak your piece. Quisleby will lend you a sympathetic ear, which is more than anyone's done for him in longer than memory can recall."

He sipped his coffee. "Stubborn, are ye? Or is it you're smart enough to know that a closed mouth is the utmost sign of wisdom? Hah!"

He snatched up the canteen and thrust it into the boy's hands. "Drink a bit and maybe we can get a few answers. No one can long conceal himself from J. McCready Quisleby." Turning away, the boy stared into the fire and drank.

"That town I seen smoking back there, way off, you wouldn't happen to be from it, would ye? Get scared and run?" He scratched his beard. "No...you're a tame little bird, but with a heart too stout I think for that…Or did you perhaps lose your parents in that hellish conflagration? Now would *that* be it?" He poked the boy's shoulder, but the boy continued staring into the fire. "Aye, I'll wager it's something like that," he said, tossing off the dregs and slipping the cup into the belt.

He stopped suddenly and turned slowly to face the boy directly. "Shock. That's the answer. Little Bird's in shock! Don't know why I didn't see it sooner." He moved close and laid a gentle hand on the boy's shoulder. "I've seen men in war looking much the same as you. And I know what it means, Quisleby does, to lose one's parents at your young age. Mine were prematurely removed from the straitened and merciless circumstances of this world when I myself was but a tender shoot." He gazed off to the horizon where the sun was lowering in a flaming sky beyond the treetops. His phlegmy voice softened.

"'McCready is,' she said, my mother, that is— a noble woman of chosen lineage— McCready is a name you'll keep, son, and do it proud. A man can carry two names as well as one.'

"Can hardly see her face anymore, but hear her yet I can, words burning into me the way they did then, starting a fire in my head. Sent me to school, she did—the best—until a stroke of misfortune by the name of Deception stole away my father's business and left us penniless. No more school, not for a long while after, anyway. No more father, either, as he saw fit to end his troubles early and exacerbate ours. A pistol shot it was took his head away. My mother, poor suffering soul, wasn't long in following, though I might add, for more natural and less damning reasons."

His attention returned to the boy. "So, as you can see, Little Bird, I am not entirely unsympathetic toward your plight. Still, we take the world as we find it, eh? Just as it is." He slapped the boy's back.

"And there's the secret of it. It's what keeps disillusionment at bay and futility leashed. Some among us are idealists, fools who make a business of optimism and who see light in the blackness of caves. Lotus eaters is what they are, always anxious to serve up their swill to anyone naïve enough to partake of it. These would-be social alchemists defy the natural laws of human behavior and flout the lessons of history. It's grandiose plans they'll create and implement for you at your expense. Noble intentions, aye, maybe, but their ambitions always fall short of their dreams because their dreams always exceed the strictures of reality. Invariably, they become self-serving servants of the people they've sworn to serve. Where, I ask you, where's the accomplishment in that?"

He tossed a stick on the fire. "And the cynics? Why, they carry their pessimism like a contagious disease, ready to breathe it into the face of any who'll listen. This particular breed, Little Bird, you want to avoid like the plague they are because while the former poison the world around you, the latter are a blight on your soul. They're half-blind and already more than half-dead, and won't be happy till they are. Doomed men prophesying doom, they would drag us all into the dismal swamps of their philosophy and drown us in the brackish waters of hopelessness. Never was there a light strong enough and never will be they can see.

"Should be a law to chain the two kinds together, the idealist and the cynic, like Siamese twins, to make a sort of balanced man, don't you see?" He roared, laughing. "Might well be the first balanced man ever." He roared again.

"And where does J. McCready Quisleby stand?" He stood up. "Why anywhere he pleases, Little Bird, any place at all, so as to keep from being a target, so to speak.

"Now—as to you! First thing in the morning, I will point

you back to whence you came. Surely you have kin waiting. As for me, Sadie will join me in my appointed rounds with destiny, a cruel destiny designed to disappoint the hopes of my dear, departed mother, God rest her soul wheresoever she may be. I might have returned you personally, but it's a long-standing promise I made to myself never to retrace my steps or look back." He stretched and yawned. "In the meantime I have a blanket in my bindle to spare, which you are welcome to tonight."

He stuffed a plug of tobacco into his mouth and stood there chewing and looking off toward the sunset. The boy watched him remove his hat and run his hand through a flowing mane of graying hair that fell over his collar as he lumbered over to Sadie, where he unstrapped his bedroll and a blanket. He whispered into the mule's ear before carrying the gear back to a grassy spot a few feet from the fire. Dropping heavily, he beckoned the boy next to him.

"Sit!"

The boy obeyed.

"Don't worry, Quisleby won't hurt you, though you wouldn't be the first if he did. You've a way about you, Little Bird—maybe it's just holding your tongue or your uncomplaining manner or your innocent youth itself that has touched my heart, and there's not many as can do that. The years have layered her over with callus, the way yours will be if you live long enough. No man is an island unto himself, Johnny Donne says, but he's wrong as water running uphill. Every man is an island, set forever apart in the treacherous sea of life." He spit a long spurt of tobacco juice. "You'll find—

"You see that?" he cried, crawling forward on his hands and knees. "See it? Got him, by God, nailed him sure!"

Probing the grass, he retrieved a grasshopper by the legs and held it up, its body shining with brown saliva. He cocked his head to keep it in range of his searching eye. "Hah! You're not the only one as can work the juice, you hop-jumping miserable counterfeit son of a kangaroo." Roaring with good humor, he tossed it away and reached over to throw some wood on the fire.

He sat back, placing his hat on his lap. "What's the matter, Sadie," he said, catching sight of her twitching ears, "scare you too? Well, pardon my bad manners, but this unexpected and unwanted intrusion into our private and nomadic existence has rendered me temporarily careless of my obligations. Allow me to introduce you to Little Bird. Now you mustn't be too unfriendly toward him because he has a particular sort of problem you wouldn't be familiar with. In any case, he'll soon be gone and we'll be on our way again. Only the two of us."

He turned to the boy. "Little Bird, meet Sadie, stubbornest, hard-headed creature this side of creation— the worst side, I might add. But she's loyal, which is more than a man can say for his own species. Sadie's a mule, you see, so when she's being obstinate, she's only being true to her nature. Now, ye can't blame a rock for being a rock, can ye? Or a tree for being a tree? Only a fool would argue that." A thin, long, spurt of amber juice whistled between his lips.

"A mule is a sterile creature, don't you know, offspring of a male ass and a female horse. And there's the shame of it, and proof there's no justice to be found on earth. You take the human race— and I wish I could give it to ye —sterile in their minds, most of them, and prolific where they oughtn't to be. No, sir, no justice for Sadie. If she had to be cast out of the blessed Garden, the least compensation she might have been given is mastery over those apple-eating sons of Satan who caused the eviction in the first place."

He struggled up to his feet and shook his fist to the sky. "Give J. McCready Quisleby a chance up there! He'll show

You how to do the job, he will all right! Give *him* a chance at the reins to teach You how it ought to be done! Give *him* the power to move the mountains and he'll show You how to clean up and bury the ills of this world!

"Ahh, it never did any good trying to reason with You," he said, breathing hard and sagging to the ground. "Never listen anyway." His face twitched as he slowly subsided.

"Now some might say there's blasphemy in my words," he whispered in his phlegmy voice, "that what I say might be displeasing or offensive to Him. But they're wrong as corn in May. He knows I'm right, don't ye see? That's the reason He don't dispatch me with His thunderbolts. If—" He fixed his squinting eye on the boy. "For a little bird in shock, you seem mighty alert to my words, the way those tender, baby-blue eyes keep following me around, watching my every move and my face when I speak."

He rose and clutched the boy by the collar. "Didn't anybody send you 'round to spy on me, did they? Try to lure me to town where they can incarcerate me, never to turn this good eye on Sadie again, or the vast beauty of this world that breathes from everything man never touched and nothing he did?"

He hauled the boy to his feet and glared into his face with one flaming eye. "Lie to me and I'll tear you asunder."

From the boy's throat leaked a tenuous crying of violins.

Quisleby cocked his head, his eye searching above, as if hearing with it. He released the boy and spun around. "Hear that, Sadie? Did ye hear it?"

Again he looked hard at the boy, then edged suspiciously over to Sadie. He stroked her neck and spoke softly in her ear. "Probably gypsies. Did ye see them, too, their wagon tracks back yonder? Sure," he said, rubbing her ear, "that must be it. And I don't like it! Fortune telling pocket-picking sons of

Deception." He cupped his hands around his mouth. "Away with ye," he shouted, "ye scavenging bunch of conniving rootless misfits. Keep clear of Quisleby!"

He trailed off mumbling curses as he drew out the flask and tipped his head back for a long drink. "Hahhh, a little brandy to sweeten the disposition, eh, Sadie?"

The sun dipped lower, flushing the sky with crimson and gold. Quisleby lay back, his eyes closed, breathing in a raspy, uneven rhythm that matched the rhythm playing in the boy's mind. For a while he lay there saying nothing as the boy's silent rhythm quickened to a choppy tempo out of which tripped a random scattering of notes that alternately found and lost each other, bright, melodic clusters fragmenting and wandering off.

"Little Bird, yours is the first human face Quisleby's observed in a long time." His eyes were still closed and he spoke dreamily, as if to himself. "Just a small part of the bargain I've made to shun this world as much as it has me, a bargain we've both found profit by. Have to admit, though, Quisleby does, your appearing uninvited and unannounced hasn't been altogether unpleasant. It's more your doing than mine, I suppose. There's a soothing quality to ye almost equal to Sadie's. Ye've struck an agreeable chord in Old Quisleby's heart, what little's left of it and not yet turned to stone."

He flung his arm over his eyes to keep the light from filtering in. "It's a strange and peculiar thing, Little Bird, but Quisleby's got a gift for seeing people as nobody else can. Give me a face, any face, and I can visualize it growing older, can see the evolutionary changes coming to sculpt the flesh and bone in accordance with the laws of its own nature. It always was one of my private amusements, ever since I can remember —to look at somebody and watch him age afore my very eyes. One thing is certain: it puts vanity to flight and takes the accent off of what's unimportant.

"I've seen women, never ogled them, mind you, just looked—well, not too much ogling anyway—beautiful women who've made their face the main focus of their lives. Made me smile as I watched them, seeing their beauty fade away and leaving before me no more than a withered hag. Oh, they'd get mad to see Quisleby smiling to himself, so smug and knowing. And how they'd look themselves over to see if a button was left undone somewhere. Finding none, they'd naturally think I knew something I wasn't supposed to. Once, one even hit me on the head, attacked me outright. Made me laugh to crying to think it was no young beauty so full of outrage batting me, but a lady old enough to be my grandmother." He laughed and went silent.

"Strange thing here, Little Bird," he said, after a while, "I've been trying to see your face that way and can't seem to do it…most unusual, most. Could be, I suppose, after all this time I've lost the gift."

Opening his eyes, he blinked against the diffused light of the dying day. Shadowy at first, he saw the boy standing above him, looking down at him, with the sunlight playing in his hair, an aura of golden fire ringing his head. He started up and edged back on his hands, squinting to see. His bad eye, white as a peeled egg, bulged.

"Icarus!" He cocked his head. "Icarus incarnate!" He fell back, his lips moving silently as if in prayer or delirium.

Sensing no danger to the man or to himself, the boy turned away from him to face the sinking sun. Music broke within his mind, as if suddenly freed from some deep and distant place, and rose on soaring strings to dissipate into the golden silence of the sunset.

"Icarus, Icarus, of course, Icarus!" He launched himself to his feet and began pacing the ground. He stopped, extending his hand. "Sadie! Behold, Icarus!"

Warily he came forward, circling the boy. "Upon what mission might ye be, hey? Or is it J. McCready Quisleby himself ye're after?" The boy turned with him. "Come, Icarus, be square with me. Would it be me ye want?" He backed away from the boy's penetrating eyes to a safer distance. Scratching his beard, which was thrust out with his face, he contemplated the boy suspiciously.

"But where's the purpose in that? Aye, that's the question. 'Tain't as if Old Quisleby'll resist if he's called upon a mission necessitating his taking leave of this spoiled Elysium field. Glad to do it. On the other hand, is a man expected to participate in the making of his own gallows, that is, supposing ye're purpose is not in the best interests of the man? Aye, there's something to think about, too."

A spasm shook his body and he stood facing the boy directly. "Make the charge against me. A man's a right to hear what he's accused of, don't he? Would ye condemn me for not involving myself in the common struggle of mankind? Is that it? Is it because I give up my calling and no longer extend my hand to the sick and needy?

"Icarus, Icarus. Ye're looking at a man who'd hoped to do just that and who's given up the dream. A man who also hoped to leave some scratch of himself on the memory of his fellow man, but who's given that up as well for the vanity it is. Think on it, Icarus, there's a fine line between helping and interfering. And who's to say where it is, eh? Many's a good intention there's been that's brought more untold misery and ruination than it had hoped to end. It's the testimony of a man who's lived long ye're listening to, Icarus. Judge if ye will, but afore ye condemn an innocent man to damnation, think back to the dreams of mankind and find one if ye can that history hasn't made a mockery of."

He spread his arms. "Well, if it's J. McCready Quisleby ye still want, come and take him!"

The boy advanced slowly, his arm out before him. Quisleby trembled. The boy touched him and he fell to the ground, howling.

"Mercy, Icarus, mercy, mercy! Ye can't take a man whose life is yet to be redeemed." He groveled, hugging the boy's legs. "It's an act of personal courage that makes a man ready and willing to go. It's a single heroic act of moral conviction that gives a man's life worth and makes it more valuable than that of a fish's." He moaned.

The boy reached down, gently touching his shoulder. Quisleby shuddered and lay still. Then slowly, his hand crept out of the huddle of his body. He felt his arm, his leg, his chest. He cocked his eyebrow and head together.

"Quisleby, ye're a fool! Ye've let ye're imagination come unharnessed. Look at yourself, cowering here before a boy who only wanted to reassure ye."

He rose, dusting himself. "When a man lives in the dark and all alone, often as not he comes to see demons where none exist." He glared down at the boy. "I can't tell whether that smile on your face is one of mischief or triumph. Then again, maybe it's just your way of offering peace to a man used to waging war.

"No matter! A man's a right to make a fool of himself now and again," he growled, "as long as he don't do it the same way twice. It's a tricky and deceptive path we follow and none runs true to expectations. The world is a labyrinth, don't you see, Icarus, like the mind of Man. Bound to find himself in a cul-de-sac on occasion. There's no shame in it. No shame in getting lost, only in staying lost. Not as there's assurance of a way out, either, but that ye keep looking for the signs, as a sort of commitment to purpose, don't ye see? ...Feed the fire!" He strode to his blanket and hurled himself down.

The boy watched the flames dance up over the new wood and sat beside him.

"Ah, Icarus, 'tis the ravings of a man who's committed his life to no purpose except madness, pure and true madness, which is not to be confused with the false madness that rules the lives of others. Consider how they use the present merely as a place from which to view the future, where, for them, fulfillment always resides. They strive for it, and when they arrive they find that it has receded to a new future place. It's a cruel deception they have created for themselves, for they have thrown away the present reality and all the riches it might give, for future illusions that give nothing but disappointment." His rueful laugh came with a phlegmy timbre.

"But that's not all, Icarus. A man living from disillusionment to disillusionment is tragedy enough, ye might think. But there's an irony in it that compounds the deception, completes it, so to speak, and makes a farce of life, for that same man, when he's advanced in years and with no future left, will look to the past and see in it a fulfillment he never knew. He draws from a kind of peripheral memory, don't you see, and says, 'Them were the good old days. I've had a full, rich life.'

"Hah! Fools lost in the madness of self-delusion. But not Quisleby. It's not the world he's backed away from; it's the people and the common strivings of the human race. There's not a day passed in the last fifteen years that he hasn't squeezed and choked out of her every pleasure she's had to offer. It's a new course he's set for himself, one that steers clear of the troubled lanes of human commerce. It's myself I seek, and madness is my Divinity, chaste and uncorrupted.

"And who's to say such a journey is not as noble as any other yet conceived by Man. I'll argue them all down on that!" He shook a clenched fist in the air. "Reason's won the day and has held it for some time. The only true way they say—they they they. But where's Reason taken us thus far? In the holy name of Reason we've colored the seven seas red with the blood of humanity. Reason it is and Reason alone that's delivered carnage and suffering in its thousand variations down through the blood-soaked ages. No, Icarus, 'tisn't true Reason men worship, but a counterfeit madness posing as Reason, logically presented and scientifically formalized. It's a false light they shine on the world, like swamp gas that lures men into the treacherous waters of hidden bogs."

He reached over and patted the boy's leg. "Ah, Icarus, the complexity of the labyrinth the mind of Man has invented to hold himself fast! And there's no escape from it in life except through madness, true madness."

He rolled sideways, squinting up. "But if Man builds labyrinths, who is it builds those infernal paradoxes from which there can never be escape? Aye, there's something to chew on. Many's the night Old Quisleby's lain out, looking up to the stars, trying to find understanding. Paradox. It's a road that doubles back on itself, an end with no beginning and a beginning with no end, a room full of mirrors that wipes out the difference between reason and madness. Hephaestus himself, that lame and master artificer of a million designs, never contrived anything like it to so confound and boggle the mind."

Gazing into the grizzled face, which was staring up again and rambling on, the boy's lips parted and the mellifluous call of a French horn issued forth. Quisleby's breath stopped and his squinting eye strained to see the boy clearly. A melodic chorus of plucking strings, sharp and lucid, struck out in a dithyrambic frenzy. Quisleby's white eye rolled with his frantic mind. He listened, then went limp. His lips moved, incoherent mumbling lost in the quickening tempo that carried the melody up and dissolved with it.

"Old Quisleby's heard," he began hoarsely, "...heard many a strange sound in the night, Icarus. But this...this belabors all powers of comprehension." His head slid sideways. "If it's Apollo that's lent ye his lyre to play in my ear, what am I to make of it? An ear hard put to distinguish between the fall of rain and the rain of rocks, that now hears and recognizes the music of the gods—what purpose is there in it? What design is to be found in the crossing of our paths, Icarus?" He sat up, moving his face in close to the boy's. "Eh? What design that brought Old Quislby out of the dark and opened his mind to thoughts he could never put words to before?" He lurched to his feet.

"Confound you! Speak and let it see light." The falling shadows mottled his face. "Well, then you listen," he growled. "No man or god exists who can long bully J. McCready Quisleby! Aye, I've seen the many faces of both, awake and in my sleep, and it's what I know of each that's driven me wide and clear of 'em. Who is it that's put the nature in a man to devour his own? Who is it that's given him a symmetry that makes a tiger a lamb by comparison? Tell me that if ye can. And more to the point, justify it!" He stalked back and forth pulling at his beard.

"Get some dirt on your hands and pitch it on the fire! And take it for a lesson. Hands with dirt on them don't ever make a war. And it's dirty hands that keep a mind clean and trouble free. And it's a clean mind that deprives the devils of a place to propagate." He pointed to the fire. "And when ye're done there, look up, take a good look at those blinking stars and measure your size against them. Consider too your ambitions and your dreams and your place in this dark and dismal universe."

A raucous chorus of music broke loose in the night, wailing

and disjointed, loud and shrilling.

Quisleby fell back. "Ye can't scare me," he shouted against the increasing volume. "It's my mind and only that playing tricks again." He stumbled over to his blanket and dropped to his knees.

"Don't you see, Icarus," he pleaded, hands extended, "don't you see that Sadie there is worth more than all in heaven and earth put together? There's not a shred of deceit in her, and none of the false promises that shine everywhere like beacons on deadly shoals. Don't ye see?" His head dropped to his knees and his back rose and fell with his labored breathing. The music settled into a sedate and soothing rhythm, wafting out to him. Slowly, he lifted his head, cocking it to find the boy. His face twitched.

"First ye come to trouble me physically, to put me out, vex my mind and disturb my peace. That ye surely did." His head shook with minute tremors as he spoke. "Now ye want to trouble my spirit. But that ye'll never do!" His clenched fists went out in front of him. "Leave Quisleby alone!" he cried into the night. "He don't want nobody! He don't need nobody! Leave him be!"

He slumped and his body shook. The music drifted in, surrounding him, placating him, wrapping itself around him in warm caressing tones. Moaning, he fell back, hugging himself.

The night stirred to life with the chirpings and cluckings that arrived with the wan light of a sallow moon. The air, damp and cool, lay heavy with the rich, green smells of new growth. From the buried embers a handful of sparks exploded softly and crackled up to glow an instant before dying in the breeze sifting in. Exhausted, Quisleby slept. The boy slept beside him.

The moon had risen overhead when the boy's eyes sprang open. He bolted up and the soft mewling of violins crept out falteringly. From out of the darkness, before he could raise his arms to stop it, a hand slipped in, clamped over his mouth and drag-carried him into the foliage. Struggling, he kicked against the dark force hauling him off through the thick brush.

Black music raged in his head as he fought to pry away the fingers. He writhed and twisted fiercely, trying to free himself from the suffocating hand locked onto his face. He tore away a piece of the attacker's garment at the same time the music went silent and the black night swallowed him.

Chapter 20

Axles creaking under its load, the wagon jostled over the rutted back roads. From time to time the boy stirred, vaguely conscious of the pain throbbing in his head. For two days he did not awaken and lay in a fitful sleep. He dreamed…

…Dreamed of a time his father had taken him to a water hole, where, momentarily submerged, he saw the silver-white water moving fluidly before his eyes. And again he heard the drum and skirling of its currents as water dumped into the hole from a pencil falls at its far end. Music played in his head, the way it did then, an ethereal melody augmenting and diminishing, ebbing and flowing in a pulsing rhythm. Then came a distortion of sound, uneven and pounding, disintegrating like a storm-driven surf on a rocky shore. Swirling darkness engulfed him, then a gradual return of light as strong hands pulled him to his mother's breast, her arms enfolding and hugging him, rocking rocking….

"You fool, you might have killed him."

The voice came through dimly and the boy's eyes flickered with the drip of cool water on his brow.

"I have told you, he struggled. He is small but strong."

The boy's eyes opened. In the dim lantern light hovering over him, he saw a woman's face. Her long hair, tied behind, hung over her shoulder and brushed his cheek. Behind her, to the right, a man sat forward, slowly rubbing his clasped hands and staring down between his feet. A silken band encircled his head.

"Look, Zara, he wakens," she said, reaching back to touch him.

"Go quickly," he whispered, "bring food."

She made a secret sign about her lips and, holding away her trailing skirt, stooped out the wagon door.

The boy eased himself up, touching the cloth swathing his head. He felt dizzy and blinked to clear his head and to adjust to the semi-dark. Across from him he saw protruding from a quilt tucked around his neck, the sleeping face of a boy very much like himself.

The man knelt forward, following the boy's eyes. "That is Yasha," he said, "my son. He is ill."

The boy did not miss the break in the man's voice nor the misty shine of his dark eyes as he spoke. His nose, hooked from the bridge, lent his face a fierce expression, and his lips, unlike Quisleby's, which were lost in his beard, were full and sharply defined against his clean-shaven face. The golden ring looped through his ear twinkled as it spun slowly with his movements.

"You have slept long, but now you will be better. It is nothing," he said, pointing to the bandage. "A small wound that will heal itself quickly." His eyes drifted back to the sick boy. "Yasha is not so fortunate."

The boy could see the young face more clearly now, the sallow skin and the hollow cheeks. The narrow ridge of his nose between the sunken shadows of his eyes, and the hair growing over his ears gave him a wolfish appearance. His breathing came at irregular intervals, shallow and almost inaudible.

The woman returned carrying a hot bowl thick with a vegetable broth. She squeezed the man out of her way and knelt in his place beside the boy. "You must eat," she said, lifting the spoon to his lips. "This will make you strong again." She spooned more out. "Good," she said, with each mouthful he took. "Good," she repeated softly.

The boy glanced to their faces, and the dirge that had begun when he first saw the sleeping boy revived and grew stronger.

"Your name is Icarus," the man said, leaning in. The boy faced him fully. "I overheard. How do you feel?" The boy smiled weakly. The man nodded thoughtfully. "You have slept long and now Marija's broth will nourish you." His eyes met the woman's and flashed away.

"Eat it all," he said, rising, "and when you are finished come outside into the daylight." He turned and crouched out.

The woman appraised the boy darkly, occasionally gazing across to her sleeping son. "The man called Quisleby," (she pronounced the 's' hard) "is he your father?" She spoke in whispers, as if from habit. "Never mind," she snapped, "I do not want to know. Do not answer."

She scraped the bowl, studying him as she had throughout the feeding. Dark eyes looked up from her half-bowed head, and her long lashes cast shadows on her high cheekbones.

When the boy had finished the last of his meal, he looked again to the sleeping boy. A funereal theme creeping out withdrew with the sound of the woman's voice.

"My Yasha," she said wistfully, her eyes worrying over him. "Like you he is very young. A happy boy always. See how he sleeps, and none of our medicine can awaken him. Each day he grows… he cannot…." She balked and lifted a glacial face to the boy. "But you do not care! He is nothing to you or your kind!" She gathered her skirt about her. "We go," she said, with a chill detachment.

Shielding his eyes against the sun, the boy followed the woman down the wagon steps into a forest clearing. Out of the crowd of watchers standing in a half-circle stepped Zara, her husband. His earring sparkled in the light as he approached. An ominous humming vibrated in the boy's throat as Zara stepped around him and pulled his arms behind to tie them with the rope he carried. "I am sorry to do this," he said, binding him tightly, "but it is necessary. Walk."

The boy passed the staring, silent faces. They parted to let him through. A young girl broke away toward him, but she was snatched back by her flowing black hair and slapped. She fell and lay quietly, her skirt flared around her. Zara led the boy along, past a number of wagons which, like his own, were embellished with strange configurations painted with bright colors. At the edge of the clearing he tethered the boy to a tree.

"You will not be here long," he said evenly, his jaw set. "Drink will be brought to you. And food. Be comfortable." He did not look at the boy when he spoke.

The sun rose to the treetops and its light danced between the leaves rustling in the morning breeze. And dancing in the boy's mind were the red, yellow and black designs he'd seen on the wagons. Whisperingly, his music came, a solemn harmony of hymnal passion, but infused with an intruding whine of sibilants that grew more forceful and persistent, until he knew that an unaccounted presence of something he knew no word to express posed a danger to him. He struggled against his bonds.

Inside the wagon Marija spoke in muffled tones through the shawl now covering her mouth. "I do not like it. This… this Icarus, he does not speak."

"He is only frightened," Zara said. "Or perhaps the blow. It is of no consequence."

"No." she answered sharply. "There is a defect in him."

"What do you mean?"

"I do not know. Once, he opened his mouth, but no words came. Instead…I thought…I do not know. It was dark, and I…I…."

Zara touched her arm. "This has been difficult for you, I know. You are tired from the long worry. But you must be strong, only for a short while more. Soon, tonight, it will be over. You will have your son back. We will have our little Yasha again."

"But how can we be sure? I could learn nothing of him. The Ancient One, she said his sign…his—"

"Hush. There is nothing to be done for it. We must trust in her word, and in her cards, and what has been delivered into our hands."

She fell silent for a moment, her fingers twisting the fringe of her shawl. She spoke then and said, "He does not look like a boy of the road."

"He must be. The man called Quisleby, he is a stranger, not the father. I heard him talking. He is a crazy man, a madman of no importance."

"But if he is only lost—"

"He is not!" His voice rose, then quickly subsided. "You have seen the dirt on him, his rags. Are these the markings of one who has a place? He is but an orphan, unwanted, cast out into the world alone. I have no doubt."

"This one is gentle, not what I had expected," she said, her voice strained. "The eyes, so knowing, yet without anger, without the malice I have seen in others of his kind. Trusting. When I fed him, his hand touched my face, as if he understood my sadness and…and my—"

"Think only of Yasha! Look, see how he sleeps? With each breath his life slips away a little more. He is our son. Who shall pity us if he dies? Who will care that his bones are buried in these fields to rot. The doctor? He who drove us away because of his fear of us? They who look upon us like a plague to be driven from their towns? All the others who persecute us because they do not understand that we wish only to roam free and to be left in peace? And you show concern for one of theirs!"

Her eyes wandered to her son and her hand reached out to

stroke his forehead. "Yes, Zara, my husband, you are right. It is as you say. The…the Ancient One, she is certain?"

"She said the signs are as they should be. She can do no more. It has been done before, she said. In the Old country, a man named—"

"No. I do not want to hear!"

* * * * *

The sting on the boy's cheek awakened him where he was dozing on the ground. He recognized her as the girl with the long hair who had tried to run to him. She stood several feet away holding a handful of stones.

"Shhh. They would beat me. No one is allowed near you."

The boy smiled to the mischievous smile in her bright eyes and she smiled back.

"You do not look dangerous to me," she said. "Why do they keep you tied up like an animal?"

The boy rose and moved toward her, but she jumped away. "Stay back!" She circled out before sitting on the ground, out of reach, with her skirt draped over her upraised knees. She appraised him curiously, suspiciously.

"But you must be dangerous. They have been whispering all morning, and they would not tie you so. What have you done? You can tell me. Have you broken one of our laws?" She leaned forward. "Are you afraid to speak? Trenina can keep a secret," she whispered.

The boy turned his back and motioned with his tied hands.

"If you tell me, perhaps I will help you." She started up. "No, I cannot," she said, falling back. "Maybe you will kill me."

Squatting, the boy faced her and watched her fondle the stones she dumped in her lap. He remembered his own bright stones at home.

Her eyes lit up. "Did they cut your tongue out? I have seen how they do it when a pig is butchered. Yasha— he is sick now but when he is well and grown up, I will be his wife—he told me that it has happened, that if someone cannot keep a secret, their tongue is cut out." She pressed forward, whispering. "Have you told a secret?"

The boy stuck out his tongue and she covered her mouth to stifle her giggles. Gradually she recovered and grew sad. "I wish Yasha was here. They won't let me see him. He would know what to do. Yasha is the smartest boy in the clan, and he knows many secrets. But *he* would *never* tell."

She meditated over her stones. "It is not fair to keep you tied, while the dogs run free. I am sorry. But you must not be afraid. My people are kind, they will not hurt you. Perhaps when you are not so frightened you will explain it all to me. It is very mysterious. I have tried to ask the other children, but they will not talk to me. Only Yasha talks to me, but he is too ill now. The others, they say I am different. But I am not. I…I do not care what they think!" She tossed the stones away. "When Yasha is well we will laugh together and not care how the others look at us."

A sprightly tune broke from the boy and quickly subsided to a throaty violin bowing down and leveling off to a melancholic resonance.

The girl brightened. "I do not know that song. But I feel I have heard it…long ago, someplace. Even Yasha cannot sing so beautifully, I think, and he sings like a bird when he is happy."

She edged closer. "If I free you, will you teach me?"

The boy turned sideways, again offering his bound hands from behind.

She touched them then pulled away. "No. Maybe you are

trying to trick me. How do I know you will not escape? Are you a devil, a serpent in a boy's body?" She recoiled with the horror of her suggestion.

The violin played again, soothingly, and she edged in. "No, if you were a devil you could not sing so. And besides, simple ropes could not hold you, not even chains. You would have the magic power to escape....

"Oh, why don't you speak?" She pouted. "If you would speak, I could make you promise...but—" She clapped her hands. "Do you have something valuable that I can hold? Then you would not run away." Her eyes narrowed on him. "No, you are poor, like us. That I can see?"

Thoughtfully she played with her hair, which flowed in dark streams over her shoulders to her lap. "When you smile like this you do not look dangerous. But...you are different from us, and perhaps that is what makes you dangerous."

She flung herself away miserably. "Oh, I do not like to see you bound so, but if you escape there will be no one for me and I do not know how long Yasha will be ill and what will I do if they find out and with no one to sing a song to my stories?" Her bright eyes shot up to him. "You can do that, can't you, sing a song to my stories, like Yasha, when he was well?"

An encouraging note throbbed out to her.

"If you sing I will free you." She faced him and he smiled across to her. "All right," she said, pulling her skirt tight around her legs, and began:

"A long time ago, faraway, in a land of hills and streams and horses and cows and many animals, there lived a little girl named Tanya."

Distantly, muted trumpets tapped in syncopation. Trombones, inflating a single note, blew in over the muffled beat of a drum. She paused, listening to the music swell in and pass like a fading echo.

"Tanya was not happy," she began again. "Each morning she would wake up to the sun and say, 'Today I am going to be happy.' But each night she went to bed as sad as ever with tears in her eyes."

The reedy sound of a melancholy oboe wavered in.

"No one knew of Tanya's sadness. All thought, what a happy girl she is! And that was because the smile on her face was something they could see. But they could not see inside her heart. Sometimes she would wander away by herself. And when she found a safe place by a stream or under the skirt of a hemlock tree, where the deer sometimes sleep, she would talk to herself.

"'I know I am wanted here,' she would tell herself, 'even though they sometimes beat me. But that is my fault. If I did not dream so, and attended to my duties as the other children do, they would not find reason to be angry with me.'

"But Tanya could not help dreaming. She loved her people, but she could not forget the old man and his blind wife and the two years she had spent with them."

The quavering of breathing woodwinds issued forth.

"And Tanya would think about them and how she came to them when her tribe had been driven from their town. In the confusion and the haste she had become lost. She searched everywhere and still she could not find them. She called and she cried, but they did not come to her. And so she wandered until her hunger forced her to the door of her people's enemies.

"At first she would not answer their many questions, even as they gave her food and comfort. She did not trust their kind faces and their gentle voices. And even when they wished to know of the laurel marking on her arm, though very proud of her tribe's symbol, she would not reply."

In the background the boy's music played a dark accompaniment to her words as his eyes wandered to the sprig showing like a blue tail beneath the sleeve of her white blouse. Behind him, his hands found a sharp rock protruding between the roots of the sycamore tree shading over them. Digging with his fingers he scraped grooves along its sides.

"It seemed strange to Tanya to sleep in so large a place on so soft a bed with no one close by to touch if she had a bad dream. It was strange to eat at a table, too, and more strange to see them pray before each meal. Each night in bed she would remember the sleeping noises of her family and the smells that had comforted her. She would think of their faces and thought she would die of loneliness. In the mornings she would look out the window for the wagons to come. That is when she was saddest of all. She missed her brothers and her sisters very much and longed to hear them laugh again and to sing the songs of her people around the campfire.

"In the evenings she would sit in the parlor with the old man whose name was Jeth and his blind wife Theresa. But because they frightened her with their difference she would not sit near them. The old man Jeth's face was wrinkled and covered with a long beard and his teeth were crooked and yellow. And the old woman Theresa's eyes looked like black holes in her white face and she seemed to be forever listening. She sat very still but her hands were always busy with her knitting."

The stone loosened and the boy twisted it in his hands to run the sharp edge across his bonds while his music brightened to a soothing, almost hypnotic mellowness. Trenina paused to listen.

"Little by little Tanya learned to trust them. Maybe it is their voices, she thought, because they are so warm, like the fire. They were kind to her, too, and never once did they beat her. And every day she sat a little closer to them, which she knew made them very happy.

"Tanya could always tell when a wagon or a cart was going to come by because the old woman Theresa's hands would stop moving before it happened. Then Tanya would run to the window, but it was never her people, and Tanya would come sadly back to her chair near them."

The music brightened and dimmed with her mood.

"Soon, Tanya was doing chores to help them. She washed the floors and the clothes and carried in the firewood. That helped her to forget her people more and more. But still she would think about them at night in bed. Then she would get terribly sad all over again. She was sure they thought she was dead. Anyway, they must be very, very far away and would never come back, she thought. And then she would cry herself to sleep."

The boy's wrists ached with his efforts. He wasn't sure the rock was cutting. Lost in her distant vision of images and sounds, Trenina did not notice his activity.

"Day by day Tanya grew more happy and she even began to hum songs. One day it was raining and Tanya could not do her outside chores. The old man Jeth was reading out loud like he always did to them at such times. It was a big book of many yellow pages with poetry in it. Suddenly he said, 'You must learn to read, Tanya.' Tanya did not know that words so beautiful to hear could be so difficult to read. But soon she was reading to them as they would sit with their heads back and eyes closed. It was very wonderful to Tanya to read to them and feel their happiness."

The music played softly around her dreamy face.

"And sometimes they would listen to Tanya's stories and make her tell all she could remember from around the campfires, and they would tell her how beautiful they were. Tanya was very happy she remembered so many, and she was very proud. And sometimes the old man Jeth would tell Tanya stories of people and of places with many strange names. He told her how people who lived long, long ago built wonderful cities with great temples and palaces and how they had spread their knowledge and their art."

The boy's music flared in a strident parade of rich, ruffle beats of marching rhythms that diminished to a hollow, distant din. One of his bonds slackened.

"And sometimes when the old man Jeth would tell his stories, his Theresa's hands would work as if with eyes of their own to make Tanya clothes of the kind young girls of the town wore. At first they seemed strange to Tanya, but soon she became accustomed to them, though they were not as colorful as her own.

"Tanya was very happy now, but one thing she still did not like was the bath she was forced to take every week, even when she was still clean and the weather cold. And one thing made her sad, too, though she could not help it: she could not call them Father and Mother, as the old man Jeth had once asked."

A violin echoed plaintively to her words as the ropes loosened.

"It was in the summer, when Tanya was in the yard scattering feed to the chickens and she was not paying attention and did not hear any sound because she was thinking of the school she would soon go to. She remembered the many books on the old man Jeth's shelf she would soon be reading and her heart was singing. Suddenly, she was surprised by someone hiding behind the coops. At first she did not realize it was her people. She did not know the face anymore. She cried out but it was too late. She—"

The boy was standing. His hands were spread wide before him and his music spilled in an effusion of mingled and contrasting harmonies.

Trenina leaped up. "Wait," she cried, seeing him step over a fallen log into the woods. "Please don't go."

He turned and paused, his music damped to a velvety arpeggio.

She hoisted her skirts to give chase, ran a short distance, tripped and fell. "Don't be afraid!" she called as he disappeared into the trees. "Please…wait!"

For a moment she lay still, listening to her heart and to his footsteps dying away. Color rushed to her cheeks, and her hair hung loose around her face. She raised her head. "He's running away!" she cried. "The stranger is running away!"

A chorus of voices preceded the men scrambling toward the clearing. It was Zara who arrived first. "Where?" he said panting. "Which way?"

"I did not do it," she protested, "I did not set him free."

Zara shook her. "Which way? Speak!"

She pointed.

He shouted back, giving instructions and crashed into the woods, out of sight.

The boy did not know his way. He squinted up at the sun through a breach in the treetops, seeking a direction. He struck out again, plunging ahead of the voices, everywhere, and growing louder.

He did not get far. At the base of a shale outcropping a band of four swooped in, taking and lifting his struggling body and raising cries amid other cries.

Chapter 21

Zara's hands worked feverishly as he bound the boy hand and foot to a tall stake anchored in the center of the field. The anger he had felt with the boy's escape obliterated the doubts Marija had sown in his heart, and he saw only Yasha's pallid face before him now as he worked coldly, efficiently. He pulled the ropes tight.

"This time you will not so easily escape, Icarus." He played out just enough rope for the boy to stretch out on the ground. "It will not be long, little one. It will not be long now."

He scrutinized his knots and stood up, scrutinizing the boy. "You have a brave heart and are stronger than you appear. That it good...good." He unfastened the gourd from his belt. "Drink."

The afternoon wore on slowly under the sun that beat down from a cloudless sky. Few people were to be seen. Now and then from one of the wagons shaded under the trees far to the side, a head popped out and vanished again. A shriek, like that of an animal in pain, shattered the afternoon stillness, and the boy recognized it as Trenina's voice before it died and returned the afternoon to the monotonous droning of insects.

The day cooled. Like shadows, women slipped from the wagons to set up their pots on the cooking fires burning nearby. A nickering horse answered another. From one of the lead wagons, the one he had slept in next to Yasha, the boy saw Marija emerge, her shawl tight over her head.

Soundlessly she approached him, head low, carrying in her hands food and water. Her long black lashes guarded her eyes as she set the dish on the ground and held the bowl of water to his lips. His parched tongue sucked at it. Kneeling, she spooned food into his mouth, as before, avoiding his steady gaze.

When he had had enough, she rose, shrouded in uncertainty and doubt. He was handsome, this boy, she thought, though not so much so as her Yasha. But he was healthy and Yasha sick; strong, while Yasha wasted away to nothing. She saw the cords cutting into his wrists and she winced with the sharp twinge of compassion she tried to keep from her heart. She bit her lip to drive away the image of a lamb with its willing throat ready for the knife.

But she could not still her anxiety. Not until she remembered that he was one of those who would leave her Yasha to die, pitilessly, forgotten. Zara was right! She would not allow this face that showed no anger, no scorn, no hate to soften her. She was not unaware of his race and their skillful art of dissembling.

Coldly she turned and began to walk away. A poignant note hummed out to her. She stopped, half-turning, listening to the ancient melody of a haunting lullaby reach out to her, wreathing her. Clutching her head shawl she scurried on, her bare feet stirring the dust.

The sun sank in the darkening red sky, as if in a sea of blood, and with the coming darkness came dark figures from the wagons to gather in small groups. The boy could not hear their voices but he sensed a peril that registered in him like the ominous beating of a drum. He fought against the ropes burning his flesh as a music of black despair swelled in his chest.

For a while all was silent again. The stars twinkled out one by one until, collectively, they saturated the sky with a milky hue. Edging over the treetops, the moon cast long, hard shadows over the ground. Lying on his back, the boy watched its undetectable but inexorable ascent. From the wagons, voices went up and he saw the faceless shapes collecting in a circle outside the lead wagon.

He struggled. Together, the voices rose, chanting words in a melodic vein that made him listen. His music crept out to find a blend to it. Strange rhythms hid within it, unfamiliar phrasings and musical expressions that seemed to embrace a range of contradictory emotions. It was intimate and alien, cruel and kind, exotic and familiar, savage and tranquil. An urgency quickened in him as he sought to determine its predominant theme, its rudimentary source and meaning. Again he pulled viciously against his bonds.

The musical chanting filled the night, mounting in fervor with the mounting full moon until it hung directly overhead, when the music stopped abruptly. Out of the silent group four figures moved toward the boy. Two carried a stretcher between them, and the boy knew without seeing that it bore the sleeping Yasha. He watched their steady approach, heard the tread of their feet, and saw as they neared that one of the figures was a woman.

In the flooding light he could see that it was Zara who knelt close by to drive several small stakes into the ground. Beside him, under the burning eyes of an old woman, the stretcher-bearers laid the sick Yasha and stole away in a stooped, loping run.

From the woman's lips fell silent incantations. Her white hair, fanning out over her shoulders from under her head shawl, lent a wild expression to the fissured imperturbability of her face. Zara's knife cut cleanly through the boy's bonds and his powerful hands held him firmly as he tied him to the stakes. Over his shoulder, past his grim face, the moon shone bright.

The old woman moved to the feet of both boys, lying side by side. From the folds of her clothing she drew strange amulets and jiggled them in her hands. She raised her arms, muttering. Her voice strengthened and her words became audible.

The group beyond began to sing again, the same chant that now regulated itself to a controlled, even pattern of measured time. From her dark garb the woman drew a bowl which she handed to Zara, kneeling between the boys. He took it and placed it at his side. Then from a sleeve she slid a long-bladed knife that glinted in the eerie light. She held it in the palms of her hands, like an offering, and spoke her words over it.

Hesitantly, Zara reached for it. Then, determined, he grasped it and pulled it close to his chest, fondling its edge with his thumb. Crouching, he took the boy's arm firmly and slid the bowl beneath it. The knife hung poised over the boy's wrist. The woman fell silent, her upraised hand also poised and ready to fall. The chanting from behind stopped.

At the instant the music roared from the boy's heaving chest, flames roared up from one of the wagons. It lit the sky as it crackled to life in a fireball of light. Zara leaped to his feet. Another wagon burst into flames, then a third. Screams tore the silent fabric of night as the clan scrambled in confusion and panic. The boy, trying to understand, lifted his head in time to see Zara and the old woman swallowed by the smoke billowing over the ground.

"Icarus!" The phlegmy voice came through the dark from behind. Smoke stung the boy's eyes as he twisted his neck around, trying to see the face he knew could belong to but one.

"Old Quisleby'll have you free," he said, crawling close, "if it's not too late." He touched the boy and squinted out his face. "Well, ye're living yet, it seems," he said, grabbing a wrist and digging into the knots.

"Superstitious heathens! Listen to them, will ye? Don't know what demon's come to visit. Ha! It ain't only one as can play hide-in-the-night."

He cursed the ropes. "It's a blessing to you, Icarus, I heard the singing-ruckus back a ways. Been hunting high and low ever since I found that sash decorating the bush near camp. Made me know you didn't just run off, but was most likely snatched by a band o' no-goods who wanted something they had no right to. You can thank Sadie for my being here, too. She wandered off this morning, most unusual behavior, and led me to within earshot.

He coughed, a long, choking, gasping spasm. "Had to fight myself to come alooking. Still not sure why I did. Perhaps 'twas the mirror you held up to this philosophical buffoon that has coaxed Old Quisleby out of his mental cul-de-sac; reminded him, so to speak, that to hit the mark of logic dead center is to miss it completely— and there's another cursed paradox to chew on in your empty moments."

Growling, he put his eye down close to the knot to find its secret. "Blasted—" He attacked it with his mouth and began gnawing at it with his side teeth. From the tail of his eye he caught the glint of Zara's knife on the ground. "Aah," he said, snatching it up, "now there's the gods aiding and abetting—for a change. But the purpose, always, the purpose is missing."

He rubbed the boy's arms and, cradling his neck, raised his head. He pointed off to the flames shooting up. "They'll be awhile savin' their wagons and putting themselves together, they will."

The wind shifted the smoke away from them and he lifted the boy, who felt his strength returning as he breathed in the clear air.

"Now, my Sadie is tethered yonder a bit." He nodded the direction. "You strike out that way. The road's not far beyond." He smiled through his shattered teeth. "I'll not be far behind ye, soon's I tend to him." He nodded toward the sleeping Yasha.

The boy stooped and laid his hands on Yasha's head. A tenuous note quavered dimly.

Quisleby nuzzled his head in close and looked up to the boy from the ground. "They'll be back for him soon enough. Go now. Don't hold back on my account, I can take care of myself. Ye've your wings back, Icarus. Fly! Fly!"

The quavering note strengthened, gradually augmenting itself to a full ensemble that lifted and rose suddenly in an empyreal climax. He wheeled, then, and fled into the smoky night. The searching eye of Quisleby squinted after him until he lost him in the dark.

Chapter 22

The boy did not find the road, but found instead a forest trail that carried him deep into the woods. Stumbling in the darkness and hampered by the heavy undergrowth, he pressed on, unafraid and determined. Wherever he found a clearing, he tried to orientate himself by the stars.

His strength soon waned and he could not think clearly. Knowing he needed rest, he was about to choose a dry hummock for the night, when he saw shimmering ahead the silver-edged outline of a ghostly shack.

It was deserted. The boy stood in the open doorway, searching in the pale light funneling through a glassless window for something on which to lie. Finding nothing, he dropped wearily to the rotting floor planks and curled into a ball to fight off the chill creeping into his bones. He fell quickly to sleep, hearing last the fluttering of wings and the scratching of scurrying feet.

But his sleep was disturbed. The memories of recent days joined the memories of his past, filling his head like a musical collage. And though he was able to understand most of its parts individually, he was unable to comprehend the whole. Here and there pieces would juxtapose themselves in a logical relationship, only to break mysteriously away again. Others remained obstinately apart, as if some connecting link, some thematic bridge were missing. A few merged in pure and perfect harmony.

He awakened to the rising sun rimming the treetops. Stepping outside, he listened to the morning sounds of birds and insects and the ticking of the trees. The air tasted damp and fresh, and a cool, fitful breeze freed him from the lingering smell of dry rot. Finding a new trail, he followed it a short distance to where it opened near the bank of a narrow but fast moving river. He threw himself down on the stony edge and drank in long gulps.

Refreshed he struck out down river. It was not only some buried instinct that told him he must now return home, but a deep longing to see his mother and his father. New images blossomed in his mind as he picked his way along, and a new music was born to fit them. And with them came words, new words to crystallize the musical concepts he had until then understood only as feeling.

He forged on, occasionally forced inland by an outcropping of rock, or where the trees grew too thick to the bank. On one such detour, as he broke into a clearing undulating with blue, red, and yellow wild flowers, he spotted a beehive hanging like a paper globe from a tree branch. He struck a vibrant note as he climbed up into the low crotch of the tree to reach it.

Deliberately his hand slipped into the mouth of the hive. A number of circling bees buzzed his head harmlessly. Gingerly he withdrew his hand to lick the sweetness from his fingers. Again he probed inside the combs, then explored several more times until he felt satisfied. He climbed down and continued on his way, still tasting traces of the last sticky glob between his teeth.

Steadily he moved through the cool shade of the thick forest. Despite scratches, bruises and skinned knees from several falls and with the climbing and sliding down the deep earth scars he was forced to cross, he pushed on. Thirsty, he stopped to drink from standing pools of water or the river itself.

Mid-afternoon, as he fought his way through a tangle of dense brush, he heard a cry. Lifting his head to seek its source, he pressed on until he found it at the edge of a bluff overhanging the river: a bear cub clinging to a splintered limb elbowed out over the water.

Cautiously he edged out on the limb until he had the cub by the collar. It cried as he tugged at it to break its frightened grip. Dragging it back against its will, he pulled it firmly to his chest, inched back and lowered himself to the ground where he set it down and ran comforting fingers through its matted fur.

A roar rent the air and shook the ground. The boy spun and stepped back against the sight of a bear, looming like a bristling black hill, her bared teeth and claws gleaming where the light caught them. He fell back, his mouth opening. The earthen bank crumbled beneath his feet.

Chapter 23

The cold water shocked his senses. Blinded in the muddied current, he righted himself and broke the surface, choking. Trying to orient himself, he fought the tug and pull of the current sweeping him farther off shore. He struggled, helpless against the surge of its power.

An eddy turned him suddenly and he swallowed more water. Gagging, he saw the sky spin dizzily overhead as he again sank beneath the surface. Kicking desperately, he rose once more, gasping for air. His senses reeled and the forested banks blurred past his field of vision. Where the sky met the water he could find no distinction.

He retched and his head cleared with the rush of cold air filling his lungs. Pulling against the water, he swam toward the rocky base of a low cliff that lifted straight from the water's edge, but the current caught and whipped him around. He foundered.

A dimness engulfed him, as if the river were tearing away his consciousness. Arms flailing, he clawed for the light above, pitting his ebbing strength against the relentless force sucking him under. His lungs burned, ready to burst, when he surfaced, strangling.

He fought to regain his lost equilibrium as the river swept his legs out ahead of him. His shoulders sank and he felt the brute force of the water closing its grip on him. In the impending darkness, something, a shadow, passed before his eyes and instinctively he reached out for it. It was solid, a log, hard and real, and he lunged for it, hooking his arm over it as it rushed alongside.

The boy held tight, letting himself be carried along. When

more of his strength returned, he dragged himself onto its solid surface and lay forward, hugging it. He coughed up more water and lay unmoving until his breath evened and his vision cleared. Feeling stronger he pushed himself up to straddle the log, and he remembered his sewing-box horse, his mother— home, and his will hardened with his urgent desire and longing to return.

With the boy firmly seated on top of it, the log swept on swiftly, its root system forward, bare and black as autumn branches. The river broadened, and the boy watched the forest glide by on either side. Feeling strong again and knowing he must get to the river bank he slipped back into the water. His grip firm, he tried maneuvering the log with his kicking feet, but his strength drained quickly with the futile effort and he hoisted himself back. He peered ahead, holding a delicate balance to keep the log from rolling and waiting for the river to bring him in close enough to swim ashore.

His music began then, flowing evenly, smoothly, a flat, monotonous sweep with heavy undertones faintly counter-pointed by the liquid chiming of bells. The river ran straight and sparkled with a silver sheen where the sun painted its light over it.

The water darkened and grew agitated as the river constricted between the high rising walls. The log began to keel; the boy's music stopped. Feeling the log quiver beneath him, and trying to understand its motion, he extruded his legs to steady its course. It lurched suddenly and began to spin and roll, throwing him off its slippery back, but he caught its now trailing roots and pulled himself in close. Moving more swiftly, more convulsively, the water foamed around his head and hissed in his ears.

Then he heard it, a hollow din echoing between the stone walls of the gorge that cut off direct sunlight. The water deepened to green. It churned and frothed around him and he felt his fear grow with the growing surge of its power. He thrust his arms into the root system for a more secure hold as the log, swinging in great, lazy circles, rushed on, lifting and falling in the increasing turbulence. The boy jammed his legs into the gnarled roots, trying to lift himself higher out of the water. Ahead, the river boomed in the deepening chasm.

Scudding and arcing in the swirling waters the log made the boy's arms ache with the strain and tension of their hold. Several times it had nearly broken free of him, painfully wrenching his arm sockets as the dipping far end raised him from the water only to plunge him unprepared beneath the surface with its reverse action. Again and again he surfaced, gagging and choking up water that had forced its way into his lungs.

But he was beginning to understand its motion now and anticipated the coming drops. He would conserve his energy and, where possible, he did not fight the pressure trying to tear him loose. He repositioned his hold, shifting hands and feet in quick, separate movements to accommodate the log as it twisted and rolled in the water foaming over the shrinking dark surface.

The log regained its course, plowing ahead root end first, and the boy felt the pressure of the water at his back pinning him against the bramble gouging his chest. Undulating, and heavy as iron, the water threatened to drown him. He could not see what lay ahead, only behind and the flying white water that lashed and stung his face. His stomach sickened with the river's spasms. Desperately he clung, feeling his heart quicken with the murderous pull of the current.

A boom, a rumble, a roar and an explosion of sound. The world shook. The log suddenly dove, taking the boy under and holding him there, crushing him in a raging silence that pounded in his ears. Instinctively, his grip tightened with the violent spin and upsurge that spewed him high above the roiling surface into the thundering air. Spear-like, the log rose to the sky as if trying to escape the fury and for a brief moment it hung there, shuddering. Still, the boy clung. Then it toppled, plunging him beneath the water. His handholds broke free, but his entangled arms snagged in the twisted roots.

He shot up dazed. Around him the river boiled and the stone walls of the canyon reverberated. Blindly he fought to keep his grip and to hold his head above the rushing torrent spuming over him. The log convulsed to the river's dictates and the boy searched for a tandem rhythm. He no longer felt afraid. The river, which had earlier struck fear into him, now tore it away, leaving him only with the instinct to survive.

The water flumed and pounded the jutting boulders and flung itself into the air in geysers of whipping spray. The log keeled and lunged in the seething roar. Into the roiling troughs it plunged, stalled, pitched and shot out again.

The boy's head whirled in the whirling water, dulling his senses and blotting consciousness. And still he clung, arms and legs, alternately or together. His world darkened in the maelstrom swallowing him. An enveloping blackness was closing in when the log careened and slammed into a rock. The stabbing roots jolted him back to light.

Quaking, the log swung 'round in a slow, tremulous roll. It skittered and yawed, sped on, then rammed another rock that completed a split down its center. The impact hurled the boy clear.

End over end the river tumbled and pummeled him, his flailing arms clawing blindly for support they could not find. His breath, whenever it could, came in short, tight gasps. The current pumped him along, barreling him, catapulting him and finally capturing him again. It echoed in his head with an intensity that threatened to tear his body apart.

Through the burning slits of his eyes, he glimpsed, looming ahead, a series of rocks projecting above the water like jagged stone teeth. The sky and the river reeled with his reeling senses. He gyrated and somersaulted in the frenzied water that buried him, freed him, and seized him again, that gushed and fomented over him as if erupting from the earth below, hurling him along and pounding him as it pulverized itself in its tumultuous course. Half-drowned he waited....

...Waited for the impact, for the sharp stone jaws that would rip and grind and shred him to pieces. Instead, he felt himself wrenched sideways, drawn into a funneling channel that pulled him down, corkscrewing him along and draining his consciousness as if in the vortex of a whirlpool.

An increase in momentum, a sharp jolt, and a sudden upsurge shot him out of the water, retrieved him and slammed him back, face down. Helpless against the drag, his body slackened. He felt the smooth bedrock grazing his chest as the undertow sucked him to the bottom of a chute in a long, precipitous dive.

Then it disgorged him.

The boy bobbed to the surface. Wits scattered, he groped clumsily in the eddying flotsam for a remnant limb. Grasping one, he clung weakly as sharp stomach spasms convulsed him. He retched.

Exhausted, he drifted to the side, where he clawed and humped his way up the gravel embankment to hard, dry ground. His eyes closed in instant sleep. In the afternoon sun his cold flesh warmed.

Chapter 24

Late in the afternoon he wakened with a cooling breeze fanning over him. He heard the echoing roar of the cataracts and he lifted his head, remembering. His music seeped out, rippling, flowing, pulsing. It swelled in power, range and scope, ringing with the wild crashing of cymbals and ebbing finally to a drifting close.

Pulling himself up slowly, he felt the torturous ache of his body. He felt the burns where his wrists had been bound, the sting of bruised and scraped flesh, saw the nicks, cuts and gouges washed bloodless by the water. He stood, choosing a direction, and set out, barefoot and naked.

The forest soon swallowed the last of the river sounds and smells and let through only the scent of foliage, the busy cries of birds flitting in the trees, the humming insects he waved away, and the whispering scamper and scurry of ground animals darting underfoot. Gradually, the stiffness worked its way out of his joints as he picked his way over the rugged terrain that sloped gently downward and away from him. Behind him the sky glowed a fuzzy pink through the treetops, sifting a random breeze.

Shadows were beginning to invade the woods when he came to a logging road. Like a jagged scar it cut a tortuous path through the forest and he followed its rutted course. Unhindered by the nettles and briars that had earlier torn his skin and slowed him, he now moved at a much quicker pace. Hunger gnawed at him. The darkness thickened.

A deep and gloomy twilight had settled in by the time he had crossed a small ravine and stumbled onto a macadam road. He knew his direction now, knew it by the position of the dying light and emerging stars and by an instinct that assured him beyond doubt. He walked the road, as if down a tree-walled corridor. The moon crept up, inviting new sounds to haunt the night. A caterwauling pierced the air from deep within the forest and, unafraid, he paused to listen.

Softly his music played to him, weaving from primitive strains new and sophisticated themes. From pristine depths it discovered subtle intricacies and detail that wound their way into the musical fabric forming and reforming itself. Images of the events of the past few days flashed in his mind, and with each came musical correlations to impart new meanings. His mind filled with sound, with the color of sounds, with nuances of tones and half-tones, and with the shadings and stresses that spoke to him in a way he had never heard before. He was an instrument played upon by the tints and hues of sound, by the variations and tonal gradations of sound shaping new configurations of the world around him.

He opened his mouth to release the music expanding within. A stillness cloaked the forest as his augmenting symphony reached out to embrace the night.

The shadowed houses splashed with a silvery light greeted the boy in a welcoming silence as he entered the town. Within, insulated against the night, the townspeople slept soundly and he felt himself breach the walls to form a kinship that brought warm harmonies to his lips. He passed the church and the muffled peal of bells chimed from him. Ahead, the schoolhouse loomed bright in the night and a medley of short, happy pieces erupted and lilted out to it. He passed the quarry, visible only where a dim cluster of lights hung together in the distance, and he sent one clarion note out to touch it.

He turned onto the path to his door. A yellow glow filled the window square. Quietly, he climbed the steps and rapped softly. He heard no sound within. Suddenly, the door sprang open. Silhouetted there, rigid and dark, stood his mother. Stunned, she swooned, then her arms went out to him and he did not resist the crush of her embrace as she lifted his naked body and buried her head in his shoulder. She swayed, rocking with him tight against her.

"Mama."

Stifled spasms of emotion breaking from her throat mingled with tender notes as she carried him into the parlor. His music whispered out, subdued but joyous, as she sat with him in choked silence, hugging him ever-tighter to her bosom. He saw the quilt on the floor beside the rocker and the crumbling logs of a low-burning fire, felt the heaving of her breast and the wet of her cheek as he breathed soothing music into her ear.

From upstairs came the stamp of feet.

Chapter 25

Early the next evening, after the boy had been put to bed, Garth sat in his chair across from his wife, a cup of coffee in his hand. "Sure be nice to know where Jonathan's been all that time, what he's been up to. Ever see a boy so beat up?" He laughed. "Looks like an Indian, all that me-cury-chrome you basted him with."

He looked over the rim of his cup to his wife, staring out to the beaded manger, glittering on a corner stand. "He's back safe, though, just like I said. Aside from the worry, no real harm done." He eased himself back, getting more comfortable. "Wonder what made him go; why he'd want to do it. Can't get a word out o' him no way." He wrapped his hands around his cup, contemplating the mystery and repeating his words.

"I want to go back to church, Everett." She did not look at him.

His mouth fell open. "Why, Beth, I thought you was against them people. Never wanted to see them again, you said."

"For the child. He needs his religion." She did not mention her prayers nor her private vow to return to God if He returned her child to her.

Garth regarded her curiously, listening to the words that dropped from her lips one after another, like heavy stones. He knew her mind was made up. "Ain't you afraid no more?"

"The Lord will watch over him. There's nobody else can."

"Now hold on there, woman," he said, jabbing out to her with his cup, "seems to me he's been kep' safe enough so far. He—"

Her cold eyes swinging on him froze his words. "Safe? With endless rumors and accusations running through town

like poison? Safe? With investigations and threats? Safe? For
how long, Everett? How long before their threats…before—"

"Threats! They don't mean no more than the hot air they're
made of. Just loose talk from idle minds." He threw up his
hand. "But I ain't arguin'. If you want to get back to church,
that's fine with me. Just so long as you remember it was you as
wanted it, not me!"

She turned away. "It's all that's left to us," she murmured.

He set his cup aside and leaned forward. "Say what's really
on your mind, why don't you? Ever since I started up goin' to
town oncet in a while, you been broodin' away in that chair,
and that was afore the boy left." His voice rose. "Can't a man
have a night to hisself, a beer or two to relax him? A man
works like a dog, humpin' till he's near dead to support his
own, ain't he a right to it? And when he comes home, comes
home draggin', lookin' for—comes home to—" He threw his
hand out to her. "—to *what?* A woman who won't even look at
her husband! Like he's a stranger in his own house. A man
starved for a little talk, a kind word so's he knows he means
something. A leper'd at least get pity."

His voice grew plaintive. "I could understand it whilst the
boy was gone, but God's sake woman, will it never end? I got
feelin's, though you mightn't think it. A gentle look oncet in a
while, would it kill you? A warm touch, a—" His fist smashed
the arm of the chair. "I don't know what you want of me!"

Chapter 26

On the second Sunday after the boy's return, they readied themselves for church. Garth stood waiting in the doorway, smoothing a black felt hat he hadn't worn in years, while his wife finished trussing up the boy in a suit he'd already outgrown.

Garth wasn't anxious to go, and he still brooded over the words they'd recently had. He felt awkward, even embarrassed, and helplessly trapped. Until that morning he had no intention of giving in to her and going and having to face people he didn't like and had no use for. At the last moment he relented, as much a concession to his guilt as to her will.

The walk seemed long under the hot skies. Skipping along, the boy kept stride between them, and though she said nothing, she was pleased with how quickly his wounds had healed. And not until she had dressed him after his return did she realize how much he had grown in recent months and how much he had filled out. He was strong and healthy and she felt reassured.

"This about where you're at when you sing out to me, Jonathan?" He pointed off. "I must look pretty small to you, standing way out there. And you look smaller yet to me." He laughed. "Give me your song, the way you do, come on."

The boy's music lifted and carried, then died away.

"Don't sound near so loud to me there," he said, chuckling again and tousling the boy's hair. Garth glanced over to his wife, trying to determine whether his improved temper had any effect on her, and saw that her grim expression did not change.

Dusty and damp, they arrived at the church in time for services. Garth removed his hat and wiped his brow as they climbed the steps. The misgivings he had felt earlier returned more strongly and, for a moment, he considered turning back. At the door his wife balked, then, with a sharp squaring of her shoulders, strode inside, leading the way.

The church was nearly full, but they found space halfway down the aisle. The buzzing stopped as they passed each pew and heads turned curiously to watch them.

Garth's face burned. He felt a sudden, almost uncontrollable urge to stand and shout at them, to ask if they'd never seen people before, or whether they thought them freaks. Instead he crowded over the boy self-consciously and adjusted his collar. His wife, sitting rigid and fixed, heard the excited murmurs and her features hardened into an expression of defiance.

Service began and a hush fell over the congregation. The minister spoke from the pulpit and his stentorian voice, warmed by the passion of his words, swept over them in soothing waves. It infused the church with an atmosphere of comfort and peace that, until that moment, Mrs. Garth did not realize she had lost.

The words flowed out to them, words of brotherhood, love and the common bond of humanity. Her hands twitched on her lap, and she felt uncomfortable with the feeling that the message was somehow personally directed toward her.

Garth remembered the minister's face, remembered it at the door some twenty-five years before. Except for the youthful glow of the skin it was no longer the same face. He noted the cruel lines time had etched on it, and how the nose stood out more hawkishly against the shrunken bones. He wondered if he himself had changed as much. He remembered the minister's plea for them to return to church and his own refusal, calling them hypocrites. He glanced furtively at the faces raptly listening to the sermon, so pious, and he remembered the snub that had destroyed their dinner and their spirits. He rankled.

They sang.

From out of the chorus rose one clear and exquisite note. Mrs. Garth clapped her hand over the boy's mouth and glared down at him fiercely. For a stunned moment silence reigned. Garth started and together they began to rise, ready to leave.

"Please," the minister called out, "Stay, Mr. Garth, Mrs. Garth. We all know, have known for some time about your son."

Her hand dropped, but the other held the boy by the shoulder, close to her side.

"You have no need to fear us here. We are in the house of God. Please, let the child share with us this gift we have heard of, this miraculous gift given by the Lord Himself."

Her eyes flashed to the faces turned toward them and found in them not the hostility and fear she had expected, but a genuine, smiling warmth and reassurance. Garth sensed the same and the tight clench of his jaw and hands relaxed. She stood undecided, listening to his voice, the sincerity in it, so reminiscent of her father's voice.

"We implore you," he continued. "Let the child join us in a hymn."

Garth fidgeted, waiting for her response. Anguished, she looked down to the boy, kneading his shoulder. She hadn't prepared for this. Now they knew. They had heard with their own ears. She could hide the child no longer. And with that thought she felt a sudden sense of relief. *Now let them hear him fully, let them hear how beautifully he can sing, and find, if they can, any danger in him!* She nodded.

"Page 16," the minister said: *Rejoice in His Mysteries.*"

Together they began to sing, a pleasing chorus of men's and women's and children's voices, mellow and clear, rising in unison with a holy communion conveyed in the harmony.

Then came a faltering in the voices as a shimmering vibrato began, low and sweet, gradually ascending, then dividing and dividing again to build blocks of harmony that embroidered, complemented and enriched each other. Somber chords lifting on spiritual wings of melody wove a mystic blend that garnered the voices and carried them up, strengthening and inspiring them until they soared in an exuberance that rang from the rafters and sang joy to the world beyond....

* * * * *

They returned home in brighter spirits than they had come with. The danger, the fear they had girded themselves for didn't materialize, and the sense of relief they felt was proportionate to the anxieties that had weighed them down. Garth was mightily pleased, not only with the good effect the experience seemed to have on his wife, but with the apparent sincere show of affection and respect the boy had won for them.

Though still reticent, Bethany Garth seemed to exude a buoyancy long unfamiliar within that household. She herself felt a sense of renewal, though she could not tell whether it was the return to church that had brought it about or the revelation of the child's difference. An uneasiness stirred deep within, an intuitive sense of having exposed herself and the child to a lurking, unnamed danger. But with the lifting of her burden and her spirits, she chose to ignore it.

"Well, that wasn't so bad after all, was it, Beth?" Garth said, smiling broadly and patting her back.

She smiled back and they spoke.

Chapter 27

Every Sunday thereafter, they attended services together, and with their coming came curious townsfolk to fill the pews. The boy sang, awing the parishioners, who wasted no time confirming to their neighbors what had until then been merely rumors.

After service several tried to approach the Garths, but the ingrained habits and attitudes of so many years made them shy and embarrassed. Though secretly pleased with the attention and acceptance, they could bear to exchange no more than a few words before excusing themselves with some feeble excuse and fleeing. Those who heard of their behavior did not understand and, among themselves, accused the Garths of being standoffish.

It was on the fifth Sunday after their return to church that the minister called them aside as they were leaving. Garth, sensing something amiss, felt uneasy.

"Mr. Garth," he began hesitantly, "Mrs. Garth, please understand. What I have to say, what I must say…is not easy for me….We have found in your being here among us a great joy, not only to hear the child share with us his precious gift, but to have you here in our presence to share in our worship of the Lord." He smiled warmly down to the boy. "It is true, we have heard and we have marveled—"

"To the point, Reverend," Garth said irritably, "to the point."

"Yes, yes, of course," the minister said, his pink skin flushing. "I'm afraid I…I must ask you not to allow your son to sing during services anymore."

Beth winced and Garth reached out angrily to draw her

away. "Wait, please, let me explain," he pleaded, laying his hand on Garth's arm. "You see, since Jonathan has been singing, word of his gift has gone out and many now come to hear, more each week, as you have observed." He read the question on Garth's face. "I am pleased of course to see my church filled; however, I'm afraid many come only to…merely to—"

"To see the show," Garth snapped.

The minister's voice deepened to a warm intimacy. "I pray this will not discourage your attendance, that you understand my position and why I have found it necessary to make this request of you." They turned. "I will be looking for you next week Sunday…."

Garth raged. "I told you, Beth," he said, kicking up road dust, "I told you. Bunch o' hypocrites, the whole lot o' them." She looked at him sharply. "Most o' them, anyways."

* * * * *

For the next several weeks all went well with them. After a stubborn and prolonged time resisting, Garth finally relented and they went to church as a family. The boy did not sing and the attention they had become accustomed to was drawn away from them. Attendance dropped and the controversy picked up again in town. Some swore that the boy sang like an angel, while others— those who came later— swore he never uttered a sound, that it was a ruse of the Reverend Hempstone 'to get the strayers back in the fold and fill the collection basket.'

At home Bethany tended her garden and did her mending and cleaning. Her anxieties subsided with her strengthened faith and she was more magnanimous toward Garth with her feelings, more open with her thoughts.

Mightily pleased, he laughed, he joked and at least once

each week brought home a "little something" for her: an embroidered handkerchief, a kitchen utensil. And she did not make him feel guilty when he went off to town for "a bit o' relaxation" on Saturday nights. Their days were cheerful and the nights pleasant, while around them the boy's sweet rhapsodies tightened their family bond.

Chapter 28

Summer deepened to late August. Having just finished their supper, Garth slid his plate away, and sat back patting his stomach. "Delicious, Beth, delicious." She smiled her demure acceptance of the compliment.

"Now, Jonathan boy," he said, leaning forward eagerly, "how's the idea of visiting a carny-vale set with you?" The boy sang out and Garth reached over to pat his shoulder. "Knew you would," he said laughing. "Comin' to town tomorra. Signs all over everywheres announcin' it." He looked up. "What say, Beth, join along? Been years and years for me."

"I think not, Everett," she said tonelessly.

"Do you good, gettin' away from the house for something asides church. Say you will, Beth. Give it your nod."

A frown touched her brow. "I've much to do," she said, rising to clear the table.

"Well, if you change your mind...tomorra night then, Jonathan, right after work. A little supper and—" His arm imitated the undulating motion of a roller coaster. He threw his head back laughing.

* * * * *

The next evening at dusk they arrived at the carnival grounds, just Garth and the boy. Ahead, colorful lights danced to the festive music pumping out of a calliope that greeted them at the gate. Remembering his wife's warning, Garth kept the boy close to him as they drifted in with the crowd. Together they walked the midway.

"What do you think now?" Garth said, sharing the boy's

excitement and seeing his head turning everywhere to gather the crying voices and the hum of machinery, the blinking lights and the mingled smells of food and animals. "Sure wish your mother would've come.

"How 'bout a nice box o' Cracky Jack or popcorn, Jonathan, before you screw your head clear off your shoulders?" He laughed and led the boy to one of the concession stands....

"Step right up, mister," a man cried out from a game called *Wheel of Fortune.* "Step up and try your luck. Nice prizes for the lad."

"What say, Jonathan?" Garth prodded, pulling the boy along with a sudden yank that almost made him drop his popcorn. "Give her a try?"

"Step right up, that's it," the thin man said. "Place your money on a number, try your luck—a nickel, dime, quarter or half dollar and win a fannn-tastic prize." He wore a soiled black bow tie, a soiled white shirt and a soiled brown hat pushed back on his head.

Garth looked down at the boy, whose eyes were glued on the dazzling array of stuffed animals, dolls and assorted prizes on the shelves behind the counter. "Reckon we can spare a bit, what do you say?" He fished a small cluster of coins from his pocket and picked one out.

"That's the spirit, mister," the soiled man said, speaking out of the corner of his mouth. "A nickel will bring you a fourth row prize—a monkey, a dove—any one of them, mister—a rabbit, a bear. Guaranteed quality merchandise made in the good old U. S. of A." The cigarette dangling from the corner of his mouth forced his head at an angle to keep the smoke from burning his squinting eye.

"How 'bout it, Jonathan," Garth said. "You say the magic number and I'll plunk it down, anywhere you think."

The boy pointed to number eleven on the counter and Garth placed the coin in the numbered square. A few feet to the right of him, a young couple deliberated secretly. The young man nodded.

"Place your money...and win for your honey," the man said, tapping the side of his soiled neck with his croupier's stick.

The girl watched her boyfriend place the fifty cent piece on their number. Her blond curls spilling out from under her bonnet framed the chubby features of her face, which resembled the Kewpie doll's on the shelf.

"Number 36 for the lady," the man said, "going for the Madonna doll. Win and you get your money back too." He spun the wheel and it sang out its revolutions. Gradually it slowed to the last few suspenseful snaps—8, 9, 10, 11.

"The little man wins!" the man called out to the passers-by as he scooped the fifty cent piece into the pocket of his apron. The girl's pouty lips reflected her disappointment and she went into another secret conference with her boyfriend.

"Pick your prize, lad," the man called. "Name it and it's yours. Fourth shelf, anything that catches your fancy."

"Well, Jonathan?" Garth said, trying to conceal his mixed pleasure and discomfort.

"The rabbit," the boy said, his voice shy.

"One rabbit coming up, so real you'll swear she'll throw you a litter." He snatched it off the shelf and clumped it down on the counter. "Your luck is running and mine ain't. And that's the way I like it. How about it, Father, try the lad's luck again?"

Garth rubbed his jaw, doubtfully. The boy was watching the girl.

"You got a two dollar prize there for a nickel play, mister. Show a little gumption and give the lad some fun and a chance to win another. It ain't every day the carnival comes to town."

"All right, since you put her that way," Garth said, digging out his money. "We'll just take you up on that. How 'bout it, Jonathan, a dime this time? Pick the magic number and I'll lay it there." The boy pointed to number 17.

Nervously, the young man next to them placed another half dollar on number 36. A few others drifted into the makeshift stand and the man made sure their money was down before launching the wheel into another song. "Let her turn…let her spin…somebody here…is sure to win." The spinning wheel ticked to a gradual stop.

The man froze for a moment, then shouted: "Number 17! The little man has done it again. Another winner!" His cigarette burned close to his lips and he spit it out and stamped on it. "Pick your choice, lad, third shelf, anything you see, anything at all."

The boy pointed to an elephant standing square on four solid legs and embroidered with a red and gold blanket molded into its plaster back. The man lifted it off the shelf and stood it in front of the boy.

"Another winner!" he barked. "Another winner here!"

Attracted by the excitement new players crowded in.

"How about it, mister, one more time? Don't want to quit when you're on a roll, now *do* you, lad?"

The boy smiled and Garth shrugged. "Well, since the boy seems to be having such a good time of it, why not?"

"That's the kind of spirit I like, mister. Wouldn't want to deprive the lad of his small pleasures, now would we?"

The boy picked his number, and the couple beside him laid their money again on number 36. Again the boy won and again the couple lost.

"Another winner!" the soiled man barked, louder than before. "Another winner here!" He edged over to his wheel and studied it a moment.

After the boy's fifth win Garth spoke up. "I think that's about it, Jonathan, don't you? You got five prizes already. Can't hardly carry more and still make the rides. Besides, your mother wouldn't look favorable on our gamblin'."

"It ain't gambling, mister. It's a game of chance," the man said, pleased with the growing crowd who were laying bets. "Perfectly legal, otherwise we couldn't operate."

Garth fidgeted, scratching his head. He hadn't only his wife in mind; he knew the boy's powers had something to do with his luck and he felt guilty.

"All right," he said finally, "if the boy agrees, I'll go along. What say, Jonathan, do we or don't we? One more time."

The boy pointed to the Madonna doll. "We do," he said softly.

The girl next to him looked shocked and she tugged at her boyfriend's arm. The boyfriend spoke up: "There's only one of them, correct, sir?"

"That's right, one Madonna doll, and only one."

"Well, sir," he stammered, "with all due respect, Lucy here has been playing her lucky number for it and, well, it doesn't seem fair if she...if he...well, sir, I've only one chance left to get it for her." He turned an empty pocket.

"I can appreciate that," the man said, anxiously watching the counter fill, "but there's no bone of contention here. Only one number can win it." He lit another cigarette.

"But what if we pick the same number?"

"Ain't only the Madonna doll you can win," he said, unwilling to lose a fifty cent play. "Got a beautiful replica of the Capitol building here." He pointed with his stick. "Any good American'd be proud to own it. Or that dish made of genu-wine pearl inlay, hand crafted in the South Seas."

The girl spoke up. "Why's he want it for anyways?" she

whined. "He's but a child and I was intending to put Her in a special nice place in our house so the Holy Mother would always be looking after us when the time comes we're married, and keep a candle burning in front of her so—"

"Look, Miss, I got customers—"

"Tell you what," Garth interrupted, "you go 'head and pick your number. If my boy here wants the same, why, we'll cancel out. It's fair an offer as I can make. Besides, your young man says here hisself it's your last try for it anyways."

Cocking his head away from the smoke curling up to his squeezed eye, the soiled man stroked his jaw. He knew odds, and the odds that they would choose the same number were remote. He knew too that the odds either would win this time were impossible. He waited and when the girl nodded, he said, "Place your money, folks."

Garth dug for the coin. Everybody except the girl waited for the boy to place his bet before laying their money on the boy's square.

Squinting with a half smile, the man spoke as his hand went secretly under the counter: "'Round she goes...'round and away...who'll be lucky and win today?"

Just as his hand reached to spin the wheel, the boy shifted his money to another number.

The man turned, smiling, as the wheel slowed to a clicking stop. His cigarette dangled from his dropped jaw and his eyes popped when he saw the matching numbers. "How in—" Dazed, he shook his head.

The crowd grumbled.

"Never saw nothing like it," he muttered, absently scooping the losers' money into his apron pocket. "Two in a row, I've seen, maybe three or four, even—but never six. Never! And I could swear that last number—"

The girl stood fixed as the man reached for the prize. Still numb, he pressed the doll into the boy's arms. After fondling it a moment, the boy turned and offered it to the girl.

Confused, she took it, unable to speak. She stared at it in her hands. Her lips trembled and her hands shook. Then her nostrils flared with the fire in her eyes. She hurled it to the ground, smashing it.

A low, throaty hum escaped him as he watched the rolling head come to rest against his foot. The girl spun on her heel and disappeared into the gathering crowd, her boyfriend racing after her.

Garth fumed. He hadn't expected this, hadn't suspected the boy's motives. He'd been thinking of how pleased his wife would be to have the statue. He started to call out after the girl, but the boy held his hands up against his chest.

"Sure are some crazy people out there these days," the soiled man said, taking in the faces of the onlookers. "Imagine, busting up a treasure like that? Not to mention the lad's generous handing it over to her." He stroked his neck with his stick. "Imagine that."

He suddenly realized they weren't listening, that they were waiting for the boy to make another bet, pressing close and ready to bet with him.

"The kid can't play anymore!" he said sharply.

"Garth, gathering up the prizes and ready to leave, stopped. "Why not?" His voice was harsh.

"Something's fishy here. Nobody can hit six in a row. It can't be done."

"You calling me and my boy here cheats?" He set the prizes back on the counter.

The man stepped back. "Nobody can hit six, I told you. It just ain't possible."

"Well, I wasn't aimin' to, but we're playin' again," Garth boomed. He pulled his pocket open, digging for his money.

The man stamped out his cigarette and lit another. "I'm telling you, mister, the game's closed to you. If—"

"It was all right your takin' a bite out o' them others, but somebody gets a nibble back and you want to run 'em out. That it?"

A voice lifted from the crowd, joined by others. "Let him play. His money's good."

"I seen it before," the man said, on the verge of panic, "a guy'll use a magnet or a—"

"Let him play!" they cried out, pushing against the counter, moving it a little.

Garth leaned over the counter. "You calling me a cheat!"

"Stay back." He raised his stick. "Get out of here. Beat it! All of you. I'm closing up the goddamned joint."

"Let him play!" The counter gave more.

"I'm warning you!" He pressed himself into a corner.

Shouts went up. The counter groaned with the crush of people against it, then collapsed in its middle. The man cried out for help.

More cries broke from those who were pinned as they struggled to untangle themselves from the mob. Attracted by the commotion, others rushed in and the stand shook. The wheel tipped and fell, hitting the soiled man cowering in the corner and still crying for help. The wobbling prizes lined up on the shelves toppled and shattered on the ground like a series of gunshots.

Garth managed to snatch up two of his own, still teetering on the edge of the stand and, keeping the boy in front of him, pushed his way backwards to the outside.

"You okay, Jonathan?" he asked, pulling him away from the crowd.

The boy's hum sweetened and he smiled. "Yes, Father."

"Good. Got a little more than we bargained for, I guess, all the way around. And it won't be something we'll be wantin' your mother to hear about, neither."

He thrust the rabbit into the boy's hands. "I'll carry the elly-phant. One for each." He chuckled. "You see that man crouch-hidin' in the corner, just like a rabbit might do? And wavin' that stick so, I thought he'd beat his own brains out with it." He chuckled again and started off, when a voice called:

"Mr. Garth!"

Chapter 29

Garth paused, watching the man approach, seemingly from out of nowhere. In his shadow followed another, slight of stature and obviously younger.

"It *is* Mr. Garth, is it not? Mr. Everett Garth?"

"That it is," Garth said, appraising the man.

Wiping the dampness from the huge bulge of his forehead, the man faced Garth directly. "I observed the performance of your son a few minutes ago, before that unfortunate brouhaha began," he said, tucking away his handkerchief and leading Garth gently by the arm off to the side. "Remarkable, Mr. Garth. A very impressive display of talent."

"And who might I be talking to?" Garth said, pulling his arm free.

"Holloman T. Beeker, Esquire." He turned. "And this is Farnsworth, Calvin Farnsworth, my associate. You've heard of us, I presume?"

Farnsworth's eyeglasses, catching light, flashed with his nod.

"Might have," Garth said, pulling the boy close and noting the fine tailoring of the man's suit and the thin cover of white hair curving neatly over the bulging dome of his forehead. "What is it you want of me, you gentlemen?"

Beeker slipped an arm around Garth's back and nudged him to a slow walk. Garth shrugged his arm off. The boy stuck close to his side, while behind them walked Farnsworth, tapping his swagger stick lightly against his gloved hand.

"I am not a man to mince words, Mr. Garth," Beeker said, speaking close to his ear. "Therefore, let me put it to you directly. Of course, what transpires here between us is a matter of mutual confidence, you understand. Agreed?"

Garth nodded.

"Good. I knew you were a man of character as soon as I laid eyes on you." He glanced around at the people shuffling by. "It's a proposition I have for you, Mr. Garth, one that may well put us, shall we say, into a more propitious financial state?"

"By which you mean money."

"Exactly, sir," he answered in a similarly stiff voice. "Surely you're not averse to the acquisition of an honest dollar." His sharp eyes flicked over Garth's clothes. "Think of what the dollar can buy, Mr. Garth. The power of it."

Garth tightened. "There's money, and there's money."

"An *honest* dollar, I said, Mr. Garth. Far be it from me to even remotely suggest anything not in strict compliance with the law, the law of God as well as the law of man. This, upon my word as an attorney, sir, one sworn to uphold the sacred trust and reputation of the bar." He pointed to one of the picnic tables set up on the grounds. "Shall we rest there? Perhaps we could carry on our discussion with fewer distractions."

Garth and the boy sat opposite the two men, a short distance from the Ferris wheel looming up against the dark sky, its winking lights orbiting with its languorous revolutions. The boy's music played to the music undulating over them, blended with it so perfectly that it was indistinguishable from it and therefore unnoticed.

Garth watched Farnsworth lay his stick on the table and adjust the level brim of his hat before folding his gloved hands before him. Here in the better light, Garth noticed that he was even younger than he'd thought, twenty-five, perhaps. He didn't like him, didn't like the stick he carried or the cocksure expression on his face or the thin lips that curled in a kind of perpetual sneer. The eyes, steady on him behind the flashing lenses, awakened an old fear in him and made him nervous.

Garth spoke: "Would this propy-sition by chance include the boy here?"

The question, so bluntly put, caused Beeker to balk. "Let's not get ahead of ourselves, Mr. Garth," he said, blotting his forehead. "First—"

"First, how'd you know my name?"

Beeker smiled. "It's my business to know what's about, Mr. Garth. Of course, I wouldn't have known you personally, you understand, if not for—" he nodded toward the game stand— "that. As you must be aware, your son has aroused no little community interest of late. Naturally, it didn't take *me* long to deduce his identity nor, being of a logical turn of mind, yours as well. Which, Mr. Garth, should indicate to you the caliber of man you're dealing with."

"When you're dealing with Beeker and Farnsworth," Farnsworth interposed, in a voice soft yet hard, as if gloved like his hands, "you are dealing with the very best, bar none." He smirked over to Beeker who did not acknowledge the pun.

Already irritable with Farnsworth, Garth stiffened. "Well, if you gentlemen's through pattin' yourselfs on the back, I'd be obliged if you'd let me in on the propy-sition. Seems ever'body knows 'cept..." he paused, turning to Farnsworth with a smile faintly insolent, "... 'cept the principal party."

Farnsworth bristled and his glasses flashed.

"Investments, Mr. Garth," Beeker said, "simple and direct. Of course, it will not be possible to disclose the many facets of this...shall we say, enterprise? You wouldn't understand, I'm afraid, because of its eso—"

"So I'm to be kept in the dark, is that it? The man which is in the center of it ain't to know how or—"

"Shut up, Mr. Garth!" Farnsworth broke in. "When Mr. Beeker addresses—"

"Now you listen you...." Garth growled, starting up, his fists clenching.

The boy's music crooned, low and ominous.

"Gentlemen, gentlemen," Beeker said, reaching across to hold Garth back, while his other hand covered Farnsworth's fist, which was curling around his stick. "It behooves none of us to engage in hostilities of this nature." He glanced around. "Perhaps, Mr. Farnsworth," he said, his voice weighted with authority, "perhaps it would be best if you allowed Mr. Garth and myself to carry on our business privately."

Farnsworth's glasses flashed.

"Best if you went along with him, Mr. Beeker," Garth said. "Nothing you got to say is of interest to me. Neither o' you. Asides, it's not me you want, I know that. It's the boy here you want to use." He gathered the boy close to him. "Wouldn't do you no good anyhow. What you seen back awhile ago was nothin' but beginner's luck and no more than that."

"I'd like to be the judge of that, Mr. Garth," Beeker said. His patient eyes combed Garth, as if seeking a weakness.

"No need to. My mind's made up." Garth was thinking of Beth, remembering his own proposal to her when he'd kept his little black book. He remembered her wrath and the marble hardness of her voice.

"The power of the dollar, Mr. Garth. The doors it can open before you; the doors it can close behind you. Consider carefully." He rose slowly.

"'Fraid not," Garth said, mellowing. "My answer's final."

"You work at the mill, is that correct?"

Garth tightened. "You know a lot."

"I have considerable influence there, Mr. Garth. You might keep that in mind."

"Are you threatenin' me?" Garth said, leaning across to him. "'Cause if you are—"

He saw Farnsworth's hands tighten on his stick.

Beeker stepped back. "No, no, of course not. I merely meant there is much I could do for you there." He took Farnsworth by the arm. "Perhaps this is all too sudden for Mr. Garth….If you should have a change of mind, Mr. Garth, I'll be in my office. Tomorrow evening at seven would be agreeable, the Bowman building."

Garth watched them leave, their heads close together as they merged with the crowd. "Some pair," Garth said, scratching behind his ear and shaking his head. "Pillars o' the community, as they say."

He lifted the boy off his seat and set him down. "Now, Jonathan, I won't be tellin' your mother none o' these things that happened tonight. Wouldn't want to worry her now, would we? Bad enough we'll be gettin' home late." He tousled the boy's hair.

"Mmmm, smell some good meat cookin', Jonathan? And lookee there, Jonathan, ice cream. How 'bout it? Any flavor you say and as many dips." The boy, clutching his prizes under his arm, purred as they moved away. "After that, a ride or two on the merry-go-round, one o' them fancy big horses you see goin' up and down. How's that sound? Ride 'em cowboy. And maybe see the freaks. Ain't seen near enough o' them here yet, have we?"

They walked into the milling crowd and lost themselves.

Chapter 30

All that week Garth talked of nothing but the 'carny-vale.' Beth listened, saying little as he relived the events at their kitchen table after supper.

"Wasn't that somethin', Jonathan, that Ferris wheel?" He leaned back in his chair and shaped a circle with his widespread arms. "Just like being on top o' the world. Not a bit scared, neither, Jonathan wasn't. And that big painted yellow horse ridin' so nice, up the hill and down the hill, up and down, 'round and 'round." The boy's voice recaptured the lively music of the carousel and pumped warmth into the room. "And how 'bout that wild creature o' Borneo, where ever that be, you 'member that, Jonathan? Half man, half beast...."

In his quieter moments Garth recalled Beeker and the promise in his words. He thought of the mill and all the marble dust he'd eaten over the years and would eat in the years ahead. Several times he had considered dropping into his office, had even started out once, just to hear Beeker out, but each time Beth's face rose before him. She'd been content of late, and their relations smooth. Upsetting her in any way was the last thing he wanted.

Still, how long would she remain sweet-tempered? How long before some trifling incident would bring a relapse? He'd seen it happen before, too many times. Wouldn't it be better, he wondered, to chance her not finding out, even to risk her anger if she did, if in so doing he could acquire the means of future independence? 'The power of the dollar, Mr. Garth...the doors it can open....'

Each day he wrestled with the problem. He vacillated. He would, he wouldn't, he would, he wouldn't. Finally he decided that he couldn't jeopardize the peace and security of his marriage. He relaxed, feeling noble in his decision. Still, he couldn't rid himself of his doubts and the nagging curiosity as to the nature of the 'investments.' Only vaguely did the suspicion occur that Mr. Beeker was not the kind of man who easily gave up something he wanted.

Chapter 31

Saturday night, a week after the carnival, Garth sat in his usual place, a small table in the corner of the tavern, partially hidden by a remnant partition with shelving on the outside to display a collection of beer vessels. The spot afforded him a sense of distance and, at the same time, provided a clear view of the barroom and a comfortable proximity to the lively goings-on he enjoyed watching.

"Welcome to the Owl," the maid said, the usual greeting to everyone. "I'm Maggy. Abbey, well, she's sick tonight, sir, and I'm here for her. Hoping to please you, sir."

Her quick smile dimpled her cheeks and put him at ease. He ordered his drink. This one was not as pretty, he thought, nor as young as Abbey, the other he'd grown used to and looked forward to seeing. This Maggy, though, had a touch of wildness in her eyes, something a little frightening. He stirred uncomfortably and drummed the tabletop with his gritty knuckles.

She returned and, avoiding her face, he slid the money to her. As she left, he observed her surreptitiously, noted the supple motion of her hips, fluid beneath the shiny black skirt that swirled about her feet when she walked. She reminded him of Beth, early Beth, with the prim squareness of her shoulders and the slim arch of her neck. Her black ringlets bobbed beneath the ruffled edges of the white period cap she wore.

He lifted his glass and drank. The beer washed the sting and burn of marble dust from his dry throat, refreshing him. Closing his eyes, he licked the cool foam from his lips and sighed.

He leaned on his elbows, his glass almost at eye level, and

with each nursed sip he felt the tensions drain away. Across the room a group of men raised their foaming mugs and began singing. Pleased with the forgetfulness overtaking him, he watched them and joined in vicariously with their carefree spirit. Laughing raucously, they applauded themselves and spontaneously broke into another song.

The room was filling fast as others filtered in, each to the same greeting of 'Welcome to the Owl, gentlemen.' Any shyness they might have brought with them soon dissipated in the jovial atmosphere as they too joined in the merriment. Thoughts of Beth crept in, and of the boy, but Garth forced them away. To think of them stifled his sense of freedom and dampened his spirits. He enjoyed the noise, the laughter and the good-natured bantering that flew across the tables.

"Babman, it's drawn and quartered you should be!"

"And to you, Wittlesdon, I say I give no quarter and ask no quarter!"

A sudden longing awakened in Garth, a hungry, desperate desire to lose himself in the world. He tried to imagine what it would be like to be free, unencumbered by responsibility, to simply get up, walk out and never return again. And no sooner did he think it when he felt guilt's arrow pierce his heart.

He saw Beth's face, rigid and tight, yet vulnerable and frightened. He knew her coldness, yes, but he knew her warmth, too, the depths of her generosity and sensitivity, her capacity for suffering without complaint. And he knew, sensed really, that passions neither of them understood ruled her, that beneath it all lurked something dark and punishing, something that separated not only her from him, but that divided her against herself, as well.

He swallowed a long draft and signaled the maid for another drink. He hung there indecisively between the opposing thoughts squeezing his mind like a vice. Surely, he thought, a man's a right to live his life free of misery, a man humpin' away his days, bustin' and haulin' stone. A right to find a little peace in his later years.

And no sooner did he think that when he saw Beth hugging the boy, waiting for him on the steps as she often had, and the conviction returned that a man's got to shoulder his responsibilities, too, to protect and care for those dependent upon him and who need him to survive, without thought of himself, his wants and desires, to be willing to sacrifice anything for his family, even his life, or he's no man at all.

The maid brought the beer and this time he handed her the money. This time, too, he found the courage to face her directly. The warm flush of her cheeks did not escape his sight, nor did her eyes, level, bright and intent, as if with an expectancy of promised excitement.

His greenish fingers stroked the wet glass. Lifting his drink, he drained half of it quickly to quiet his mind. His eyes wandered to the far corner where, perched in a metal cage, a stuffed owl stared back at him through the smoky blue haze.

A seedy stick of a man held a fiddle in the air, its old varnish glowing like his bald head in the light. He clamped his chin over the box and played from a crouch with a tapping foot. His elbow flew and cheers went up with his music. Voices broke out as they sang to his accompaniment. They pounded the tables and cried for more.

Another man, meek in appearance as a parish clerk, rose glassy-eyed on unsteady legs. He smiled foolishly, then leaped out on the floor and broke into a jig. They clapped and stomped. They called for Maggy, who obliged by setting down her tray and standing with her hands on her hips, ready. A smile lit her face and deepened her dimples. Then she tossed back her head and hiked up her skirts. She kicked out her feet and together, arm in arm, they swung to the fiddler's music and the roaring approval of the crowd.

Toward the end of the dance, Garth noticed a man enter the tavern, almost sidle in, it seemed to him. Through the layers of blue haze he saw the man lean over the bar, as if whispering to the bartender, who wiped slow circles with his bar rag as he listened. Garth did not recognize the man, was sure if he had he wouldn't have forgotten the broad shoulders he'd seen only on mill workers. He especially wouldn't have forgotten the skull-like head that seemed to stretch his skin and flatten his features.

The dance ended and Maggy scurried over to the bar to pick up a tray of refills. The fiddle squawked again and Garth's attention was drawn back to the crowded tables where the patrons crowed their self-congratulations, slapped each other on the back and, tipping their glasses, began another chorus.

Emptying his glass and feeling mellow, he debated whether to have one more before leaving. Maggy approached, making the decision for him.

"Compliments of the house, sir," she said, holding out the glass streaming foam down its sides. Her smile flashed.

Flustered, he smiled back. She was gone before he could manage a 'much obliged.' Warmed by the atmosphere and by the beer setting him aglow and tingling his cheeks, he eased back on the settle.

He was almost finished and ready to leave, when Maggy rushed up to his table. "Sir," she said in a hushed voice, "if I might ask a favor...."

Garth looked up, surprised.

"You're closest, sir. If it wouldn't be too much bother...."

"Why...sure now. If you'll...if I can be—"

"A barrel, sir. Tipped in the back room. A keg, with beer in it, large and too heavy for me. If it wouldn't be too troubling—"

"'Course," Garth said, rising a little unsteadily but anxious to please. "Just point the way," he said, following after her quick steps through a door at the far end of the wall.

It was a storage room, not too large and dimly lit. Tables and chairs were stacked haphazardly; buckets with mops, crates and broken odds and ends of equipment lay on the floor along the walls and on shelves. Garth glanced around, bewildered.

"I don't see...where's the keg, Miss?" he said, looking at her questioningly.

She backed away, her face sober and frightened. Her hand went to her shoulder.

"Miss?" He reached out to her. "You feelin' all right...? What's...what's wrong, Miss?"

"Don't, sir. Don't touch me. Please!" she cried. Her arms crossed, clutching herself.

"Why, Miss...I only...."

Falling back, she tripped over a box. Instinctively he caught at her and her dress tore away at the shoulder.

She screamed.

Panic jolted him. Alarmed, he retreated, his hands up as if trying to hold back something physical. "Miss! I was only tryin'...just wanted to—"

She screamed again, flung open the door and dashed out.

"Wait, Miss! The keg. You don't under—" He withered in the wake of her trailing cries.

Stunned, he staggered out into the bright light, blinking dumbly in the silence. His jaw fell. He tried to speak, to call the girl back, to explain.

A voice boomed out, a wild cry, and, as if in a dream, Garth saw a man flying toward him. Unprepared, his stomach caved with the skull-like head that drove in like a battering ram. Shouting erupted, filling the room with noise again and drowning out his feeble protests. The skull whipped up and slammed against his jaw. Garth reeled along the wall and fell over his table. The man sprang up and pounced on him. Trying to recover his senses and his balance, Garth struggled to hold the man off. The crowd pressed in around them, cheering the man whose fist now shot out and snapped Garth's head back.

Pain ignited Garth's temper. Bellowing, he brought his fist down on the skull like a club. The man's knees buckled and he clawed up for Garth's eyes. Garth reared and hammered home a second blow that collapsed the man's legs. He raged over the crumpled man, pummeling him with his fists until dragged off and pinned by the crowd crying for his blood and for the law.

They came soon enough, handcuffing him and dragging him howling off to jail.

Chapter 32

It had all happened so quickly. He didn't understand. He paced his cell, grinding his teeth and squeezing his fists.

"I'm tellin' you," he pleaded through the bars, "I've done nothin' to rightfully put me here."

The jailer sat at his desk with his back to him, writing in a book.

"I've...I've a wife. She'll be wonderin'."

The jailer nodded and continued writing.

Garth rattled the cage door. "I'm talkin' to you, old man, damn it. Let me out o' here! You've no right to hold me!"

The jailer swung around lazily in his chair. He stared at Garth out of the deep wells of his tired eyes, as if any anger they might have ever possessed had long ago expired. His face hung, hound-like, and he spoke with a drawl. "Convince the judge, not me."

He said it with a finality that foreclosed any further talk and Garth subsided. The jailer shuffled the papers on his desk and dimmed the light over it. He lifted his feet on another chair and let his head slump over his folded arms.

Garth flung himself down on the wooden bunk, an oak board suspended from the wall at each end by chains. His mind was frantic. He thought of the stranger who had caused his grief and his hands tightened on the chain behind his head. He thought of Beth and the worry that would keep her awake all night and his stomach sickened. Finally he thought of the girl and the events of the evening, and considered what he might have done, what he should have done.

The cell closed in on him. A fear crept into him as he realized his tenuous position. He curled up on his side, trying to force sleep on himself, but sleep was long in coming.

When it finally did come, it did not bring the hoped for peace and forgetfulness he might have expected, but instead brought dreams to torment him:

He found himself in a shadowy room, with bars on the window. And the girl was there, Maggy, smiling at him over her bare shoulder. Falling back, he swung 'round and lunged for the door, but it was locked. Furiously he rattled it, calling out to the men, who were laughing and singing and could not hear him.

Frightened, he backed away to the darker recesses until he bumped into something, someone. It was Maggy again, sitting down and crying into her hands. She tilted her face up to him and he bent down to comfort her, to pull her into his arms. Her lips beckoned, drawing him in, when suddenly her face changed to anger, her face changed to Beth's. An owl suddenly screamed out of the darkness, clawing at his eyes, tearing at—

A short cry caught in his throat and he bolted up, sweating, trying to locate himself. Remembering, he lay back again, exhausted, and drifted off into a restless sleep.

The sun shining through the barred window did not awaken him. Not until the key clinked in the lock did his eyes snap open. He sat up suddenly on one elbow, recognizing immediately the man entering the cell. The key turned behind him.

"Beeker."

"Yes, and hoping you're of a better temperament today, Mr. Garth, than you were upon the occasion of our last meeting." He nodded his ponderous forehead toward the vacant bunk opposite Garth's. "With your permission."

Garth gestured, still at a loss, and Beeker lowered himself with great deliberation. He held his hat over his knees. "Now then...."

"You are here to release me, Mr. Beeker? To call off—"

"One moment, Mr. Garth. I am *not* here to represent you."

Garth's voice rose sharply. "Then what *are* you here for?"

"That's a nasty temper you have there, Mr. Garth. Little wonder you find yourself in the difficulties you do." He started to rise. "Perhaps I'd better—"

"Wait...Mr. Beeker," Garth said, quickly subdued. "Is there anythin' you can do for me? Somethin' to help get me out o' here?"

Beeker eased down. He sighed. "I'm afraid it's all a bit more complicated than that, Mr. Garth. It seems several rather serious charges have been laid against you, not the least of which is your alleged assault upon one Miss Margaret Townsend, better known to you as Maggie."

"Hold on there. I've done nothing. Just a drink and...and trying to help—"

"*A* drink, Mr. Garth?"

"Two drinks. At the Owl." He held his head. "Maybe...well, a man's a right to that, surely."

"That's what *you* say. Unfortunately, others stand ready to tell quite another story. None of it favorable to you, as is my understanding."

"I tell you, Mr. Beeker, I never laid hands on that girl, never touched her."

"Never touched her? Careful, Mr. Garth, I warn you."

"O' course, only when I reached out to catch her."

"To catch her? For what purpose, Mr. Garth?"

"To keep her from fallin'!" He grew flustered. "What's a man to do, let a girl fall flat on her face?"

"Calm yourself, Mr. Garth. I put these questions to you the way the prosecutor will. Except that I have been far more gentle with you than you may expect *him* to be."

"Pros—"

Beeker held up his hand to quiet him. "For instance, he may ask why you chose the most reclusive corner of the tavern to sit in. Was it easier there to work your devious charms on an innocent lass?"

"Why…why, I always do. That's—"

"Always work your devious charms?"

"No—sit there!"

"So. Then this is not the first time."

"Now hold on there—"

"And when you found your advances rebuffed—and your senses already altered by a mild inebriation, which you've already admitted to—you could not control your passions. You followed her into the back room—"

"No, no!"

"She resisted, tried to escape. You tore away her dress and—"

"Stop! It's a lie, a black lie." His voice crumbled as he crumbled to the bunk, holding his head.

"Of course it is, Mr. Garth, but what's a jury to think? A man who disassociates himself from all except the lovely young lady who is compelled to serve him in a dim corner. A man who leaves his wife and child at home while he haunts the Owl each week—to what end, Mr. Garth? A man who speaks to no one, and of whom little is known: Where does he come from? What is his past? A man friendless, without known kin, outside his immediate family, of course. And reliable witnesses to swear against him—what's a jury to think, Mr. Garth? I ask you again, what *is* a jury to think?"

Shaking, Garth leaped up, his face rigid. "See the girl, why don't you! She was sick, ready to faint, I saw it. She can vouch as to the truth o' my word."

"Ah, yes, her. Well, it seems that the party in question is somewhat confused by the events of the night. However, one

must expect that sort of reaction from an assault victim—
hysteria. Not uncommon. In any case, Mr. Garth, she's already
sworn out a complaint against you."

"She—It's lies! Lies, lies, lies! A whole pack o' them."

Beeker's equanimity grew inversely proportionate to
Garth's agitation. "There, there, Mr. Garth, shouting at me will
do *you* little good. I suggest you save your energies for the
trial."

"Trial?" Garth eased himself down. He felt lightheaded and
woozy. Everything was happening too fast. "The man...the
stranger who attacked me....?"

"Ah, yes, the man who is also pressing charges against you
for injuries suffered at your hand. I'm afraid, Mr. Garth, you've
made a hero of him in the process, as well. Is there perhaps
someone else you might think of, someone who could testify in
your behalf?"

Garth squeezed his face. He felt the walls closing in. "For
the sake of God, man," he whispered hoarsely, "how's anyone
to defend hisself against lies?"

"One way, Mr. Garth, is to tell the truth as you know it
and—"

"I have. I swear I have! But who will believe me....?" His
voice trailed off.

"...and hire the best attorney you can afford, as a sort of
insurance that truth will out, don't you see?"

Garth's rueful laugh, unexpectedly breaking, momentarily
ruffled Beeker's composure. "How's a man hard put to rub a
few coins together for a night's relaxation to afford a lawyer?"

Beeker breathed a long, weary sigh. "Yes, I see," he said,
rising heavily to his feet. "Well, perhaps something you've laid
aside you may have forgotten? For a rainy day, you might say.
Or a possession of value you might convert to cash?"

"I told you, man, there's nothin'." He mashed his fist into

his other hand. "Nothin'."

"It's twenty years you're looking at, Mr. Garth," he said grimly, "a veritable death sentence at your age." Garth flinched visibly. "Twenty years at least. Not to mention the various and sundry other charges laid against you." His eyes rolled up. "Resisting arrest, destruction of property, assault and battery, public intox—"

Garth sprang to his feet. "You've got to help me," he cried, clutching Beeker's arm. "You believe me, don't you? You know it's all a pack o' black lies. Just lies and lies!"

Beeker glared at the hand, and Garth withdrew it. "Lies?" His tone was flat, reasoning. "For what good reason, Mr. Garth? Cui Bono? For whose good?" His eyes, cool and steady on the wilting Garth, were uncompromising and hard, and at the same time reflected an infinite patience.

Garth shook his head. "I don't know…don't know. Maybe she's just a crazy girl."

"And I wouldn't be surprised if your little fracas at the carnival didn't return to haunt you." He stroked the smooth felt of his hat and his forehead glistened.

Garth started with the sudden recollection. "Mr. Beeker, you approached me…a propy-sition, you said…."

Beeker's pendulous face opened with surprise. "But my good man, you've never heard it. Said you weren't interested, I believe."

"Whatever it is—however I can be of help…."

"Yes, well, it may be too late for that." He edged for the door. "Of course…" he saw Garth's face brighten "…if I had your word, as man of honor, that you promise to be amenable to my proposals, I might consider handling your case personally."

Garth grasped his hand and wrung it with both of his own. "You have it, Mr. Beeker! If you can make 'em see the truth, convince 'em, I'd be eternal grateful."

Beeker pulled his hand free. "Now then—Gifford!" His stentorian voice rang with authority. "The door."

The jailer shambled over from his desk and searched out the key from his ring.

"Gifford, get Miles here immediately for this man's deposition." He turned to Garth. "Your statement."

"Mr. Beeker...one favor. My wife...if you could get word to her, tell her—"

"You can tell her yourself, Mr. Garth. As soon as Miles has your account of the event, I'll have you free. An hour or two." He stepped outside the cell. "Saturday next, three o'clock, the Wainscott Inn. You find that convenient?"

Speechless, Garth nodded.

"Good. Use the side entrance and ask for me. I strongly suggest you do not disappoint me, Mr. Garth." His tone was as intimidating now as it had been reassuring moments earlier. Meticulously he donned his hat and smoothed his coat sleeves. "Reciprocal trust, Mr. Garth. Don't violate it."

Not only true to his word to have him released, Beeker had even provided transportation home for Garth. Garth's great sense of relief was marred by the knowledge that his wife would be distraught by his absence. She would be relieved to see him, he knew, then she would grow angry and, finally, she would question him.

Chapter 33

She was standing in the window when he arrived, partly hidden by the curtain. The boy ran out and Garth swooped him up and carried him inside with music playing gaily around them. Beth stood motionless, facing him. She looked wretched, haunted, and he knew she hadn't slept all night.

"Beth, it's all right. It's all right now." He approached her, speaking softly, and put his arms around her. "I'm safe. No need to worry more. I can explain."

As he had expected, her distress diminished with the reassurance of his presence and was followed by flashes of anger born of her anxieties.

Then came the questions as he unfolded his story of how he had been minding his own business, quietly enjoying his beer the way anybody would, when a brawl broke out; how he had tried to help break it up, only to find himself drawn into it (He displayed his bruised jaw) and finally mistaken for one of the instigators; how he had been forced to spend the night in jail until the facts could be sorted out and his innocence proved. Yes, proved, thanks to a fine gentleman, one Mr. Holloman T. Beeker, who took an interest in him and believed him....

"...No, don't know why...no, no payment, just the milk o' human kindness, I guess...o' course, still some technicalities to iron out...no, don't know what kind, not being a lawyer myself...yes, he is, one of the best...next Saturday..."

Questions came intermittently during the week, and Garth improvised answers that were not only plausible, but reasonably convincing. Saturday came quickly. He had been given an early quit without loss of pay by the foreman and, although he wasn't told why, he knew that Beeker had arranged it.

Under the curious eyes of his wife standing in the doorway, he dressed in his best clothes. "A man can't go to town dressed like a beggar, now can he?" he said to her questioning gaze. "And how often do you get to see an important figure like Holloman T. Beeker, Esquire?" He brushed past her out the door.

Chapter 34

Punctually, at the appointed time, he arrived at the Wainscott Inn and, feeling mildly apprehensive, entered as instructed, by the proper door. He stood waiting in the foyer, fumbling with his hat and peeking around the corners looking for someone to direct him. Seeing a partially open door ahead and no one around, he sidled over to it. A quick glance over his shoulder and he stuck his head inside the room.

His eyes opened in amazement. Never had he seen a dining room, or any room, of such massive dimensions. The walls, where they were not alive with the rich, lustrous glow of rosewood paneling, were hung with brocaded draperies. His eyes wandered over the empty tables, taking in the silverware glittering on the white table linens; the water goblets sparkling with refracted light; the chandeliers blazing overhead with blossoms of gem-like glass.

Most impressive was the wood: banisters, doweling, beams and posts. Even the crown molding running the walls near the ceiling was meticulously wrought and polished to a glistening finish.

The smell of stuffy tradition and grandeur pervaded the place, and he could feel the power of wealth and its wall of impenetrability. It reminded him of what he imagined a royal dining room to be and, at the same time, felt he was in the sumptuous interior of a grand sailing vessel.

"Solid oak?" he muttered, touching the door.

"Pardon me?" an austere, sober-faced man said, coming in from another door and carrying a tray of neatly stacked gold napkin rings.

"I'm s'posed to—"

"Mr. Beeker, yes, he's expecting you," he said, with a hint of disdain touching his brow. "Around there." He nodded toward an elaborately ornate cabinet. "First door and to the right."

Garth palmed the sweat from his forehead as he tread silently across the plush oriental carpet. The door loomed, massive, and like everything else, apparently hand-carved, a frightening symbol separating his world from Beeker's.

He raised his arm to knock, but instead let his hand fall to the burnished knob. He took a deep breath and pushed the door open.

Beeker turned a surprised face up to his own surprised face. He hadn't expected to see Farnsworth there, had, in fact, completely forgotten him.

Farnsworth's eyeglasses flashed. "In civilized countries it is customary—"

"Now, now, Calvin," Beeker interrupted, patting Farnsworth's arm, "no need for formalities, not among friends. Sit down, Mr. Garth. Be comfortable." He gestured to the seat across the conference table.

Garth stepped in awkwardly, girding himself against he knew not what, except that he had an unsettled feeling in his stomach, the kind he felt whenever he had to walk home across the open road in a thunderstorm. He pulled a chair out, farther down from the one suggested, and sat on the cushioned seat, convex in shape, which was less comfortable than it had appeared.

"Mr. Garth, you're looking much better today than you did upon the occasion of our last meeting."

"Yes, about that—"

"Of course, of course you want to know how we stand in the matter. Certainly, I understand your concern. But first, would you like a refreshment? I can ring. Tea, ale? Anything you like. You've come a long way."

"No...thank you."

"I see. Well! I've gone over your deposition and those of several others. I must inform you right off, Mr. Garth—it wouldn't be fair of me not to—that the evidence against you is, ah, quite formidable."

Garth tightened.

"However, we must not be discouraged. I have launched a rather formidable counterattack myself. Naturally, I can't divulge all my secrets—a lawyer's stock in trade, don't you know." He chuckled over to Farnsworth, who allowed a trace smile to cross his lips as he continued staring across at Garth.

"Suffice to say, Mr. Garth, that I am presently conducting a thorough investigation, not only of the girl in question, but of the man—what's his name, Calvin?"

"Blescoe," Farnsworth said, his lips barely moving, "Ramsey Blescoe."

"Ah, yes, Blescoe...to determine if a connection exists between the girl and him, don't you see. Bound to be something else we'll turn up in the process anyway. Never has been a closet I couldn't find a skeleton lurking within, something we can use to negotiate with, if you follow my meaning." He pushed away the papers spread before him.

Garth's brow furrowed. The news didn't sound good to him, and the knowledge that Farnsworth was involved in his case compounded his misery. He was growing steadily annoyed, too, with Farnsworth's eyes trained on him like hard, shiny bullets behind the lenses that were much thicker than he had realized.

Beeker drew out his handkerchief and patted his forehead. "Unfortunate happening, this...this Blescoe fracturing his skull."

Garth started.

"At ease, Mr. Garth. If your statement is true—and I have no reason to doubt your veracity— this diabolical miscreant deserved it. And more." He saw Garth's hands go down to his hat on his lap. "In any case, we'll no doubt have another suit on our hands. But don't worry, Mr. Garth. You can trust *me*. Eventually I will extricate you from his abominable situation."

His face broadened with a wide paternal smile. "These things take time." His great head tipped forward, as if heavy with thought and he stared down at his fingers playing lightly on the polished table. "Now," he said, slowly lifting his eyes, "as to the other matter—"

Garth tensed.

"You are the natural parent of the boy, one Jonathan Garth, observed with you by Mr. Farnsworth and myself at the carnival some days back?"

Garth nodded. "That's right," he said, a deep worry creeping in as he thought of Beth.

"An impressive display of talent, as I mentioned before, Mr. Garth. Had you noticed it or any sign of it previous to that evening?"

Garth tried to pull himself together. "Tell the truth, I can't say but what you seen was no more'n dumb luck."

Beeker studied him a long moment. "Then have you ever noticed any sign of this...this dumb luck before?"

"Not as I recall," Garth said, matter of factly, "no, sir." He saw Farnsworth reach down and bring up his stick and felt a simmering anger as he watched him stroke his gloved hand with the silver head.

"No matter, Mr. Garth. I'm prepared to risk a given amount of capital in this venture and, if necessary, suffer the consequences should it prove to be nonproductive. You will find, Mr. Garth, that I am a man endowed with certain talents myself, not the least of which is an unerring instinct for finding the jugular of opportunity and, if need be, of men as well. In time, I think, you will discover this for yourself."

Garth's mouth soured. He felt as ridiculous being lectured as he did sitting in the chair that forced him to sit erect and balanced on it, like a woman. "This here matter...."

"This matter, yes. You're not a man to beat about the bush. Good. It is a matter of investments." He weighted the 'investments' and allowed it time to sink in. "Investments which—if all works out as I confidently anticipate—investments which will bring us all great rewards."

Though looking at Beeker, Garth was distracted by Farnsworth, who had laid his stick on the table. "Rewards?"

"In a word, Mr. Garth, profits." Beeker leaned forward. "Does that perchance go against the grain in any way?"

"Well, o' course, I never agreed to anythin'...that is, is this all above board, so to speak...I mean—"

Farnsworth's voice cut in, cold and sharp: "Are you suggesting that Mr. Beeker would engage in anything criminal!"

Embarrassed, Garth stuttered.

"Of course he isn't, Calvin. Obviously this is all new to the man, a highly moral man, I might add, seeking answers to his questions. Understandable, Mr. Garth, and to your credit. As to your question, let me assure you that it is, in your words, completely above board. Profits, especially great profits, are often thought to be ill-gained and obscene. This is a misconception held by the uninformed and the envious."

Beeker leaned farther across the table, as if trying to close the distance between Garth and himself. "No, Mr. Garth, profits are nothing more than a tangible exchange for hard work and knowledge, a kind of compensation for intelligence and foresight properly focused. And more often than not, risk is involved. It is not simply a matter of stepping in and walking out with bundles under one's arms. No, indeed, Mr. Garth," he said, leaning back and wagging a finger. "Money must be put up. The greater the would-be profits, the greater the sum risked. It's an economic law, Mr. Garth, as certain as the laws of gravity. And it is entirely legal!"

Garth listened, nodding slowly, skeptical, yet swayed by the logic of Beeker's argument.

"What I propose, Mr. Garth—"

"Will I have a say as—"

"Manners," Farnsworth's voice stabbed out. "Let Mr. Beeker finish."

Garth jumped to his feet, shaking his fist across the table. "I told you before—"

"Please!" Beeker said. "Sit down, Mr. Garth!"

Garth hovered over the table, glaring down at Farnsworth, who, except to grasp his stick, did not move. Garth withdrew slowly, as if tearing himself away. He shoved his chair out of the way and stomped to the far wall where he grabbed another and dragged it back. He sat heavily and crossed an ankle over his knee. His hat lay under the table where it had rolled.

"Let's have no more of that!" Beeker said.

"Well, if that…if he don't mind *his* manners—"

"Mr. Garth! …I agree, Mr. Farnsworth is sometimes abrasive, but it is what makes him a particularly effective attorney. You should be aware, also, I think, that I have placed him in charge of your case. He is an invaluable asset to me— and to you, Mr. Garth." His eyes slid to Farnsworth, who had shifted his position and sat slowly rolling his stick between his gloved palms.

Sweat broke out on Garth's face. He avoided looking at Farnsworth and his stick and tried to keep his attention on Beeker, who was leaning toward him again, his shoulder thrust forward with the same suggestion of aggressiveness that now tinged his voice. Garth felt the chill of it the way he had when Beeker had given instructions to the jailer.

"Directly to the point, then, Mr. Garth. I propose to use your son as...as a kind of financial advisor. He—"

"But he can't speak, can't say a word," Garth interrupted, immediately aware of the anger flashing from Farnsworth's lenses.

"He did well enough with you at the carnival," Beeker pressed.

"True enough, but—"

"Can he read?"

"No...well, I guess, yes. How good I can't say."

"Can he write?"

Garth squirmed. Beth's face rose before him, haunting him. "Never did yet as I've seen."

Beeker meditated. He stared down to the table, his fingertips massaging his forehead. "Well," he said, looking up sharply, "he can indicate. In any case, Mr. Garth, I intend to lay out an investment program—stocks, bonds, futures—that sort of thing. Are you familiar at all with such matters?"

"Feller works at the mill's got some stock—pigs and such he works on the side. 'Cept for that, I'm not too knowin'," he said, irritated by Farnsworth's frosted face fixed unwaveringly on him.

"I see. Well, no matter. It's a simple affair, really. You will merely bring the boy here at an appointed time, and I will ask him to indicate from certain charts and lists those items I wish clarified. Most of the ground work will be done by me and, of course, Mr. Farnsworth. I will utilize your son only as a kind of last-minute consultant." He smiled warmly across the table. "One meeting per month should suffice."

"Mr. Beeker—with all due respect—"

"Ah, yes, you're wondering of course how your share will

be determined. I've considered that. First, of course, my bill for legal services on your behalf will have to be satisfied. And you must realize you are risking nothing at all. Any losses incurred will be entirely my own. Under those circumstances, I believe two percent is fair. How does that sound to you?"

Garth looked surprised.

"That may not seem like much, Mr. Garth; however, I assure you, when dealing with large sums, two percent is a considerable amount of money."

Garth nodded, trying to keep up. "Yes, sounds fine, but with all due respect...I know as this is all legal, you being a lawyer and all, but is it...is it...." He searched for a word.

"Ethical?" Farnsworth sneered. "How dare you insinuate—"

Garth lunged across the table, wrenching the stick away and half-dragging Farnsworth out of his seat with it. "I've had a belly full o' you!" he cried, raising the stick to strike. Farnsworth fell back, shrinking in his seat behind his hands.

"Mr. Garth!" Beeker shouted, reaching out to him. "Mr. Garth!"

Garth hesitated, fighting the impulse to smash Farnsworth's head. He raised the stick higher, then suddenly grasped it with both hands and brought it down sharply over his own knee. He flung the pieces across the room. "You can keep your investments, Mr. Beeker! And him too. I want no part of it." He spun around to leave.

"Wait, Mr. Garth, listen to me." He shot an angry glance to Farnsworth. "Your point is well taken. Please, you're a reasonable man, sit down. Believe me, this proposal is not so self-serving as it may appear. As you must know, I am entrusted with the funds of many in this town. I am also an advisor to several bankers, the men responsible for the savings invested by the people, good people, like yourself, your neighbors. And several companies hereabouts—"

"Well, you'll have to help 'em without *me*! Use some o' that *intelligence* you was talkin' so big about." He reached for the doorknob. "Or use *him*, he's so good," he said, pointing out Farnsworth, sitting on the edge of his chair fixing his glasses and visibly shaken. He strode back suddenly and Farnsworth froze in place. Garth dropped and retrieved his hat from under the table, dusted it, jammed it on his head and started out again.

"Mr. Garth," Beeker called out, "your case. Remember, it's twenty—"

"I'd rather rot in jail forever than have dealin's with the likes o' *him*." He flung the door open.

"Despite this outburst, I will temporarily delay legal action. You have until three weeks from today, Mr. Garth," Beeker called after him. "Same time. Think carefully!" His voice boomed with the slam of the door.

Chapter 35

A week after Garth's meeting with Beeker, the school year opened and again the boy stood before his mother to be smoothed, patted, straightened and lectured. She pushed the hair back from his scrubbed face and saw the excitement in his eyes, heard it in the quiet song he sang. She had not slept well that night and his music soothed her frayed nerves. She tucked his lunch under his arm.

Outside, the air was fresh and crisp, though warming rapidly with the climbing sun. The road stretched long before them, and the thought of trudging it through another winter troubled her. She knew he could make his own way easily enough, but the memory of his disappearance still haunted her. Even Garth's angry insistence that he be allowed to go alone could not shake her will.

Tripping along beside her, the boy sang with an eagerness that helped take her mind off the permanent ache in her joints that even the daily applications of horse liniment could not relieve. The air cooled her perspiring face.

When they reached the mill the boy stopped. He sang out, and when Garth did not appear, his music dropped steeply to a baritone pitch.

"Probably too busy today," she said, looking forlornly to the barren heap of stone in the distance.

From her window Miss Lapham saw the woman approaching with her son. As before, she watched her take him under the old maple tree and kneel before him to dust him, button him and tuck in his shirt.

All summer she had been uneasy with the feeling that he would not return in the fall. She had thought of him often, had even considered riding out to see him, but the intimidating image of Mrs. Garth stopped her.

The boy ran up the drive and she breathed relief. When he stepped into the room others called out his name and he sang softly back to them. His face was alive and animated as he took in the familiar faces and the new ones gawking at him. Miss Lapham expressed no emotion, except for a demure smile that quickly vanished as she directed him to one of the larger seats farther back.

She was surprised at how much sturdier he looked. He seemed more confident, too, more self-assured, and when he gazed out to her, she noticed his eyes had deepened to a darker hue, almost to a blue-green. But the smile had not changed, nor the affection reaching out from it in a kind of strange kinship that both pleased and unsettled her.

Her pupils erupted noisily again and she called for order. She stiffened and called again, but they either did not hear or would not obey. Her ruler cracked like a whip against the desktop, driving the impish genies quickly and timidly back into the bottle of conformity from which they had been released several months earlier by the magic of the recess bell. Together, her voice and her face assumed their customary chill as she launched into her welcoming speech, filled with warm promises and dire threats.

Chapter 36

Except to tell his wife that his case was still pending and would take time to resolve, Garth had told her nothing of his meeting with Beeker. "You know these lawyers," he said, feigning a levity she sensed was false. "Ever'thin' takes time with 'em. Slow as molasses in January."

She listened, noticing the subtle agitations he did not realize he conveyed. He was hiding something, she felt sure, but what? And for what possible reason?

"Somethin' else, too, Beth. Made up my mind about it. Not goin' to spend no more time in town. If a man can't sit and enjoy a beer or two without being accused of crimes and clapped in jail overnight—well, they seen the last o' my business." He glanced over to her, searching for a sign he had pleased her, but she gave none.

Privately, Garth worried. As his anger diminished, Beeker's threat returned to torment him. He paced, schemed, swore he would never give in. But he hadn't only himself to consider. With him in jail, who would look after Beth and the boy? How would they live? Besides, Beeker's argument had made a lot of sense. *Gave reasons I couldn't dis-pute had I tried all day.* Beeker had given him three weeks. He made up his mind.

"Beth," he said, fairly confident with the half-truth he was about to mouth, "Beth, it'll be your birthday soon. Good idea, I think, if I take Jonathan into town with me. Let the boy pick you out somethin'. As a kind o' surprise." He beamed at his suggestion.

"Why, that's nice, Everett," she said, lowering her eyes. "When will you go?"

"Saturday should be fine. Work's light, so I can get off a bit early. Give us more time to browse. If you can have him ready...."

The nervousness her ear detected in his laugh puzzled her. "All right, Everett," she said, sidetracked by his thoughtfulness.

* * * * *

Saturday came, dull and dreary, and Garth and the boy hurried along to beat the rain. They arrived perspiring but otherwise dry, and slipped into the side door of the Wainscott Inn. Garth did not wait for anyone to meet them, but went directly through.

"Ever see anythin' to match it, Jonathan?" he said, still slightly out of breath.

The boy's eyes swept the room. "No, Father."

"No need to answer, Jonathan. And no need to let anybody here know you can talk. Best you save it for home."

The boy paused to peer into an aquarium along the wall, but Garth prodded him on. "No time for that now, Jonathan. We're expected."

This time he knocked before opening the door.

"Ah, Mr. Garth, come in, come in," Beeker said, half rising and beckoning them over.

Garth entered slowly, pushing the boy ahead and glancing around.

"Right over here," Beeker said, gesturing to the chairs next to himself. He noted Garth's tenseness. "Mr. Farnsworth can't be with us today. It appears a new complication has arisen regarding your case." He spoke as if nothing had happened the last time they were together. "Never mind him, though. He has a job to do and you can rest assured he'll do it well enough. We can get on without *him*, I'm sure."

"Makes no difference to me either way," Garth said, removing his hat.

"So!" Beeker exclaimed, as if seeing the boy for the first time. "So this is Master Jonathan Garth, is it? And even more handsome in the light of day." He took the boy's hand and shook it warmly. "That's quite a grip you have there for one so young," he said affably. The boy smiled, remembering Quisleby's advice to 'Put a little force to it.'

"They tell me you make pretty music, Jonathan. Would you honor an old man with a brief demonstration?"

"He's a bit shy," Garth said, taking up the hard-bottomed chair and placing it between Beeker and the boy. They sat.

"Yes, I see, well—" He shuffled through a sheaf of papers. "Jonathan," he said, "your father and I want to do something for this town, want to help it on its feet, so to speak. To do that we need your assistance. Now, you're not going to be withholding your guidance from us, are you?"

The boy glanced first to his father then shook his head.

"Good, that's the way to have it." He tapped the bulge of his head, as if trying to organize his thoughts. "Now, Jonathan, it so happens I observed you the night of the carnival, witnessed the remarkable feat of your picking several winners in a row. Your father here seems to believe it to have been sheer luck. I, however, believe you possess an instinct of sorts, perhaps innate but undeveloped in the rest of us." He turned to Garth. "Is the boy understanding me, Mr. Garth?"

Garth studied the boy a moment. "He understands."

"Good. Well, now then—Jonathan, you are interested in the welfare of the people of this community, are you not?"

The boy nodded.

"And you want to see them prosper, do you not? ...Of course you do. So do I. And so does your father. Now, we wouldn't want these good people to forfeit their life's savings to the vagar—that is, we wouldn't want them to lose everything they own through those misfortunes of fate which afflict men's lives and which are beyond their control, now would we? ...Of course not! Well and good. And if we could intervene to prevent such misfortunes from befalling our fellow man, don't we have a moral obligation to do it? ...Good! I'm glad you agree."

Garth stirred uncomfortably. And inside the boy's mind a melody stirred, sluggish and dull and undefined.

"We are all of us here interested in promoting the well-being of our friends and neighbors. And that is how it should be." He swung his head to Garth and saw his troubled face. "Mr. Garth, let me repeat, we will be in strict compliance with the law, rest assured. My sole interest is in fulfilling my duty as a man entrusted with the financial interests of the public. Naturally, one should always be compensated for services competently performed." He scanned the two quickly.

"Now," he said, thumbing through to a particular page, "Jonathan, I am laying before you a sheet. Names of certain companies you no doubt have never heard of, but important to us all. Extremely so." To Garth, he said, "You see, Mr. Garth, these are the companies in which this town has invested the bulk of its earnings and savings. As these companies go, so goes the town, if you see what I mean."

Nodding, Garth cocked his head to read the names.

Beeker turned to the boy and said, "Jonathan, I will ask you simply to peru—to look this sheet over and point to those you think will bring in the best profits in the near future." The boy's eyes fell to the sheet.

"How many do you want him to pick?" Garth asked.

Beeker meditated into the steepled fingers of his hands. "Say, for a start, three. After all, Mr. Garth, you may be perfectly correct in your assessment of the boy's performance."

The boy's finger quickly pointed out three, and Beeker pulled the paper in to check them off with his pencil.

"That will be fine, Jonathan, just fine." He studied the items and frowned. "You're sure these are what you mean?" he said, pushing the list back. The boy nodded, and Beeker picked up the paper again, uncertainly. "All right. If you say so." He shuffled the papers and stood up, extending his hand.

"Mr. Beeker..." Garth began, accepting the handshake as he rose.

"Ah, your commission."

"No, not that," he said quickly, glancing down at the boy. "Actually, what I mean to say is...well, it was necessary to take a bit o' time off the job, so as—"

"You won't be 'docked,' as I believe you call it, Mr. Garth. I'll attend to that small matter."

"Thank you," Garth said, hating his own subservience. "And if I might ask as to...to that complication you mentioned...."

"Oh, that. I wouldn't worry about it. I'm sure we'll work it out, but that remains to be seen, doesn't it?" He patted the boy on the head. "Fine young man you have here, fine young man. I'm sure you're proud of him." He turned serious. "Three weeks from now, Mr. Garth."

Garth hesitated at the door. "One thing more, if it's not too much trouble," he said, "do you think we might make it a later time, so as to avoid posing a problem with...to make it easier at home?"

"Of course, Mr. Garth. Six will be fine if it's agreeable to you."

Garth led the boy out. "What did you think o' him, Jonathan? Like to be a lawyer someday?" The boy's music came dark and ominous and Garth laughed. "Lawyer and liar. Sound pretty much alike, don't they?" He laughed again.

"Well, like anythin' else, sometimes you get a bad apple—not saying o' course Mr. Beeker's one—but like 'em or not, who is it we run to first when we're in trouble? And it's them what keeps the disorderly affairs of men better than what they might be. Most important, though, keep in mind, it's the town we're doin' it for. And no need to be repeatin' none o' this to your mother, neither! Some things she just ain't up to handlin' yet."

The boy sang softly as they stepped outside into a light drizzle, and Garth felt much the same kind of relief he'd felt when released from jail.

"Now suppose we take care of the important thing we come to town for. Got any ideas for somethin' your mother'd like…?"

Chapter 37

In school the singing began as before. At first nothing unusual occurred beyond the unusual, but after a short time Miss Lapham thought she detected a pattern to the singing that she'd been only vaguely aware of before. As Garth had before her, she began to keep track of the comments made in class, especially during current events discussions. And, like Garth, she soon noticed that good news, either true or later proved true, was always accompanied by pleasant music, and that bad news brought the opposite. Of her discovery she spoke to no one except William, her fiancé.

"It's true, William, I swear it," she said, after school one afternoon. "Unbelievable as it seems…." Her voice trailed off.

William Hathoway slouched uncomfortably in one of the student seats. He watched her. His narrow gray eyes with a touch of humor to them, saw her primp nervously as she spoke, saw the delicate features of her face that made him want to take her and hold her. Her words worked through to him finally and he pulled himself up, suddenly remembering:

"Now that you mention it, Martha, there were rumors this past summer. Something about the boy winning at a game of chance, I think, or—I'm not sure. So many stories have been told. Didn't you hear? At the carnival when it was in town. I understand he created quite a stir."

"Oh, my God, William," she said, lowering herself into the seat next to him and taking his hand. "What are we witnessing here?"

He laughed, a pleasant, indulgent laugh meant to comfort her. Why not just forget it, Martha? It's coincidence. Nothing more than that. I think you're allowing yourself to—"

"There's something else, William," she said, seeming not to hear him. "He's so…so changed somehow. So different. I mean, he always was, I know, but now…it's something about him, as if he's there and not there…as if part of him is gone. Or something else has been added, something I can sense but can't see or touch. It's very strange. I can't pinpoint it. I feel closer to him now, it's true, yet more removed. Like…like the feeling you get when someone close to you dies." She clutched his arm. "William, am I going mad?"

"You're thinking too much, dear girl, making entirely too much of this. You need a rest, a—"

"And lately…lately he's been asking for books.…" She stared down to the floor.

"Asking?" He bent forward to see her face.

"With notes."

Gently he lifted her chin and turned her face to his. "I didn't know he could write."

"Nor did I," she said, "not until his first note little more than a week ago. He wrote only two words: religious books. At first I didn't understand, was surprised he could write at all. And the script, so perfect. I was stunned. I gave him a book, one from my shelf and he became so excited I knew that was what he wanted."

She searched his face. "William, he's asked for three books so far. And each finished faster than the previous one. Today I gave him another. Why, William, why? What does it mean?"

"Martha, listen to me. The child is simply fascinated with the books themselves. I seriously doubt that he's actually reading them. Maybe having them makes him feel important. More likely, he only likes to look at the pictures."

"They hadn't but a few at most."

"Well then to hold them, feel them, carry them around. Children are like that, you know. It makes them feel grown up."

Her petulance pulled her mouth down at the corners. *William, you just don't understand at all!*

"On the other hand, you may be right," he said, sensing her pique and not wanting to lose her affection. He touched her hair lightly. "Martha, last year when we talked about leaving here, you said you'd think about it. Why not go now? Away from all this, from this town, its petty problems, the...the responsibility of a thankless job."

"It has its rewards." Her voice was flat.

"We can go to New York. Or Chicago, if you like. Even California. There's no opportunity for me here. Oh, they tell me what a fine job I'm doing, how valuable I am, but will they pay me a decent salary?" He snorted. 'Patience, my boy,' they tell me, 'patience. Rome wasn't built in a day, you know.'

"Believe me, Martha, this town is a closed corporation run by a few shrewd characters who put their own selfish interests first. I can get just so far with the bank. I'm young and ambitious. But what chance do I have for a promotion working next to the president's son and two more waiting in line? ...Martha?"

"I belong here, William," she said, moodily preoccupied. "My roots are here. When Mother and Father were alive—"

"They're not anymore," he interrupted, his jaw tight. "You've done enough here, giving seven years of your life to people who not so long ago wanted to fire you and maybe tar and feather you, too. You know what goes on in this town. Haven't we seen enough of it, heard the scandals—"

"Would it be any different elsewhere, William?" She turned her face slowly toward him.

"Martha, I can get a job. A good job. I have the experience. We wouldn't have to be part of this...this—Martha, we can be married!"

"William," she said, imploring him, trying to make him understand, "I can't. Don't you see? Not until—not yet."

He lurched to his feet, startling her, and she saw him standing above her, tall and slender and tense, his handsome face hardened with frustration.

"Almost five years now, Martha." His voice was strained. "How much longer?" His hair, the color of straw, fell forward and he brushed it away angrily.

"William...please. Let me think...a little time, just a little more time." She took his hand and squeezed it.

"Time? ...All right, Martha. All right...."

Chapter 38

For the next several days Martha Lapham carried out her duties in a distracted sort of way. Thoughts of William intruded constantly to disturb her. She felt confused and miserable. It was not so much what he had said just before he'd left that tormented her, but the weary tone in his voice, the resignation in his final words that made her fear his patience was near exhaustion, that she would lose him.

On the last of those several days, as she strolled between the aisles, upset and worried because William hadn't called on her, one of the children raised his hand and stood to speak:

"Miss Lapham, ma'm, did you notice Jonathan's singing? How he can tell that when we say something that if it's going to be true, he can tell if it is true?"

Such was the clear and simple insight of a child that cut across logic and reason. The class broke up noisily. Miss Lapham stiffened.

"Utter nonsense!" she seethed. "Sit down and let us hear no more of it!" She revolved slowly, ominously. "Be quiet, all of you. Back to your work. Immediately!"

But they had heard and believed, and now they would listen to confirm that belief. They carried their tales to their homes. And once again the townspeople were obliged to weigh the new developments at the school. Outwardly, they did not take seriously the new stories coming home to them. After all, they'd heard it all before, had even held an investigation and made fools of themselves. They laughed at the 'fortune teller' residing among them and made jokes about it.

But now and then a housewife would pause amid her washing, her tongue rolling inside her cheek, to reflect on something her child had said; or a man digging in his yard would stop to wipe away the sweat, and then, with his chin resting on his hands over the long-handled spade, his eyes gazing down to the broken ground, he would ponder the meaning of a story his child had related at the supper table, perhaps days earlier.

The Few, however, rallied fresh to their cause. In the town square or anywhere else they could gather a crowd, they urged rooting out 'the evil flourishing under our noses.' And after a while some who had scoffed earlier were beginning to doubt their own hard sense. They listened with even greater interest when, in place of 'fortune teller' came the word *anti-Christ.*

The rumors rampant in town did not get by Garth. Once he even managed to slip unnoticed into the fringe of a crowd and listened to the exhortations of a speaker who urged the trammeling 'of the pestilence in our midst.' Garth gauged the mood of the crowd and he worried.

He mentioned nothing to his wife, but he could not hide from her the subtle alteration of his mannerisms, the averting of eyes, the false note in his voice. When she questioned him he blustered, grew angry and denied her speculations. He gave excuses: the hard day at the mill; the pain in his back; the weather. He saw misery surface in her eyes again. It invaded her soul, invaded the house, invaded him. He lost himself in his newspaper.

Chapter 39

On Saturday afternoon Garth washed, changed clothes and sat down to dinner. For a while he said nothing, then, "Almost forgot, got to see the lawyer again today," he said, off-handedly. "How 'bout it, Beth, I take the boy in with me. For a little company along the way, you might say. Let him see the lights, too." Bolting down the last of his food, he saw the slow and deliberate lifting of her face, her dark eyes shining in eerie contrast to her putty complexion and graying hair.

"Lights?"

"Sure," he said, forcing a laugh. "Let him see some o' the Saturday night hustle-bustle."

"I think not, Everett. It will be late."

"For God's sake, Beth, let go a bit. Just to take in the sights. I'll be with him ever' minute. Not goin' to let him get lost, if that's still a worry to you. Don't you trust me, his own father?"

She stared down at her plate.

"And listen to him sing there, so sad. Can't you see he wants to go? Don't have no school tomorrow, neither."

She scowled. "Take him."

"No need for that attitude, Beth," he said, relieved. "It's only for a while. And give you a little o' the evenin' to yourself."

* * * * *

They arrived at the inn a few minutes late. Beeker, in a buoyant mood, welcomed them in and seated them personally. After a brief flurry of small talk he settled down to business.

"Right from the sheet, Jonathan," he said, sliding a paper in front of the boy. "Let us pick, say, four this time—to buy. And," he slid another sheet over, "from this list, say, four to sell." He winked at Garth.

The boy studied the columns and made his selections.

His troubled face perusing the sheet, Beeker asked the boy once again if he was sure. Nodding to the boy's nod, he tucked the papers into a folder beside him on the table and pursed his lips, thinking. "Now, Mr. Garth, if we might have a minute or two alone...."

Garth understood. "Jonathan, go on down the hall till I come out. Look over them fish in that tank you been dyin' to see."

Hesitating, the boy looked to his father and Beeker and moved away reluctantly.

"Mr. Garth," Beeker said, drawing an envelope from the folder, "we've had a bit of luck. Not much to be sure, but enough to be encouraging." He handed the envelope over. "There's twenty dollars remaining here, after a small deduction toward your legal fees, of course. And there'll be more where this comes from if all goes well." He saw Garth staring down at the envelope.

"It's all there, Mr. Garth, as agreed upon. True, we might have done considerably better, but caution was the order of the day. Perhaps this time we can dare to be a bit bolder and—Is something wrong, Mr. Garth?" he said peevishly, his expression irritable. "Isn't it enough? Is *that* what's troubling you?"

"No," Garth answered, as if just coming to. "That's fine, just fine. Only thing is, I hear talk circulatin' in town. 'Bout the boy, you see and—"

"Ah, yes, that. I know. Damn nuisance it is too. Fools is what they are, these people. Well-meaning, but fools all the same. Nasty brutes when they want to be." He tapped his forehead. "I've been meaning to attend to that matter."

Garth felt encouraged. He didn't like Beeker much, feared him, in fact, though he would have died before admitting it to himself. He couldn't help feeling in awe of the man, his absolute confidence, the secret power that threatened to burst the bulging wall of his head.

"You still attend church services with your family, is that correct?"

Garth nodded, wondering if there was anything Beeker didn't know.

"I suggest none of you attend for two weeks. That should give me time to get this matter under my control." As if reading Garth's mind, he said, "Nothing of what has transpired here is known to your wife, am I correct in that assumption? Neither this business venture nor the rumblings in the community?"

Garth nodded dumbly, amazed at the man's awareness.

"She does of course know of your difficulties with the law—though not entirely, I presume? ...Yes, I see. Well, you might explain to her that your presence in the church will, in some manner unknown to you, adversely affect your case, which, incidentally looks promising for you at the moment, the Blescoe assault charge notwithstanding."

Garth shook his head, trying to keep up with the flow of information.

"As for this trouble in town, well, *I'll* soon put a stop to that, I can assure *you!* We have other means beside the law at my disposal to—" He pushed his chair back and rose suddenly, thrusting out his hand. "Well, no matter, Mr. Garth," he said, pumping his hand and sliding an arm around his shoulder as he led him to the door. "All will be well shortly. You have my word on it."

He opened the door. "Now, shall we say...three weeks from

today? …Good. Same time then."

His head spinning, Garth stood blinking at the closed door. As if for the first time, he saw the envelope in his hand. Folding it, he tucked it carefully in his pocket and proceeded down the hall to get the boy. He did not see Farnsworth slip silently across the hall behind him into the room he had just left.

Chapter 40

At school Miss Lapham was finding it increasingly difficult to control her pupils. Good news, whenever confirmed, caused them to erupt like miniature volcanoes. She shouted for order, her ruler cracking over the desktop. She threatened everything from paddling to expulsion. And when the music indicated an unhappy turn of events, she worked doubly hard to relieve their melancholy. She knew of the rumors flying about town and was painfully aware that her pupils were the source of most of them. She grew frightened.

She expressed her fears to William, but he was of little help and offered almost no comfort. She felt abandoned. He told her she was foolish to assume responsibilities not hers, said that she had lost her perspective.

She folded her arms and turned her back to him. He apologized; she forgave him. She confided that the boy had exhausted her supply of religious books and now wanted philosophy books. He scoffed good-naturedly and smiled as he visualized the works of Plato in the hands of a child. She misunderstood, thinking he was laughing at her. She ordered him out. He protested. She insisted. Reluctantly, he went.

When he was gone she sat down and cried, though she did not know why, exactly, only that everything seemed so confused, her life so complicated and uncertain.

* * * * *

Just after the first heavy snowfall in mid-November a strange thing happened. It was a twist of logic that puzzled William and Martha then and even several years later when, in a far-off city, while lying in the muted darkness of their room beside their own silently sleeping child, they again found themselves pondering the question and deliberating its source. Though none could ever say how it began, all were soon of the conviction that the boy did not merely foretell events but indeed *caused* them.

In town the Few were fired with renewed zeal, and though constrained from holding meetings, their secret appeals lodged themselves in the minds of the people, who nodded their heads thoughtfully, recalling stories their children had told, and subsequent events.

"Yep," a man said, "that boy was singing the bad news days before old man Potter's cattle sicklied up and died. Put the hex on him, he did."

What they did not know was that Garth, observing the ill-tended cattle on his way to the post office, commented on the probable outcome in the presence of the boy.

And one day in class, shortly after Garth had spoken of the derailment bound to happen 'if nobody fixes the track bed outside of town,' the boy sang in harsh, brassy tones and everyone waited for 'something' to happen.

Each day brought new events, each of which brought new converts to the Few, whose ranks were beginning to swell.

In late November one of the town's two churches burned down. Though the boy had not sung of this, its destruction was attributed to him. To have a church burn, the house of the Lord, was a particularly ominous sign. And again, with greater frequency and conviction, the word *anti-Christ* passed their lips.

On the last day of that month a blinding snow out of the north ushered in winter. Mrs. Garth sat brooding into the fire across from her husband. At her feet the boy sat singing a melancholy refrain into the pages of the book open on his lap.

Her voice came whispering, plaintive. "Something is wrong, Everett. Very wrong."

Garth lowered his paper and regarded her curiously. "I don't gather your meanin', Beth. You're not comin' down sick?"

"Today...the last few days, I've been seeing people... watching me." She turned her head slowly to him. "Alongside the school, staring when they think I'm not looking ...And the dreams. They're back again, Everett, worse—"

"That's all?" he said, feeling her anguish reach across the room, seeing it distort her face. He chuckled, trying to make light of the matter. "Why, dreams is nothin', Beth you know that. Just superstition to believe in 'em." He folded his paper and slapped it on his knees. "As for the other, heck, probably no more'n folks like yourself waitin' to take home their young'ns. Been some pretty bad weather, you know."

"No, they come alone and go alone, most of them."

"Just imagination workin' overtime, Beth. Probably always was 'round there, bringin' supplies or fuel or somethin' for the school. You just never noticed. Could be a dozen reasons. Anyways, most it can be is curiosity. They know he sings, and you're his mother. That's all there's to it." He felt a deep pity for her and wanted to go over to her, to touch her and comfort her, but he knew she would not be receptive.

Grim and silent, she stared into the fire.

"Look," Garth said, waving his paper and tapping it against his hand, "this here's what we got to worry 'bout. Them soldiers is gearing up over there to march. And I see war acomin'."

The screaming of brass burst forth from the boy and the beat of a hundred drums shook the house. Trumpets wailed and cymbals rang and crashed around them. In a sudden sweep of her arm, his mother had his head, smothering in her lap the sounds convulsing his body under her hands. Dumbfounded by the unleashed fury, Garth sank back in his chair.

"You see, Beth," he said in a forced whisper. "You see?"

She turned piercing eyes on him. "Everett, get us out of here! For the sake of God, man, help us!"

* * * * *

For days news of the dirges spilling from the boy spread through the town and, days later, when the world was plunged into war, no one was surprised. The anger that had united the people against the boy was now rendered impotent by their awe of him. If he had the power for this, they reasoned, what power was not within his grasp.

In town a new chapel was erected in the assembly room of the town hall, and the people crowded in nightly for prayer meetings. Christmas was not far off, and in its coming there was hope.

After the declaration of war Garth came finally to full understanding of his part in the boy's prophesies and their effect on the town. He avoided expounding any more of his theories and ordered his wife to burn his newspapers to discourage the boy's renewed interest in them. When she regarded him suspiciously, he said, "Too much bad news in the world. No need for it in the house, too."

* * * * *

In school the boy's music dissipated the drabness of the gray skies outside. Only when one of the children conveyed an item of bad news or asked Miss Lapham to point out on the globe the location of a battle raging in some far part of the world did the music sink to an elegiac melancholy. Christmas, rapidly approaching, brought with it new excitement and a flurry of classroom activities that temporarily relieved Miss Lapham of the nebulous worries plaguing her.

Gradually, as the days wore on, the boy's music lifted in pitch and tempo, sweetened and warmed, and with it came a relaxation of the tensions in town. The war, far off, left them relatively untouched, and the townsfolk settled into their daily routine of surviving the hard winter. They said nothing of the boy, and whenever their excited children attempted to relate a new incident, they showed no interest.

Secretly, however, they worried, and some spoke of 'getting out altogether.'

Chapter 41

The days passed languorously across the trough of winter and with their steady climb to spring came a rise in spirits. The threat the boy had posed now seemed far behind and the townsfolk looked forward to sunshine and the rebirth of the world.

Bethany Garth felt particularly grateful for the coming days that would make her daily trudge almost a pleasure by comparison. She was miserable with the cold that tightened her face and stiffened her aching joints. But she was relieved too that no one came now to the school to stare at her, to worry her and add to the anxieties her recurring nightmares brought. Garth himself, though complaining of the bitter weather he had to work in, felt more secure with the absence of new rumors in town and with the six hundred dollars he'd received so far from Beeker and had stashed away.

The boy continued to mystify and baffle Miss Lapham, who scoured the library shelves for books to feed the boy's insatiable reading appetite. She told William about it:

"…history books, and now economic books. Is it possible, William, is it possible he's actually reading them?"

He shrugged, looking up to her from the student seat he slouched in. "A better question is, Martha, does he understand them?"

She frowned and gazed back out the window where the warming sun glazed the snow and crusted its shrinking edges to sparkling lace. The glare hurt her eyes and she turned away. "I've tried to question him, to ask what it is he's seeking. I've offered to help…but he simply—oh, how can I describe the strange expression on his face, in his eyes, the way they seem to look right through me. Lately he's so changed. William, he makes me uncomfortable. He actually…he…."

"Frightens you?"

"Oh, William, if I could only make you understand. He's not dangerous or frightening in the usual sense, but, yes, he does frighten me…and his singing, his music—I've never heard it so complex before, so ponderous. Sometimes I find myself wanting to scream when I hear it. Or cry."

"William stroked the hard line of his jaw. "And the children, how do they react?"

"Why, they're absolutely enchanted with him. It's Jonathan this and Jonathan that. Oh, occasionally one of them will say something derogatory, something no doubt heard at home. Then they have to contend with the Perkins boy. Remember him, the redhead?" She smiled, forgetting for a moment. "And his ally, Leroy."

William smiled, too, recalling the story of their school yard fight. "He doesn't frighten the children, then?"

"They're only children, William. They don't understand."

"No, they wouldn't, would they?" he said, a wan smile crossing his pale face. "Children accept things they don't understand."

"But why should the people be afraid of him, William? He's done nothing to them."

"For the same reason you're afraid of him, Martha." To her questioning look, he said, "Grown-ups always fear things they don't understand."

Chapter 42

Spring arrived warm and sunny. It was on one of those early days that Garth, scheduled to meet Beeker, strode to town with the boy at his side. "What's wrong, Jonathan? No song to give us today?"

"No, Father?"

"Any partic'lar reason?"

"I'd rather not say, Father."

"Those is mighty high-sounding words comin' from the son o' plain country folk. You been readin' too many o' them books, I think."

"I'm sorry, Father."

"No need to be sorry, boy. But I wish you'd aim a little more conversation my way, the way I see you do with your mother. Always talkin' quiet with her, but never seem to have too much to say to me, 'cept 'yes, Father' and 'no, Father.'"

"I'm sorry, Father."

"There you go again....Come on, son, what's eatin' at you? You can tell me."

"I can't put it into words, Father. I can hear them, hear the words talking to me, but they're not clear to me. They're like faces I can't clearly see. They are so many, but they are coming together and I'm beginning to understand. It's like the clouds parting to let the sun shine through, Father. Father, I think I'm afraid. I—"

"Now now, no need to be scarin' yourself, son. It's okay, we'll let her go for now. Look around, drink in the beauty of the world. Listen to them birds achirpin'. And don't that fresh air do somethin' to you, so new and clean-smellin'? Them trees out there, too," he said, pointing. "Remember how gray they was? Now look at 'em, buddin' so tender green, just like these fields spreading out all around us." He laughed. "Green just like my hands," he said, turning his palms up before him.

They walked on, the boy silent, and Garth from time to time looking askance at him.

As usual, Beeker greeted them with enthusiasm. His broad smile lit his face and his words flowed without pause. He rubbed his hands, rubbed their backs and escorted them to their chairs. Then he settled down to business.

"First, Jonathan," he said, slipping the papers from his folder, "I wish to tell you that I'm mightily pleased with the superb job you've done over the past months." He slid the papers across to him. "Mightily pleased.

"Now, Jonathan, ten from each will be sufficient. And those commodities on page three—we're heavily into those. Cast an eye over them and give us your expert opinion." He drew an envelope out of his pocket and pushed it over to Garth. He laid two fingers on the edge of the table and winked.

Garth nodded, half-smiling, and took the money. He felt the pleasant thickness of it as he folded the envelope in one hand and slipped it into his side pocket. His expression was casual, noncommittal, but his heart pumped. He still was not used to the feel of so much money, nor to the idea that the enormous sum of two hundred dollars could be made without lifting a finger. Mentally he calculated his earnings, but his pleasure vanished with the undefined guilt that arose to taint it.

"Well, Jonathan," Beeker said, drumming his fingertips on the table, "may we have the verdict?"

The boy didn't stir, and his music played darkly in his head. He saw his mother's face before him as he brooded down to the papers.

Beeker leaned forward and poked him. "Jonathan?" Puzzled, he turned to Garth. "Is the boy all right, Mr. Garth?

Would he perhaps want some water or soda?"

Garth nudged the boy. "Jonathan, you ain't showing proper manners. Your mother wouldn't like that. Now do as the man says and give him what he wants."

The boy continued to look down. He shook his head.

Beeker straightened in his chair. "Mr. Garth, what does this mean?"

Garth felt the tension pass from Beeker to himself. "Jonathan, do what I say and give the man them names he needs."

Again the boy shook his head.

"Is he often obstinate, Mr. Garth?" Beeker said, throwing a baleful look his way.

"Hasn't been hisself all day, now that you mention it," Garth said, swinging to face the boy directly. "Jonathan, no matter what you're thinkin', you got an obligation to fill here, same's I do. Now do like the man says and get it over with so you can get out and look at them fish you like so much."

"Mr. Garth—"

Garth held up his hand. He took the boy's face, lifted it toward his own and saw his eyes, so doleful, and the jaw set with the same resolution he'd so often observed in his wife. "Jonathan, this here's—"

The boy wrenched his face away violently, and Garth withdrew. Stunned, he turned to Beeker, who was mopping his brow with his handkerchief.

"I guess this will have to wait," Garth said, his mouth dry. "Seems the boy is havin' some kind o' spell."

"This can't wait!"

Taken aback by the sudden fury in Beeker's voice, Garth said, "If he won't talk now, maybe in a few days—"

"Now, Mr. Garth, now!"

Garth turned slowly back to the boy. He shook him by the

arm, not enough to hurt him, but enough to convey his anger. "I don't want to tell you again, Jonathan, so do it! Point out them companies he needs so bad!"

Despite the pressure, the boy would not be persuaded and Garth turned helplessly to Beeker. "Guess we're just gonna *have* to wait. Somethin's got into him I can't figger out yet."

Beeker leaned forward, his face crimson. "Jonathan, you listen to me. I want that information and I want it now!"

"Hold on there," Garth said, gathering himself. "No need to bully the boy any more than he's already got from me. If he won't talk, then we got to give him time."

"Mr. Garth," Beeker said, visibly straining to control his temper, "he must speak. The timing of these issues is of vital importance. The consequences of misjudgment could be catastrophic for everyone, for this town. Don't - you - understand!"

Garth squirmed. "Well, 'course I do—now. Still, it seems, under the circumstances ...what can I do? If the boy won't talk—"

Beeker reached over suddenly and grasped the boy's wrist. "If you propose to withhold this information at a time like—"

Garth's hand locked onto Beeker's wrist and tore it slowly away, crushing it. "Don't you never touch this boy again," he growled, "not 'less you don't like bein' in one piece." He threw the arm back.

Grimacing, rubbing his wrist, Beeker drew himself up, perspiring. "I anticipated something like this sooner or later, Mr. Garth. Yes, you needn't look so surprised. Not from the boy, no—from you! Either way it makes little difference. You'll have to *make* him see it my way, however you do it....Shall we call it a little unresolved matter in your past?"

Garth smiled. He rose, motioning the boy up with him. "Well, Mr. Beeker," he said sarcastically, "I been doin' a little thinkin' on that matter myself. It just so happens I don't believe there's any danger in it for me. I don't know how you done it, workin' up that trouble at the Owl so as you could pretend to be helpin' me—you and that mouse you got workin' for you— but I know you done it somehow. Took me a while to figger it out, being worried so much, 'bout how you come up to me at the carny-vale and being so handy after they locked me up, then takin' my case for no pay." He took the boy's arm to leave. "I'm not bright, Mr. Beeker, but I'm nobody's fool, leastwise not for long. Got myself enough money now, too, if'n I got to get another lawyer to bring the truth to light."

"Congratulations, Mr. Garth, but the matter I'm referring to goes back considerably farther than that."

Garth scowled. "What matter would that be?"

"Does the name *Shepherd* mean anything to you, Mr. Garth? Home for orphan boys?"

Garth stiffened. "Why, so what if it does?"

"So what, Mr. Garth? So what? Now that's a peculiar response from one who's spent eight years of his life there."

"Lots o' boys has. That was a long time ago."

"Yes, well, but how many have left under similar circumstances?"

Garth glowered. "You know a lot, Mr. Beeker. An awful lot that ain't your business."

"Everything's my business, Mr. Garth. Everything, that is, that affects my fate and fortune."

"So I run away. I wasn't goin' to stay no place where they beat and abuse a person. I'd had enough o' that from my own father."

Beeker smiled wryly. "I'm touched, Mr. Garth. Mother dead, cruel father, cast into an orphanage and subjected to inhumane treatment. A runaway alone in the world at sixteen. Sad, very sad. I'm truly touched."

Garth stood agape.

"Still, Mr. Garth, none of it justifies...murder." He let the word hang in the air.

A tremor visibly rocked Garth. "You must be—murder! Why, I never...there's—"

"Please, Mr. Garth, don't compound your troubles with lies. I have it all, you see, the whole story. It wasn't easy, understand, the time lapse and all that." He reached into a pocket of the folder. "A gentleman, headmaster of the home by the name of ..." he unfolded a paper "...Bascomb. Horace Bascomb."

Garth felt himself beginning to reel. He held the boy's shoulder and reached for the back of the chair. "He...he was the worst! Bullyin' and tormentin' and beatin' with Hicks. 'Hicks wants a taste o' you,' he'd say, and then start thrashin' with it. I still got the scars." He looked pleadingly to Beeker. "Couldn't take it no more. I...I hit him and he fell and I fell on him. He begged and I hit him again and he begged harder, the way other kids begged when that stick come lashin' down. And him laughin' all the while... The more he begged, the more I hit till I see his face bloody and not beggin' no more. I run then. I wasn't sorry, still ain't." He ran his wrist under his nose. "But I didn't mean to—didn't know I—"

"Killed him?" Beeker said, watching him disintegrate. "Well, murder is murder, Mr. Garth. There's no excusing it."

Garth twisted his hat. "That was a long time ago, Mr. Beeker. Surely—"

"There's no statute of limitations for murder, Mr. Garth."

Garth quaked. His eyes implored Beeker.

"And, Mr. Garth, in spite of what you believe your current standing with the law to be, I am of the learned opinion that you are enmeshed in grave matters indeed." He leaned forward on the table, lacing his fingers. "You have a history of violent behavior, Mr. Garth. Now I ask you, what *is* a jury to think?"

Garth extended his hands helplessly. "What can I do, Mr. Beeker? What can I say?"

Beeker leaned back, firming himself. "You can put yourself in my hands, Mr. Garth. I have considerable knowledge of the law and am well acquainted with its workings. Even under such dire circumstances as those threatening you now, I am quite capable of seeing to it that your best interests are served. However, I must have your full cooperation. Is that agreeable to you?"

"You know how to squeeze a man, Mr. Beeker," he said, misery carving his face.

"Let us call it mutual self-interest, shall we? Now, you can show your good faith by making your son tell me what I must know."

Garth looked down to the boy. Shame burned his face. "Jonathan? You heard. I know you understand. Tell the man."

The boy squeezed his arm but did not move.

"Just put the pencil to them papers on the table. Won't take but a second."

Still the boy did not move.

"Jonathan! Hear me. I'm in trouble, boy. Big trouble. It's only you as can help me out." He pushed the boy. "Go 'head now. Do it!"

The boy looked up, a low tone humming in his throat, and Garth hauled him by the arm up to the table. "Now write!" He crammed the pencil into the boy's hand and pressed it over the paper. "Write, damn it, write!"

The boy's hand hovered a moment, then dropped the pencil.

Garth swung the boy around at the same time his hand flashed out and cracked him across the face. He stood rigid, horrified by his act and by the imprint of his hand burning on the boy's cheek. His eyes teared with the boy's. For a long moment he hung there in choked silence before turning slowly to Beeker, standing now with his hands on the table.

"Do your damndest, Mr. Beeker," he said softly. "Hang me from the nearest gallows, if you will." He laid his arm gently on the boy's shoulder and guided him away.

When they reached the door, Garth swung around and tossed the envelope across to Beeker. "Do your goddamndest," he said, turning and leading the boy out.

Chapter 43

After three short balmy weeks spring ended abruptly with the onslaught of cold, high winds and a fury of torrential rains that rushed down the mountain sides and flooded the valley. The roads not washed out turned to bogs and the fields became lakes. Ceaselessly, endlessly, the rain drummed on the rooftops, and the black clouds roiling interminably out of the northeast kept the world in perpetual dusk.

People huddled in their parlors or stared dismally out of rain-streaked windows to the dreary world outside, with thoughts of the boy creeping back into their minds. Those who dared venture out, sloshed their way to the chapel to pray for their lives and their livelihoods. Whenever any of them chanced to meet on the street, they were silent, and only their eyes revealed the thought that lay behind them:

'The boy! The boy!'

The Garths, too, looked forlornly out, waiting, wondering. And all the while the boy's music played, dark and grim and foreboding.

For over a month the rains came. Night and day. Slanting, driving, raking rains. It closed the shops, the roads, the businesses, the school. It sealed windows and doors and isolated the people from each other. Lightning ripped the skies and the houses shook with concussions of thunder rolling and reverberating over the watery land. Rising rivers and streams, spilling over their banks, lost themselves beneath the deepening water. In their homes the people prayed for an end to the deluge.

And one day, as suddenly as it had begun, the rain stopped. People awakened in their beds to the unaccustomed silence.

They called to each other and offered up prayers of thanks. Sleep deserted the night as they rejoiced and planned anew.

At the break of dawn they rushed outdoors to greet the new day. Filling their lungs with the exhilarating freshness of cool air, they waited for the rising sun to disperse the gloom and bathe their faces in warmth.

The receding waters drained off quickly and soon the land began to dry. Laboring from dawn to dark, farmers hastened to plant what could still be grown. And where ever people met, they slapped each other on the back and joked about Noah and how they had feared of never seeing 'a piece o' blue' again.

With the growing heat of day, rivers and streams shrank from the banks they had so recently overflowed and settled back into. The sun, unusually hot so early in the season, sucked the moisture from the soil, and only the shaded and deepest hollows showed any signs of the spring floods that had devastated the land.

All threw themselves into their labors with renewed hope. In the valley, tillers lifted great wet clumps of earth and broke them down for planting. In town the shops bustled in readiness for the rush of business, already on the rise.

Cleaning in a burst of energy, women tore their homes apart. Everywhere, windows were thrown open to let in the light and let out the must. Even the children joined in, giving up their playtime without complaint when they were told to wash down the muddy walks or to drag furniture from flooded homes to dry in the sun.

Because the earth still held much water and the sun was strong, the germinating seeds took hold and the crops began to flourish. Grasses emerged everywhere and spread, lush and green, and the livestock fattened in the golden light.

Spirits ran high: 'Not gonta be half so bad a year's we thought, neighbor.' And together they smiled and squinted up to the bright sky. Peace descended over the land and the town and the Garth house.

It was not to last.

With the passing days the deep blue skies faded and whitened. The heat grew intense. People loosened their clothing and looked uneasily upward, afraid to wish too much, for the memory of the 'Second Flood,' as they called it, was still vivid in their minds.

At night they lay on their beds, naked on the sheets, waiting in the stillness for a breeze with the smell of rain on its breath. Windows remained closed during the day to hold what little coolness the night had afforded, and to keep out the grit and sand lifted by the dust devils spiraling over the land. Except for those driven by necessity, no one ventured out.

Gradually, their fears surfaced, showing first on their faces, and then in their tempers which flared at the slightest provocation under a flaring sun. Occasionally, thunderheads billowed dark over the distant mountains to the north, then drifted out of sight, carrying their hopes with them.

"Hell's own fire," said Joseph Fletcher, the town's unofficial historian. "Three score and ten I can 'member, and never did see nothin' like it. First the floods, now this."

He did not speak the dread word. No one did. In the fields a farmer picked a plant and felt its leaves crumble to dust in his hands. He stooped again for a handful of earth and watched it sift between his fingers and blow away like powder. He spoke—it could no longer be ignored or denied—and soon all were speaking it: Drought!

And again the words, smoldering like fire in their brains, came back:

'The boy! The boy!'

Wells ran dry. On the land the crops withered and burned. Each day the sun grew hotter in a blazing sky and baked the earth until great fissures opened along its yellowing crust. In the distance the shimmering mountains gleamed like hot steel against the molten sky, and the river between dried to a bed of bleached gravel and rock. Brush fires erupted everywhere, with nothing but the sweat and beating hands of smoke-choked men to contain them. Any foliage yet unscorched was soon devoured by scavenging stock whose bones surfaced and poked up under glistening skin-tight hides.

And again, like a fever sweeping through the town, the words arose louder, more insistent:

'The boy! The boy!'

Chapter 44

For a long time after his last meeting with Beeker, Garth worried. Each day, at any moment, he'd expected to be carried away in handcuffs. Every unusual sound alerted him, made him sweat. Several times, late at night after his wife was asleep, he'd started to pack his bag, ready to run, the way he had from the orphanage so many years before. And each time he gave it up.

Ashamed, unable to bear the thought of abandoning his family and leaving them alone and unprotected, he resigned himself and waited to be taken. But with the passing weeks he became gradually convinced that he was in no danger, that Beeker had been bluffing or feared implicating himself somehow and could gain nothing by prosecuting him.

As his preoccupation with his personal problems diminished, he became more aware of the temper of the town. He'd heard the grumbling, seen the grim, suspicious faces and felt a palpable danger to himself and his family.

One evening as he sat down to supper, shirtless and miserable with the heat and the anxieties plaguing him, he made up his mind:

"Beth…" he began, balking, "…uh, how's the well?"

She stared morosely into her dish. "Holding."

"Looks like this heat wave don't never want to break. Kills a man's appetite, too." He pushed his plate aside and glanced at the boy, smiling at him across the table. Drawing himself up, he looked at his wife and spoke directly:

"Beth, we're clearing out."

Her fork slipped from her hand and clattered to the floor. She raised her head slowly and he saw her face loosen, saw the deep wells of her dark eyes filling. Her chest heaved and though he knew her relief, he didn't know the true depth of it. Neither did he realize that not since her release from the institution, so many years ago—though she didn't show it then—had she felt so profoundly unburdened.

The boy slid off his chair to retrieve the fork, while his music broke, quickened and brightened.

Garth felt encouraged. "That's right, Beth, clearin' out, lock, stock and barrel, once and for all."

Her voice whispered out: "When?"

"Well," he said, scratching into the hair on his chest, "they been cuttin' me shorter and shorter hours at the mill. I see the handwritin' on the wall, but I still want to pull in all I can. So...I figger maybe another week, ten days. I can pick my time."

"Everett, now—tomorrow."

The boy's music dropped an octave and played softly in the background.

"Now, now, Beth, we waited this long, and if'n I can take a week to squeeze a few more dollars out o' the job we—" He saw the lines in her face deepen. "Okay, then, a day or two, Beth. You can start gettin' things ready, packed and such. But I'm gonna need a bit o' time to get on down to Deerfield and find us a place to live. Nice little town 'bout a hundred fifty miles south. Spent some time there way back when. Maybe rent a truck there, too. Soon's I get back we'll load up and I'll give the house over to a real estate man. Not worth much but he can send us whatever she'll bring in...How's it sound, Beth?"

Her eyes glistened.

"How's it sound to you, Jonathan?"

"I like it, Father," he said, and sent out a flutey trill of birds.

"And, Beth, you needn't fret over the cost," he said, smiling broadly. "Managed to set a bit aside you know nothin' of. Kinda as a 'mergency fund."

He saw her anxious face and he rose and went around to her. He laid his green-hued hand on her shoulder and bent close to her ear. "A new beginnin', Beth. We're a little smarter now, a little wiser, too, maybe. The world's full o' new beginnin's. Why not for us, as well."

The boy's music flowed sweet and soothing, and wrapped them with a feeling of hope.

Chapter 45

Two days later it came, a pestilence that struck down the livestock and left them carrion in the barren pastures. Meetings were hastily called. Nerves raw, the townspeople fought among themselves, arguing for and demanding solutions. Suggestions went up and were as quickly beaten down. They proposed, challenged, bickered. They cried out to each other. Tempers flamed. They accused, cursed and damned. The disease spread and ravaged the land while overhead the sun blazed relentlessly. And over and over, burning in their brains were the words:

'The boy!' Throbbing, chanting, 'The boy! The boy!'

Sensing the explosiveness of the situation, Garth knew he couldn't wait. Not wanting to alarm his wife, he hid his fears. That evening after the boy had gone to bed, he said, "Best I get movin' now, Beth. No sense waitin' 'round any longer. Already checked the train schedule." He came to her, sitting on the edge of their bed, and kissed her forehead. In her own excitement she failed to notice the urgency in his moves. "You try to get some good rest. I shouldn't be gone long. Just hope that train's on time."

He started out, then paused a moment to peek into the boy's room. In the dimness he saw the glow of his body on the bed. He stepped in, changed his mind and hurried downstairs. Outside, the early morning air was still and hot. The pulsing stars lit his way.

Before dawn broke, Bethany Garth worked eagerly, filling and packing and stuffing carton boxes. She had debated keeping the boy home, despite Garth's admonition: *May be best the boy go to school till I get back, to avoid any eyebrows goin' up with wonderin'.* And though she could make better use of the time spent trekking back and forth to the school, the stack of borrowed books waiting to be returned decided for her.

The school calendar had been extended because of the floods and the days shortened because of the heat. Inside the schoolhouse Miss Lapham, now Mrs. William Hathoway, listened raptly to the boy's steady undercurrent of music. He had been singing since he'd arrived, perfect rhythms and harmonies imparting a sense of completion, like the final movement in a symphony.

She shivered as she listened to the quiet composition infiltrating her mind, touching her strangely with nuances of sound that seemed to carry meaning, and meaning within meaning, beyond meaning. She felt the music enveloping her, permeating her, suggesting thought and feeling she could neither comprehend nor define. She felt its dizzying influence escape her senses as it transcended audible sound, consciousness and time.

Just before noon, approaching the sweltering height of day, news broke of the town's economic collapse. The banks failed, businesses teetered on the edge of bankruptcy. Savings and investments plummeted or were wiped out. Whole lifetimes and the labor of lifetimes were forfeit and ruined in a moment. Panic spread. Rumors raged.

* * * * *

No one could ever remember, or did not want to remember, who called it out. Whoever it was, found in his words the power to move men, to bind them to a purpose. They rallied behind him, swelling the street with their numbers as they strode in a blaze of light and fury toward the schoolhouse.

The boy had not eaten his mid-morning snack, but sat off

by himself, motionless, singing in a low, brooding key, with an endless stringing of threnodies coming from some cavernous place deep within. As she had all morning, Martha Hathoway listened to the hypnotic phrasing and watched him closely.

He stirred finally. Slowly, his eyes came 'round to meet hers, and in that stunned moment of their locking, she felt the power of his gaze yoking them together, paralyzing her with its force and intensity, as if the essence of his being were penetrating her, infusing her. Faint, shuddering, near to swooning, she could not tear her eyes away until he had averted his own.

Expressionless, the boy continued singing to the images flashing before him, felt the dark sensations of his music fingering down to unexplored depths, dredging the abyss of his soul, gathering and capturing in its webbed embrace the nuances and abstractions of knowledge and experience. Then, elevating, his music molded itself in new intricacies to the faces, the voices, the places crowding his mind. Words and ideas translated themselves into a composite, total and complete in geometric forms of white light, and his music, shaping itself to the final configuration, merged with it to create a final synthesis.

Damp with foreboding and the heat, Martha Hathoway heard the sounds, dimly at first, like the rumbling of an approaching storm. Lethargically she moved to the window and looked up hopefully to the sky, seared white by the blinding sun.

An explosion of voices rounding the building startled her. She fell back. Dazed, then alarmed, she rushed to the door and slammed it against the thunder of feet trembling the stairs. In a moment the door burst open and she staggered before the glut of bodies pushing in past her.

"The boy!" they shouted. "Where's the boy!"

From the rear, more cries went up: "The boy! Give us the boy!"

Amid the shocked and silent faces, they heard him, saw him. His music ruptured and a high shrieking of brass rose against tumbling strings.

Crying out, Martha Hathoway flung herself between them and the boy, clawing at the lunging mass that swept her aside and trampled over her to the middle of the room.

The music wailed to a screaming chorus joined by a chorus of the children's screams as the boy turned for the first time to face the roar and the outstretched arms grasping for him. His hair shone a platinum, haloed brilliance in the white light falling in through the window, and his great, darkening eyes were wide with wonder and sadness as the mob descended upon him, wrenching him unresisting from the seat, hands on all parts, dragging him out amid the shouting and the music that flowed in torrents, engulfing them all.

Lifting him high, they handed his sprawling body along. Clamoring, they thronged down the path, their cries drowned in the thunder of percussion and the insane and disjointed rhythms that clashed in ringing dissonance. Falling on him, they swallowed him up with their numbers, and were themselves swallowed up in the raging din.

An instant of silence. Then, filtering up through the swarm of bodies blanketing him came a single, sustained note, pitched high and clear, pure, sweet and divine—suddenly choked off.

Chapter 46

When Martha Hathoway regained consciousness, the room lay silent and empty. She touched her head, and her lips shaped the name of William. But William, her husband, was gone, she remembered, gone off to war after a single night together.

Using a desk for support, she climbed unsteadily to her feet. Her eyes passed over the room to the seats askew and overturned, to the strewn papers and books, and the globe flattened on one side. She heard again the insane cries and the insane music and remembered the madmen raging hot-faced over her. She saw her torn dress and touched her bruised cheek. Her heart tightened and her breath came short and gasping.

Hesitantly, trembling, she staggered to the open door, where she leaned against the frame, holding her side. There, within the shadowed circle beneath the tree, she saw the shadowed woman kneeling in the dirt over her son's body, broken and still, a dove torn to pieces by dogs. She saw the white hair cascade down to veil her face as she bent low to kiss him, something Martha Hathoway could not recall seeing before.

Gently, Bethany Garth lifted her child in the iron cradle of her arms, as she had in the yard so long ago. Swaying under the crush of day, she gazed down at him, at the lolling head and the lifeless legs dangling limply over her arm. Tenderly she eased his head to her breast, like that of a nursing infant. For a long moment she stood unmoving, then, stiffly, she went down the path, her feet lifting a trail of dust until she disappeared over the hump in the road.

No music played now. No sound came at all, except the faintest whisper of wind in the dry grass.

Martha Hathoway's hand wandered to her abdomen, where she sensed a stirring, almost imperceptible, like the leaves beginning to stir high in the treetop.

End